A
Question
of
Negligence

Other books by Hugh McLeave

FICTION

The Steel Balloon
The Sword and the Scales
Vodka on Ice

NONFICTION

Chesney
McIndoe: Plastic Surgeon
The Risk Takers
A Time to Heal
The Last Pharaoh

A
Question
of
Negligence

HUGH McLEAVE

? ? ?
? ?

Harcourt Brace Jovanovich, Inc.

New York

A
Question
of
Negligence

1

? ?
?

Donovan carried two mugs of tea into the cubbyhole the surgeons used as a locker room, her rubber boots scuffing on the jute of the threadbare rug. One she handed to the older of the two men; the other she placed pointedly on top of the steel desk for the young house surgeon. He picked it up, swallowed a mouthful and grimaced at the taste. "That's the way they make it in Scotland." David Wilkinson, the registrar, grinned. "Sweet as a sheep's eye and strong enough to trot a mouse on. Isn't that what your professor says, Sister?" Above the surgical mask which lay under her chin like a muffler, Donovan's face remained neutral. "When do we start on the next one?" Wilkinson asked.

"Professor has just rung to say he'll be with us in quarter of an hour," Sister Donovan replied in her Glasgow brogue. "But we can start when you're ready."

"And, presto, he'll appear to perform the tricky work," Wilkinson put in. "Who's giving the gas?"

"Dr. Rothwell." Sister Donovan hesitated a minute, glancing warily at the house surgeon. "I wish you'd have a word with Professor about him. He's getting awful bad again."

"I've given up trying. The old man likes him, and that's the way it is." He toweled the sweat off his forehead, face and neck and drew the jacket of his surgical pajamas over his undervest. "Another jag, I suppose," he

3

muttered. "What is it this time—hash, goof balls, French blues or just plain LSD? You never know with these gas-men. We're the only firm in the hospital that has two patients in theater at the same time, one on the slab, the other on the gas wagon."

"It's not funny, Mr. Wilkinson."

"I know, Donovan, I know. But we have to live with it. We just do what we did the day before yesterday and every other time—keep an eye on the patient and see that the oblivion needle hasn't gone too deep, and all our handiwork will not be in vain." Rothwell's drug addiction was hardly the worst of his problems.

Donovan picked up the mugs. "Five minutes," she muttered tersely. When she had gone, the young house surgeon picked up his reprints from the *British Journal of Surgery, Lancet* and other medical journals; his eyes darted over them nervously, as though he were cramming for the toughest examination of his life. Wilkinson's lip curled with amusement as he pulled on his skullcap and tied the tapes of his operating gown and yashmak. He remembered his first session with the great Murdo Cameron. What a rough ride that had been! And not much better now.

"OK, Dr. Wells?"

"I was just boning up on the case."

"Case!"

"Sorry, I forgot." In the two days he had worked with Wilkinson, the senior surgical registrar had dunned into him that Professor Cameron detested the word "case." They were patients, all with names and personal histories. Never Abdominals, Fractured Femurs or Ventricular Septal Defects.

"Try not to be too clever, and no medical bull—he smells it."

4

"He'll be the first I've ever met," Wells said, perhaps too confidently. "What's he really like? Is he as good as they say?"

"For the umpteenth time, wait and see." Wilkinson was not trying to dodge the question; he found it almost unanswerable, although he had assisted Cameron at operations for more than ten years as house surgeon, registrar and senior registrar. How could he describe to a raw beginner from medical school what Cameron signified as a surgeon, let alone as an individual? How could he explain why some days he felt like chucking a scalpel at the Professor of Surgery and others he would go through fire and brimstone for him? He might have whispered, like so many others, that the Cameron of this morning seemed a shadow of the Cameron he had known a year ago, even six months ago. He might have warned him to keep his head down and his mouth shut, but why frighten him? If he lasted long enough, he would answer the question himself. Wilkinson kicked off his slippers and plunged his feet into the green rubber boots. "Come on. We've got some cutting to do before the great man makes his entrance."

Professor Murdo Cameron finished dictating his letters, pulled on his white coat and made for the A Block Theater on the north side of the hospital; he walked down the broad concrete corridor that split the original old building in two, his nostrils wrinkling at the odor of steam and boiled cabbage from the kitchens mingling with iodoform and carbolic; he traversed the long waiting room, its rows of seats bought as a job lot from some Baptist church, where outpatients attended their call from the cubicles that passed for consulting rooms. What a trade! he reflected, glancing at the queue which the staff of St. Vincent's never seemed to whittle down to manageable size.

5

And this passes for a teaching hospital, training physicians and surgeons, scattering its medical degrees all over the world! Who could elicit a patient's history and arrive at a diagnosis in five minutes? Who could even hear himself think when the stud partitions dividing these consulting boxes were so flimsy that you could hear someone two doctors away venting his urine specimen?

"Professor Cameron—one moment, please." He turned and noticed a middle-aged man hurrying toward him; he took in the Homburg hat, waistcoat, watch chain, and well-shined shoes. You rarely met them that well dressed in the East End of London and hardly ever at St. Vincent's. "You remember me, Professor—Harry Brooke?"

Yes, he remembered. Brooke (né Bruch) who ran a restaurant in Dock Street, where the hospital staff went to repair the stomach scars caused by their canteen food.

"It's my boy, Bernie. He's bad, Professor, very bad. I spoke to you about him two months ago at the restaurant. He's so bad he can hardly draw a good breath, one good breath. I wrote to you about him. You remember?" He was pleading.

Cameron nodded. He had mind of the boy. Livid face, pigeon-chested, no wind. Obvious heart defect, probably a hole in the wall of one of the upper chambers. He recalled something else. "But, Mr. Brooke, you live up Golders Green direction. Didn't I hear that somebody operated on your son in a clinic there?"

"Right, Professor, quite right. But they hashed up the job, and Miriam said, 'Now, Harry, if only you'd got Professor Cameron for the operation, our boy would be better than one hundred per cent by now.'"

"He had a good surgeon, I'm certain. Some patients just don't respond."

"He would with you, Professor. You will take a look at him, won't you?"

"Sorry—not unless he's referred to me by a consultant at your own hospital."

"But what if I paid and you saw him privately?" He stopped when he noted a bleak expression settle on Cameron's face. "I meant to say, I would donate anything you want—up to a thousand pounds—to any charity you like. I'm not a rich man, but I will do that."

"Money doesn't enter into the question, Mr. Brooke. I have a hundred and sixty surgical patients on my waiting list. Four months' work. Your boy would push one or two of those back a day or maybe a week, and I can't do it."

Brooke was nearly weeping; he supplicated with his hands. "Look, Professor, I'll make it two thousand . . . all right, three thousand, but that's as far as I can go."

"This isn't a bazaar, Mr. Bruch." Unconsciously Cameron gave the name its guttural German or Scottish ending. "If I did your boy, he'd have the same free treatment all of these people get. No more, no less. But I can tell you that for that amount of money the best surgeon in the country will even take out his own stitches and get you the best room at the finest clinic in London."

"I don't think you understand, Professor."

"I do, Mr. Bruch. Only too well. Good-bye and good luck." Cameron shook his hand, turned and walked on. He objected to having his ear bitten by patients or their relatives, to having bribes even under the name of charity dangled in front of him. He felt little compunction for Brooke; at least he could pay to push his son up the queue. Three thousand pounds! Thank God he had a few hundred in the bank, or he might have wilted. It would have bought a new autoclave for the North Block Theater. But, damn it, he had his principles. His eye lit up when he saw Stroma, his daughter, emerging from the corridor leading to the obstetrics wing. She spotted him at the same time and waited until he caught up. She kissed him on the cheek, and his eyes flickered up and down the corridor to ensure no one had noticed this demonstration of affection. Stroma laughed at his embarrassment.

"How are things in the Almoners' Department?"

"All go, like yours. I've boarded out twelve children this morning. The mothers are in Obstetrics. And I found a problem for you. Would you have a word with Sarah?"

"What's wrong with Sarah?"

"It's a small thing, but important to her. She didn't want to bother you, but it would help if you talked to her about it."

"I'll go on my way to theater." They parted company at the corridor leading to Cameron's two-room flat. As Stroma left, she said, "You won't forget tonight."

"What's happening tonight?"

"Daddy, we fixed it two days ago. You're taking me to dinner, and I'm standing you another type of theater, then we're driving to the cottage for the weekend. Even if you're called out to Buckingham Palace, you're not spending another weekend in that crumby little flat. You need a rest."

"Sorry, darling. Of course I remembered. I've been looking forward to it for days. My mind must have been on something else."

Stroma realized he had not remembered at all. Tonight had been a reminder that tomorrow was her twenty-second birthday. He never seemed to recall that date, and she had often wondered if his wife's death on the night she was born had something to do with this lapse. She gazed after the tall figure striding through the swing doors at the end of the corridor. He had too much on his hands and mind. Her own thoughts switched back to the day nine months before when she had started in the Almoners' Department after taking a degree in sociology at Oxford; he had paraded her around the whole hospital, introducing her to everyone from the gate porter to matrons and consultants. He was so proud that she had chosen a job in his hospital. Would he have shown so much pleasure had he guessed that she had applied for the post not so much out of a social conscience as to be near him, to look after him? That he would have resented just as he spurned her suggestion that he should coast along and delegate more to his staff; he scoffed at the notion that his skill and stamina were not as good at fifty-two as, say, ten years ago. No one outside St. Vincent's would have disputed the fact. To them he remained the great surgical pioneer and teacher. But inside! They did murmur, too softly, of course, for the professor's ear, that he was over the hill.

As Cameron reached the flat, he caught sight of Sarah in her dust cap and charlady's apron, her slight, bowed figure engulfed by the mass of laundry he had left that morning. She hesitated as she spotted him, and Cameron noted that her eyes were red from weeping. "I've put Chula's milk down for her, sir," she said.

"Thanks, Sarah. Now, what's the matter?"

"Not to bother you with it, Professor."

"Come on, then—let me guess. Your niece or grandchild?"

"Neither, sir. It's Boodles. The vet says she's got to be put down. It's a kind of growth, and her only nine. I just can't believe it."

For several minutes Cameron quizzed her about the bitch of indeterminate breed who shared her bed-sitter and absorbed most of her affection. Illnesses, pregnancies, accidents, eating and sleeping habits—he might have been taking a patient's history. "You can stop worrying, Sarah," he said finally. "We'll do what we can for Boodles. Bring her in tomorrow. No, wait a minute. . . ." Saturday he had promised to Stroma. Well, if she had to miss dinner tonight before the theater, it was too bad. "I've just had a thought. I might fit her in this evening. We'll find her the best private kennel in the experimental wing, and I'll do the surgery myself. How's that?"

Sarah was crying openly with relief as she thanked him. Patiently he gave her instructions about taking the dog to the X-ray Department in the animal wing, then resumed his march toward the A Block Theater.

Donovan brewed him a mug of tea while he scrubbed up; he then tied the tapes at the back of his gown and powdered the inside of his rubber gloves with talc. Donovan helped him into them. She had known him for twenty years and for fifteen of those had served as his theater sister. Now she briefed him on the progress of the vagotomy operation. "How's the new callant getting on?" he asked.

"He's a bit halakat and he clashes too much, but he might learn," she replied. Donovan flattered herself that only with her would the professor lapse into Lallans. A Scots word or two meant he was feeling in a good mood, or, alternatively, something was irritating him. It depended on the word and the inflection. She swung open the Perspex doors, and he padded up to the table, thrusting his mask high on the prominent bridge of his nose and muttering a good morning to everyone.

They dropped into position around him; Holroyd, the younger theater sister, checked the instruments on the tray; Rothwell glanced instinctively at the electronic scribble on the oscilloscope measuring heart and blood-pressure readings; Wilkinson stood opposite the professor, ensuring that young Wells had assumed the right position to hold the retractors. They had opened the stomach and drawn back a flap of the liver so that Cameron would have a clear sight of the area in which he would carry out his most intricate work—the end of the food tract, where it joined the stomach. The surgeon had to locate the web of vagus nerves, where they branched off over and under the food tract to serve the stomach and the liver. He would have to identify and snip the nerves leading to the stomach that controlled gastric acidity so that the duodenal ulcer would have the chance to heal. This vagotomy demanded great skill with the hand and knife as well as long experience in cutting only the necessary vagus nerves. Cameron's big hands began to probe for the nerve strands; he uncovered each one deftly, slipping rubber cuffs between them and the food tract, then calling for cutting forceps to sever them.

"What do we know about this patient?" He posed Wells the question in an offhand voice.

The house surgeon started his recital. "Referred from Dr. Studhold in the Department of Medicine when conservative treatment for gastroduodenal ulcer proved negative. The patient had a history over three years of hunger pains relieved by nutrition and antacids. The trauma was located usually in the epigastric region. She also had gastric reflux, anorexia and had lost about a stone and a half in weight."

"You certainly know your textbook, laddie," Cameron grunted, and young Wells's eyes smiled with pleasure above his mask. However, Donovan, Wilkinson and Holroyd all flicked looks at each other; they had caught the bite in the word "laddie." Cameron, they knew, abhorred jargon. "You mean," he continued, "that this woman had pain under her ribs on the right side between meals, she had vomiting spells, didn't feel like eating and lost twenty-two pounds?"

"If you put it that way, sir."

"Go on, what else do we know about her?"

"She's twenty-eight and married, sir," Wells said. He had lost a little of his self-assurance.

11

"Name?"

"Mrs. . . ." The house surgeon faltered; the small group hunched over the figure on the table froze as they waited for him to remember. "I'm sorry, I've forgotten."

"Forgotten, eh? Then I hope if you're ever a candidate for surgery, your surgeon can at least remember whom he's operating on. I don't suppose you know what her husband does or how many children she has."

"No, sir. I didn't think that was relevant to the diagnosis or the operation."

"At Vincent's we think everything about our patients is important. Even those tissues which you are damaging with the pressure on those retractors."

The house surgeon realized he was gripping the retractors until his knuckles showed white; he eased the strain on the instruments. They hadn't lied, those who told him that Cameron cracked the whip and could be a crusty old swine. Well, he might be a brilliant operator and a tin god in this hospital, but they could keep both as far as he was concerned. This grimy old prison with its crush of National Health patients from the slums and dockland led nowhere. Certainly not to Harley Street or the private clinic he had set his sights on when his six months as a house surgeon had ended.

"You're throwing a shadow," Cameron barked at him. He moved quickly, too quickly, out of the line of the arc lamps over the table; he collided with Holroyd, who stepped back involuntarily and knocked a tray of suture needles onto the floor. The atmosphere in the theater had become as taut as the nerve fibers Cameron had just cut. Now the surgeon was turning to the incision he would make to widen the stomach outlet. He called for a scalpel.

Holroyd went to slap the knife into his hand. Their long association had made this drill an automatic-reflex

12

action. This time, however, something happened. The tapered handle of the surgical knife missed the outstretched palm; its sharp point nicked his glove at the web of his middle finger, and blood began to ooze out. But Cameron did not appear to have felt the knife hit his hand. Or the cut. The scalpel spun downward into the cavity, where he had been operating. Holroyd reached for it, retrieved it with some effort and discarded it, choosing another to hand the surgeon. Cameron was, however, gazing at his bloody hand, the left one, which he favored when cutting. For several seconds he stared, as though he could not credit what had occurred. He flexed his fingers and clenched his fist several times, then braced himself. "All right, let's get on with it," he called, and made the slit at the lower end of the stomach.

In that tense moment no one had noticed that the knife had fallen point first on the line where the stomach joined the food tract and had pierced the flesh. In her haste and embarrassment, in her desperation to redeem the knife, Holroyd had enlarged the cut, which measured about three-quarters of an inch. The team was now concentrating on another area of the abdomen, and no one spotted the tear. The surgery continued in silence, without further trouble. Cameron closed up; then they wheeled the woman back to the recovery ward.

Before his next operation, Cameron went to a telephone to make arrangements for the surgery on Sarah's dog, giving Wilkinson and Wells time to drink another mug of tea. "Now you know as well as anybody." Wilkinson grinned.

"As you say. I've only one question: How the hell do you stick it?"

"I've often wondered myself. But you either hate him or you love him, and it's the same on his side. In my case it's a bit of both. There's another reason. You won't find more than a handful of surgeons like him around any more."

"Thank God for that. Those were the worst two hours I've ever spent."

"Well, he believes in being hard on the doctors and easy on the patients. You'll get used to it."

"Used to it! With that petulant old bastard I won't last a week."

Both men almost dropped their mugs when they heard the shout from the door. Cameron stood there, his face wooden, his blue eyes boring coldly into the house surgeon's. "You may be right in saying I'm a petulant old bastard, Dr. Wells. But you're wrong when you think you won't last a week. You haven't lasted a morning."

"I'm sorry, Professor."

"Sorry's a word that's always used too often and too late. If you report to the medical superintendent, he'll find you another firm while you're on contract here." With that, Cameron turned and strode back into the operating room. Wilkinson, trailing behind him, had rarely ever witnessed him so angry.

In the evening Cameron strolled around the recovery ward to inquire, as always, about the patients he had done that day. All five were making progress, though he stopped by Mrs. Fowler's bed when he noted the upward kink in the temperature chart. No more than a degree. Nothing to worry about; nothing to keep him in the hospital over the weekend.

When he returned on Monday morning, they told him the story and he listened, sad and perplexed. Just when the woman seemed to be recovering from the surgery, she collapsed suddenly and began vomiting blood. It was three in the morning, and Casualty was coping with five accident victims. By the time the duty surgeon arrived, Mrs. Fowler was dead. They had tried, unsuccessfully, to resuscitate her. Later that morning Cameron read the autopsy report; it revealed that the bleeding had sprung from a small, infected wound at the junction of the stomach and the esophagus, a wound consistent with a scalpel cut.

Again and again, in his mind, he played back each cut and stitch of the operation. He could recall nothing untoward, except that he appeared to have gashed his own hand.

2
? ?
?

Harley Street was emptying as the young man walked slowly along it, peering at the numbers over the doors of the consulting rooms. Receptionists were closing their appointment books and specialists drawing their Rolls-Royces and Bentleys away from parking meters, heading for home or for a weekend in the country. Every now and then the man would pull a note out of his pocket to remind himself of the name and number on it. Finally he stopped in the middle of the street at a Georgian building, which had a name plate reading "Dr. A. Gregor Maclean." He rang the bell, and a few minutes later a girl with reddish hair, blue eyes and an Irish tilt to her chin appeared on the step.

"I'd like to see Dr. Maclean, miss," the man said diffidently.

She noted the cheap suit and tie, the bare head, plebe-

15

ian face and rough hands, which fingered a letter. "I don't suppose you have an appointment."

"No, but I brought him this." He held out the limp, fingerprinted letter which, she saw, was addressed to a Mr. Stanley Fowler. "Read it, miss," he prompted.

She ran her eyes quickly over it, concealing her surprise, then handed it back to him. "I don't see that this had anything to do with my Dr. Maclean," she said curtly. "Are you sure you're searching for Dr. Maclean the psychiatrist? There are several consultants of that name in Harley Street."

He nodded. "Just for his advice, like. I'm the husband of the woman mentioned in the letter—before all this happened, I mean. My brother was a patient of the doctor and said he'd be bound to help. Let me see him for a minute, miss?" He put all his appeal into the request.

The girl pondered. In fact, Deirdre O'Connor spent much of her time brushing unwanted clients off this step. Maclean twitted her about her Harley Street complex, how she looked first for the Rolls or the mink coat or the diamond pin in the Old School Tie before admitting patients. However, she understood her psychiatrist well enough to realize that, left to himself, he would always pick the wrong cases—the hopeless, unmoneyed failures who would stick to him for life, playing on the compassion and sympathy that he, as a psychiatrist, should not have felt. She had long ago run her personal rule over Dr. Maclean and decided that things would work better if she did the selection, he the psychiatry. She prided herself on her Irish sixth sense about trouble; it began like this, with a casual knock on the door, and finished up a thunderclap. This was trouble.

"I'm sorry," she said. "It's already after hours, and the doctor has had a very trying day. He still has a patient, and immediately after that he goes to the Royal Society of

Medicine to give a lecture. I'm afraid tonight is absolutely out of the question."

"Tomorrow, then?"

"He doesn't consult on Saturdays, and I've filled his diary for the next three weeks."

"I can't wait that long," he said dismally. "He told my brother, 'Any time.' Can I hang on, miss, if you don't mind —on the off-chance, like?"

She could hardly shut the door in his face. "Please yourself," she said, and he followed her inside, where she disappeared into a cabinet by the side of Maclean's consulting rooms on the ground floor. She had another trick, however: reappearing a moment or two later and announcing, "In a quarter of an hour I shall have to close the office and leave, and then you must go." He nodded, his face gloomy, though with no suspicion of her subterfuge. Deirdre realized that the garrulous lady in the adjoining room would continue her blather for at least another hour; she would return to lock up after this man, Fowler, had departed.

On the other side of the consulting-room door, Gregor Maclean was praying for the last patient to empty her mind; he, too, estimated another hour. On the chaise longue sprawled the elegant, if full, figure of Lady Blye, her voice droning with the relaxed refinement she deemed appropriate to sessions with her psychiatrist. It might have shocked her to learn that she was indulging in a form of sex substitute, lying fully clothed on a couch, baring her soul to a doctor she hired by the hour; she would have been outraged to hear that she always demanded the final appointment because she had the subconscious desire to sleep with Dr. Maclean.

The stale narrative and the monotonous intonation bored Maclean, who was musing for the umpteenth time

17

that week, "I must order Deirdre to clear my list of these rich hostesses and socialites who prey on me because their hormone tide is on the ebb or their husbands have found a stand-in." Lady Blye, for instance. The only interesting fact she had ever permitted herself to reveal was her neurotic gourmandizing; every time Lord Blye turned nasty or spent the night with someone else, her consumption of *petits fours* and soft centers soared, and with them her weight and chances of keeping her husband happy. In his notebooks she had two hundred hours of free association, most of it drivel. "A fair mileage," he reflected as his ballpoint halted and he wondered if she would become the first recorded case of the patient hypnotizing the psychiatrist. That would make the correspondence column of *Lancet*.

The flea came to his rescue. Impudently it leaped from some corner of the couch onto the frill of crêpe de Chine which outcropped from the valley between Lady Blye's alpine breasts. In the curtained penumbra of the consulting room Maclean strained to observe the brown parasite; he could imagine its powerful saltatory muscles flexing for the next leap, the mandible ready to bite, the upper lip salivating at the smell of blue blood. The history of that flea he could guess; it had arrived with Bob Hearn, the East End carpenter he was treating for depression, had liked the place and had stayed. Would it be a match for the awesome lady? He crossed his fingers for it.

Again it jumped, landing this time on the crosshatching of the well-fleshed neck; from there it hopped to the fine skin behind the right ear, where Lady Blye sported the scars of two face lifts. Maclean almost shared its moment of pleasure, almost imagined the ecstasy as it buried itself in the sweet flesh.

"Something's bitten me," Lady Blye screamed, slapping her neck and forgetting the confessional whisper.

18

She turned, wide-eyed, to Maclean and noticed he was smiling.

"Probably only a flea," he murmured.

"A flea?" she repeated incredulously.

"Yes. *Pulex irritans.* Not the bubonic type. Most likely you picked it up from one of your dogs, or horses," Maclean said amiably, trying to keep a stiff tongue in his cheek.

"My dogs and horses haven't got fleas," snapped Lady Blye. "It's an insult to suggest that they have." Her dignity demanded an apology, but Maclean did not utter one. The lady leaped off the couch, throwing hauteur aside, and ran to the door; she barked at the astonished Deirdre to bring her wrap. "And you can cancel my appointments," she shouted. "Disgraceful!" Out she swept.

"What's wrong with her?" Deirdre asked.

"I couldn't bring myself to rape her," Maclean said blandly.

"I'm serious."

"Well, you won't believe it, but she was bitten by a flea, poor woman. No psychiatrist will ever survive that sort of blow to his prestige. Ten minutes and the whole of Harley Street will have it and use it to dine out on. Anyway, I've had my fill of these society misfits. Say we're booked up when she rings."

"When she rings! Do you think she'll be back after that affront?"

"Sure of it." He handed her Lady Blye's crocodile handbag. "Her subconscious wouldn't have overlooked this if she'd been serious. But I'm still out."

Deirdre was not smiling. "They pay our rent," she muttered.

Maclean opened his mouth to reply, when he spotted the man in his waiting room. "Not another," he exclaimed.

"I've already told him you can't see him," Deirdre said quickly. "You've had enough this week." She motioned to the door that led through to the basement. Maclean was not listening; he was studying the man's face and walked into the waiting room.

"You look like somebody I know. Let me see—Fowler, Dick Fowler, wasn't it? You some relation?"

"His brother. I'm Stan."

Maclean beckoned him into the consulting room. He pressed a button, and the curtains slid back; he sat Fowler in an easy chair and pushed a box of cigarettes at him.

Fowler was thinking that legends sounded better than they looked. His brother hadn't told him that the great Dr. Maclean was built like a brewer's drayman, only fatter. He'd been a drunk himself once, Dick had said, but now he could laugh about his own cure for alcoholism and run parties for reformed soaks and anybody who wanted to join them in drinking fruit juice and synthetic wines. He had no time for the homemade dog leads, woolen mats and fretwork of the occupational therapist; he discovered what interested his patients and made it his interest. So he often quit his consulting room to hunt for antique books or furniture, or to see a cricket match at Lords or the Oval. "The couch is for the nobs," Dick had told him. "I was given the treatment at the ringside of the International Sporting Club, all on the Health Service." His brother had given him another slant on Maclean. "Watch that Irish miss. She's sweet on Mac and looks after him like a tigress." Well, he had side-stepped her and now sat face to face with the great man.

"Trouble with Dick, is it?"

"No, Dick's fine. Got a good job as a checker in the docks. He said I should show you this letter."

Maclean fished in the envelope and drew out the letter. It carried the embossed heading of St. Vincent's

Teaching Hospital in the East End, not far from the hospital where he himself acted as psychiatric consultant. First he read it quickly, then let his eye scrutinize it. Fowler watched the big, jowly face change its expression; one hand reached into the baggy pocket of his jacket and produced a snuffbox, which he flipped open to take a pinch. He read the letter a third time. It said:

"Dear Mr. Fowler, I should like to commiserate with you on the recent death of your wife. I felt doubly sorry because, in my opinion, which is widely shared here, Mrs. Fowler need never have died.

"You may not know this, but the mortality in this type of operation for duodenal ulcer is very low. The surgery performed on your wife is described as vagotomy and pyloroplasty—that is, the severing of the vagus nerves leading to the stomach and the enlargement of the stomach outlet.

"In the case of your wife, the surgeon pierced the esophagus with his knife as he was resecting the vagus nerves. This, in my opinion, proves negligence or incompetence. It was this mistake that caused your wife to suffer a rupture of the esophagus and the consequent infection that brought about her death. The post-mortem carried out the following day clearly revealed that there had been a surgical mishap. The post-mortem examination records are available, as are the clinical notes of the physician who attended your wife.

"I am writing to you because, as the husband, you have the right to demand an inquiry through the Board of Governors of St. Vincent's. For your own peace of mind and for the good name of surgery in general and this hospital in particular I hope you will decide to adopt this course."

The typed letter bore no signature; the envelope carried a Central London postal frank. No other clue, Maclean thought. But the hospital note paper, the medical terminology, the impression that its anonymous author had witnessed the operation and even had access to the pathology report, all indicated that the poison-pen writer held a fairly senior position in the hospital.

"A bit of a facer, Stan. You don't happen to know which surgeon did the operation?" he asked the young man, who sat with an inch of ash on his cigarette butt, too apprehensive to reach for the ash-tray.

"They said it'd be Professor Cameron."

"Cameron! No, that I can't believe. If Cameron made such a slip, he'd be the first to admit it and take his punishment. I've known him, on and off, for more than twenty-five years. I sat in as his anesthetist when he was operating on casualties from El Alamein in a tent in the Canal Zone and saw him do twenty-six operations in sixteen hours, and he had the best pair of hands I've ever seen. We could have sold the shrapnel in the theater for scrap metal. I just don't believe it."

"That's what I thought, sir. My wife—she had so much faith in him. We was sure she'd be OK with him operating."

Maclean well understood. Professor Murdo Frazer Cameron, whom he had known since his undergraduate days in Edinburgh, had an international reputation for surgery. Hadn't he built up the Department of Clinical and Experimental Surgery at St. Vincent's from a hole-and-corner affair to a teaching center that drew students from all over the world? Hadn't he and his staff pioneered thoracic and intestinal surgery, open-heart operations and organ grafting? On the other hand, he knew that Cameron had the name of being a hard taskmaster, one of the school that demanded nothing but perfection in technique and staff work. Maclean had often seen him heave aside viciously the occasional scalpel that had offended him by its bluntness; he had watched him vent his temper on some luckless theater sister guilty of no more than handing him the wrong forceps; house surgeons, registrars and even consultants had taken the rough edge of his tongue for some slip.

Every good surgeon had his enemies, his rivals. But Maclean found it difficult to acknowledge that someone at St. Vincent's hated Cameron so vehemently that he would try to persuade a patient's next of kin to indict him for negligence.

"They say I should make an official complaint, Doctor."

Maclean's thought orbited back to the timid man who faced him. He had two children to bring up, and his wife had died through the ineptitude of some surgeon, so far as he had been informed.

"I can't advise you what to do with this letter. What I can tell you is that the medical profession will close its ranks on the affair. It will be almost impossible to prove negligence."

"My wife's sister thought I should take the case to *The World*, the newspaper, and let them fight it for me, but Dick said I'd be better to see you first."

The World! Maclean had met only one man from that paper. One was enough. During the trial of Neil Archer he had acted as defense psychiatrist and had tried to persuade the advocate, Paul Lippman, to plead that his client was paranoiac to save his life. Archer, they knew, had almost certainly murdered the socialite Julia Colethorpe. *The World* had paid for the defense, and its assistant editor, Stanley Barcroft, had toiled deviously to ensure that Archer was hanged and his paper got its money's worth. Lippman fought for an acquittal, lost, and Archer was hanged. Maclean's black eyebrows beetled at the thought of Barcroft or someone of his ilk stirring up a scandal that would crucify Cameron.

"I'll tell you what'll happen if you do," he said. "They'll use you and this letter and pay you a few hundred pounds. But the publicity will make life difficult for you as well as for the doctors concerned, and you'll finish up worse off."

"I must do something. Dick says we shouldn't let them get away with it."

"Tell Dick from me to give his aggression a rest. What have you got? A letter from someone who is too scared to sign his name, accusing one of the best surgeons in the country of doing something that a palsied man with six fingers on each hand would find difficult. The hospital wouldn't even listen, and the courts would kick you out if you sued."

"I'll do what you think I should do."

Maclean reflected for a few minutes. If he did nothing, that letter would sooner or later arrive on the desk of some news editor; Cameron would face an official inquiry set up by the Minister of Health, from which no one would emerge unscathed. Even if Fowler did not take it to Fleet Street, the poison-pen writer would seize the next chance to accuse the surgeon through another patient. To become embroiled in some hospital feud held no appeal for him; he had more than enough bother of his own. Could he, however, sit back and let someone cut Cameron to pieces professionally? He had known and respected him too long, and he owed him too much to do that. He must also think of the humble figure who had trusted him with his problem. Didn't he deserve some redress if his wife had really died through incompetence or negligence? His hand paused for a moment on the way to the buzzer.

What if Cameron were guilty? He might get his own loyalties crossed seeking justice for a patient while exposing one of his friends. If that worried him, he might as well bracket himself with those doctors who conspired to hush everything up. Guilty or not, Cameron obviously needed help; and medicine surely meant more than squatting at the head of a couch hearing confessions from self-indulgent neurotics. He punched the buzzer.

"Deirdre, make Mr. Fowler a cup of coffee, and give me a direct line. Oh, and would you get this letter copied?"

She tossed her head in disgust, put his telephone over, then reached for the instant coffee she reserved for the nonpaying patients. If that was how he wanted it, the high rents in Harley Street would soon force them to look for consulting rooms in some East End slum, where he would find plenty of patients like this one.

3

He caught Bob Moulton as he was leaving the front entrance of the Ministry of Health for Waterloo Station and Wimbledon. He could hear him wheeze asthmatically, as though he had just taken the sixteen floors to his office at a run or had gone short of adrenaline for his spray. Moulton, who looked after teaching hospitals, had begged Maclean to treat his wife when no one had seemed capable of pulling her out of postmenopausal depression. If he could help, he would.

"Murdo Cameron—I know him well—what about it?"

"I just wondered if anybody had complained about his work recently. Officially, I mean."

"Now, Gregor, we're very good friends, but you know as well as I do that apart from prize fighters, jockeys and actresses there's nobody more litigious than one of your own profession."

"I'm not trying to damn Cameron, but to help him. And what you tell me will go no farther."

Moulton still sounded dubious. Did security bother them that much at the ministry? His sigh crepitated over the line. "It didn't come from me, but as a matter of record there were two complaints in the past four months. A colostomy in a sixty-year-old man. Seems they omitted to place holding sutures between the mesocolon and the peritoneum, and he died of internal strangulation. Then a woman of forty-one, a heart case with mitral stenosis. The valve might have been handled too strenuously, and she died of heart failure. But I don't need to tell you what these surgical accidents are—it's always difficult to impute fault. We only heard about the complaints unofficially. They didn't get beyond the Dean of the Medical School at Vincent's."

"Why is it then, Bob, that you have total recall on a couple of hairsplitting cases which can happen any day of the week somewhere or other?"

"Simple. In both cases someone in the hospital had written a nice, chatty letter to the nearest relative—unsigned, of course. All the details, all the jargon. They might have been written by Cameron himself in collaboration with the pathologist who did the PM."

"Did he defend himself?"

"Cameron defend himself! He sent everyone to hell and suggested they could take the case to the General Medical Council or the courts. I almost wish they had—

he's a testy old swine. But they didn't. He's so brilliant that he'd have to shoot somebody before they removed his illustrious name from their staff."

Maclean put the phone down and looked at the sketch he had doodled beneath Lady Blye's last words while he was talking; it showed an angular, boyish face with flat cheekbones, a long nose and a shock of hair.

What had happened to Cameron since those days at Edinburgh University Medical School?

He had tutored Maclean in surgery after his own graduation, while he himself was studying for his Edinburgh fellowship to the College of Surgeons. The psychiatrist could still picture him running a piece of thin twine or thread through a waistcoat buttonhole and tying knots, one-handed, with astounding dexterity. "It's the feel and tension, Alec. When you can stitch two bits of tissue paper together with a needle and twine without splitting them, when you can run a seam with a curved needle through a piece of sausage skin without tearing it, when you can peel a grape with a scalpel and not damage the flesh—you're on the way to being a surgeon." His own hands appeared incongruously large in a gangling youth, and he never stopped training them to perform surgical tricks. While he tutored, he would sit picking up pins and various other small objects with a pair of forceps, acquiring an uncanny knack of manipulating these surgical pincers like an extension of his fingers. He gave Maclean hints on passing exams. "What do exams prove, except the ability to pass them?" he snorted. "So never read outside the curriculum. Only tell them what they've told you. Read the books they've been brought up on. They don't want originality; they don't want to know how much you know, only what they themselves know." He himself did brilliantly, leaving Edinburgh with the Lister Gold Medal for surgical research, the Syme Medal for clinical surgery

27

and the Hunterian Award for clinical pathology. A just reward for the long nights he spent alone in the dissecting room, drilling his mind and hand to recognize every piece of flesh and fiber of the human body.

What had happened to Cameron, the humanist with a horror of even essential animal experiments?

Maclean recalled his spellbinding denunciation of Nazi pogroms, one of the final speeches he made in the Edinburgh Union debates. Twenty years in England had eroded the soft edge, had stifled the West Highland lilt and the curious accent; but the psychiatrist could still evoke that voice in his mind. The University of Edinburgh had pleaded with him to remain as a lecturer, but for his own reasons Cameron had turned his back on Scotland. He had rapidly made a name for himself in London Hospital as a surgical registrar, spending his sabbatical and annual leaves in Berlin watching Sauerbruch, and making the pilgrimage to the Mayo Clinic to see the famous surgical circus and men like Judd and Balfour. His contributions to the surgery of the chest, the thyroid, the pancreas and the esophagus appeared in medical journals, gaining him a reputation and one of the consultancies in St. Andrew's Hospital. When he returned from the Middle East after the fighting, he applied for the vacant chair at St. Vincent's and became the youngest surgical professor in the country.

Though Maclean needed no other motive for running to Cameron's aid, he remembered the surgeon's kindness when he himself was hitting the bottle. Cameron had offered him room in his house when he was trying to get over the guilt of his wife's death in a car he had driven when he was too drunk to remember anything; he had also lent him enough to pay his debts while he was breaking the drinking habit. Maclean also felt the strange challenge the man might present—a psychiatric patient who was worth more than all the effete, upper-crust layabouts who left only the impressions of their bodies on his consulting-room couch.

But how to help? He might tackle the surgeon bluntly about Fowler's complaint and reveal the existence of the third letter. That approach, he realized, would invite a proud rebuff. There was no pride like Highland pride. If he took the problem to Dr. Charles Prior, the Dean of the Medical School, he might initiate the sort of inquiry he was hoping to avoid. No, somehow he must spend enough time at St. Vincent's to make his own diagnosis. He knew of one man, at least, who would co-operate at St. Vincent's. But a strange doctor, especially a psychiatrist, wandering around the wards would attract suspicion. Would Paul Fiegler, the consultant psychiatrist, wonder why a colleague was trespassing?

Fiegler? Now, that was a thought.

He picked up the phone and dialed Fiegler's consulting rooms, fifty yards away in Harley Street. In more than thirty years the Austrian Jew had made no concessions to the English language; he had brought the uvular *R* and glottal stop with his light baggage in the late thirties. They fascinated his better clients, though at St. Vincent's, as at other hospitals, they did not care much for Mittel-European psychiatrists and dismissed it as an act.

"Gregor, my dear old chap, what can I do for you? I hear you had a spot of bother recently with some insects."

"Yes, half an hour ago. It was only *Ctenocephalus canis*," Maclean murmured blandly.

"Oh, I thought it was . . ."

"What I said, a dog flea. Or it might have been *Ctenocephalus felis*, the cat flea. And, as you know, I haven't had a dog or a cat on my couch for years."

Fiegler worked his glottis in a chuckle. "The lady in question phoned my secretary."

"I wish you and her much happiness. It's not what I rang about. You know we were discussing your article on group psychotherapy and psychodrama in the *British Journal of Psychiatry*, and you mentioned you had an interesting group going at St. Vincent's. I'd like to sit in on a few sessions."

"We'd be highly honored," Fiegler said. "We have a couple of groups going four days a week. If I'm not there, Thornton, my registrar—he knows your work—he'll take care of you."

Maclean thanked him. Now he had his excuse to get in and out of the hospital. It remained only to square Deirdre, but the mention of Cameron's name would quash her objections.

4

? ?

?

On Monday afternoon Maclean spent two tedious hours sitting through the psychodrama class at which Fiegler presided. All the types conformed with casebook classics: the bluestocking writer of children's stories, who had an innate dread of growing up and of meeting men as well as a skein of repressed sexual desire which no one would ever tease out of her subconscious; the assistant bank manager, his mind sundered by latent homosexuality, who was retreating so far between his ledgers that the figures were holding a dialogue with him and he was losing contact with reality and with his staff; the neurotic divorcée with a history of deprivation, who was desperately trying to hook the fourth member of the group, an American with an Oedipal fixation, which had rendered him easy meat for three previous wives, all of whom had tired of mothering him. Fiegler acted as prompter, confessor and analyst. As the session wore on, his accent grew more glottal and guttural, the eyes, floating behind the pebble lenses, more intense; this, with his pointed beard, black Merino jacket and sponge-bag trousers, stamped him as the most extraordinary if not abnormal member of the group. Maclean only just resisted laughing out loud at him. While he expounded, Fiegler had the habit of curling his quiff of gray hair around his left forefinger; with his right forefinger he was dialing some imaginary telephone number, stopping every now and again as though he were listening to the engaged tone. And he had spent three years on somebody else's couch to rid himself of his complexes! One of these days, Maclean thought, they'll find complexes are as contagious as the common cold.

"Well, what do you think, Gregor?" he asked when the small circle had broken up.

"Interesting," Maclean said evasively. He needed Fiegler. "But they're lifers—people eternally in search of problems. You win this battle with them and they take off for the sound of gunfire somewhere else. Yet I'd like to see how the experiment works."

He made his excuses and escaped, thankful for the flush of wind blowing up from the Thames and for the late-afternoon sun. He had a call to make on the medical superintendent, but before that, he wanted to have a look at St. Vincent's, the environment in which Cameron worked. He had not seen it for five or six years, so Deirdre had obtained the cheap leaflet the governors issued to patients. However, he had no need to refer to that. Any medical man could size up the place from a look at its buildings.

Its nucleus, the three-story, red-brick building, had

obviously begun life as a Poor Law Institution for the Halt, the Infirm and the Destitute of the East End; its penitential architecture and rabbit warren of wards and treatment rooms had invoked the curses of four generations of doctors. "What do I do, hand the porter a silk thread so that I can get out again?" Maclean mused as he strolled around. The late Victorians had made their contribution, an inelegant graft of gray sandstone like an open-ended square, which served as courtyard and reception center. Behind, and to the flanks, buildings of glass and concrete had sprouted as and when the governors had received funds to complete them; these teaching and research units, the surgical block, the microbiology and maternity wings, stood out in bizarre contrast to the older buildings. No one, doctor or patient, had ever broken stride to study or admire the architecture of St. Vincent's.

Maclean took off down the huge concrete corridor that bisected the main building; from this, like nerves from a spinal cord, the wards, consulting rooms and diagnostic departments radiated. It was something of a wry joke among doctors. Often the traffic jammed in this great gallery as food trolleys met staff wheeling patients up and down. Even the kitchen lay off the main passage, not far from the swing doors leading to a pair of operating theaters; the last thing many patients remembered before their enforced oblivion was the tang of ether, iodoform and carbolic mingling with the smell of overcooked roast beef, cabbage and mashed potatoes, a staple item in the diet. More than one accident case had expired in that corridor because the ambulance bay had been sited at the end farthest from the casualty theater and the concrete floor had a pronounced slope.

Maclean recalled headlines about the hospital that must have ruined the breakfasts of its governing board: the operating theater's ceiling that had collapsed during a demonstration to visiting surgeons; this and that ward shuttered against some microbe that had proliferated in the aged bricks and plaster; some row about the shortage of nursing staff or the reliance on immigrant nurses and doctors. One patient wrote to a newspaper to complain that she had to call an Indian nurse to translate her symptoms to an Indian doctor who spoke hardly any English. But, as Maclean well knew, concrete, glass, plastic, sterile wards, electronic diagnostic equipment, well-laundered nurses and doctors, did not make a hospital. That depended on the quality of the medicine and therefore the doctors. And St. Vincent's had several men of international reputation.

Above all, they had Cameron, whose presence Maclean could see wherever he turned in the hospital. Joseph Lister, the great surgical pioneer, had his statue in the forecourt; William Harvey, the great physician, had his around the back square, gazing toward Obstetrics. The psychiatrist wandered into the six-story experimental-surgery block, which Cameron had designed, then financed by barging in to see the Chancellor of the Exchequer. There he noted that Professor Cameron would perform a heart operation in front of a gallery of students the following afternoon, in the Shaldon Theater. Since he had not seen Shaldon, he wandered into the low monolithic building facing Experimental Surgery. This also testified to the surgeon's knack of squeezing money out of people. "I just put a knife to this man's throat, and he coughed up quarter of a million," he joked, with some truth; in fact, he had operated for goiter on Harry Shaldon, the shipowner, who had endowed the block of surgical and teaching buildings. Thyroid Hall, as the wags christened it, contained two of the best operating theaters in Europe, with a superb teaching gallery and two lecture halls into which closed-circuit TV had been run. This was

Cameron's kingdom; students from all over the world came to watch him operate, to hear him expound his technique, or merely to lionize him. The students who elbowed into his sessions soon gave up note taking and just looked and listened; his surgery might have been programed by a computer, yet he could intersperse his work with teaching and comment in that soft, rapid voice. His asides became legends. To one inexperienced house surgeon: "Drop a few bits of tissue on the floor if you like, laddie, but don't lose any organs." To another, holding rib retractors too fiercely: "We're resecting the lung, not bisecting the patient."

Daring and courage characterized his work. Early on, he had thrown his reputation behind cardiac surgery with heart-lung machines and blood-cooling techniques and had pioneered kidney and, later, heart grafting. Much of this he did in the face of opposition from physicians in his own hospital as well as in some of the Royal Colleges. He brought the hospital renown it could never have won otherwise. St. Vincent's might lack the prestige, the tradition, the money, of Guy's, Barts, Westminster or St. Thomas's, but it drew the visitors. It always nonplused the British Council and other bodies who played host to foreign delegations that they insisted on spending a day in that ramshackle environment near dockland. It was Cameron they came to see, often squashing themselves among his gallery of students and peering through the plexiglass dome over the operating table.

Maclean remembered and agreed with Bob Moulton's comment on the third letter and the attempt to dethrone Cameron. "Vincent's without him! It would revert to the overcrowded slum it was before. Nobody's going to fell Cameron with three paper darts tipped with poison."

Maclean finished his tour and made his way back to see his old friend Dr. Joseph Sainsbury.

5

? ?
?

No one ever fathomed exactly how Joe Sainsbury managed to cope with the problems of administering the hospital and the medical school; even he admitted to fumbling through each day, buttressed by copious draughts of black coffee and enough cigarettes to fill three or four ash trays and leave saffron stains on his fingers that pumice stone could not efface. Everyone agreed that he made a brilliant medical superintendent, for he excelled at juggling several crises at once, and emergencies are, after all, the quintessence of hospital work.

He had joined St. Vincent's the day he got his demob papers in 1945 and had married one of the nurses from the obstetrics wing. "Where are Joe and Jean spending their honeymoon?" someone asked. "Probably on a bed in a delivery room," a doctor had quipped. They did, in fact, spend their honeymoon in the hospital, pinned there by a flu epidemic which caused a staff crisis and kept them both working. They merely moved from their hospital rooms into the flat Joe had acquired with the job and forgot about their holiday.

He and his wife knew everything and everyone at St. Vincent's; in the course of a day he could handle several burials, the odd bigwig having treatment, a group of foreign doctors and the often impertinent queries of Fleet Street. His flat overlooked the front courtyard, but as Jean often remarked, it could have sat astride the main corridor for all the privacy they ever enjoyed.

Maclean knew them intimately. He had met Joe at Aldershot during the war, and Jean had been a friend of his dead wife's. As allies in the hospital, he could hardly have chosen better.

When he entered the office, Sainsbury had the telephone wedged between his ear and left shoulder, which allowed him to smoke, take notes, listen and talk. He also mimed his conversation as if the person were sitting in the room. He waved the psychiatrist to a chair, cupping his hand over the mouthpiece and whispering, "I heard you were in the hospital this afternoon—with Fiegler! Don't say the Freudians have finally hooked you."

He turned to the phone, rasping into it as though too many cigarettes had truncated his vocal cords. He shouted, "No, I told you he couldn't go into a general ward—we've nowhere to display the ermine and coronets, and he'll be touting for converts and turning visiting hours into a press conference. Shove him into the empty private room in D Block, and we'll meet the cost out of the contingency account if he must have state medicine." He paused. "No, I don't give twopennyworth of stool samples if he'll like it or not." Banging the receiver into its cradle, he turned to Maclean. "What's this with Fiegler? You can tell me upstairs. Jean has the kettle on and has baked something special for you—against the day when this madhouse brings us screaming to your day bed."

"What's the flap?"

"Lord Blatchford, one of those Socialist peers who thinks he invented medicine for the millions and wants to be seen by the press and TV slumming it in one of our crumbier general wards while he has his stomach out."

"Why Vincent's when he can walk round the corner from the House of Lords to Westminster or Thomas's?"

"Ah, but he wouldn't have anybody but Cameron ply

a knife on him. They're great buddies. He also happens to be on our Board of Governors."

"When's he booked in?"

"A fortnight's time—when he's stoked up his energy on a friend's yacht in the south of France. Why the interest? You don't know him, do you?"

Maclean shook his head, following Sainsbury out of his office, along the main corridor and up the stairs leading to his flat. "Through the air lock," Sainsbury said as they stepped into the space between the double doors. "We had it fitted to stifle the screams and keep out the smell of cold roast lamb and carbolic."

Jean wheeled in a tea trolley. "They told me you were wandering around the hospital."

"I didn't bother to get Deirdre to phone you. I knew she would."

Jean laughed and cut him a slab of fruitcake. "She merely asked me to keep an eye on you, but she did sound worried about something."

"When have I known her that she wasn't?"

"Well, it's mostly about you. I often wonder why you two . . ."

"Jean, would you stop trying to break up a couple of nice people," Joe put in.

Maclean shrugged his shoulders. "I might get round to it one of these days, when you can find me a replacement for the best psychiatric receptionist, nurse, housekeeper and moral conscience in the business. Anyway, my problem can wait. I came to see Joe about his."

"Me? I've got all I want. I've got three hundred and thirty-six beds, and each one of them gives me a pain in my ulcer. What's the new one?"

"Cameron."

"Cameron!" They both echoed the name and gazed at

each other as though it rang like an ambulance bell in their heads. It needed no flash of insight to guess that it occupied much of their conversation.

In silence, Joe welded the glow from the stub of one cigarette to a fresh one; his wife refilled the teapot and bent to straighten the rug, which looked all right to Maclean; through the double doors filtered the boom of some indistinguishable summons on the tannoy. The psychiatrist had met it before, this confused loyalty. Ask any detective about a crime on his own manor, ask any doctor about trouble in his own hospital, and they both felt shamefaced. But go up the road to the next police station or the next hospital and they will spare no detail about the other man's bother. A peep-peep-peep cut peremptorily across their contemplation; it came from the gadget clipped like a fountain pen to the breast pocket of Sainsbury's white coat. He picked up the telephone and transferred whatever crisis had occurred to an assistant.

"Has he been to see you?" he asked, and Maclean shook his head. "Then you've been listening to gossip."

"No," Maclean replied. "Neither here nor in Harley Street. I give your security system at Vincent's full marks."

"Well, what makes you think Cameron's a problem?"

The psychiatrist plunged into a pocket and brought out an assortment of papers, which included restaurant bills, a rates demand and a couple of bus tickets. Smoothing out Deirdre's copy of the anonymous letter, he passed it to Sainsbury, who scanned it earnestly before handing it to his wife.

"A crank," he said. "Somebody who didn't pull senior registrar or consultant, somebody who got the bad side of Cameron."

"And the two previous letters? The same crank? Weren't they taken seriously enough for the dean to emerge from his cabinet and make a visit to the pathology lab?"

Sainsbury threw up his hands. "I'll say this much for you, Gregor—you're lost in your cuckoo country among the head cases and the theatrical hypnotists. You've done your homework—but take it from me, this is some character with a grievance and a twisted mind."

"If it is, he's got his facts right. Somebody made a slip in that operation. And some people say that Cameron is getting very temperamental."

"He's still the surest set of hands in the surgical trade. Go and see for yourself. And if he's temperamental, which of these surgeons isn't? You know the breed better than I do . . . always something . . . they've found God or they'd cut up their kith and kin for a few bob."

"All right, Joe, I can believe you and push off and look after my Harley Street couch with much less wear on my head and feet. But this letter—I know a man in Fleet Street who would pay five thousand pounds for the original and hire a lawyer to stir up trouble, all to fill a few pages of his sheet. Can you imagine it finishing up as one of those official inquiries with copies to the Minister of Health and the House of Commons library?" He paused for a second, then went on. "It could ruin Cameron, which is what worries me. There's one other small point which explains my interest in Blatchford. What happens if Cameron makes a fatal slip there? You can't take that chance."

Sainsbury sat squeezing the cleft of his upper lip between his yellow finger and thumb. It was Jean who spoke. "Joe's trouble is that he likes and respects Cameron, but he still has to think of the hospital. Tell him, darling, and get it off our chests."

"We've had our doubts. Quite a few people have. It's not the letters so much, but he's not the man he was." He stabbed his glowing cigarette at Maclean. "I still say he's better than ninety-nine and ten-tenths of the others, but there you are. He might just have made those mistakes."

"I hope not."

"Don't most of us. We couldn't do without him." Joe walked to the window and watched the traffic through the courtyard. "You've got to have loyalty to somebody or something," he said dejectedly. "It's bad enough to sit by and see that slipway out there in the corridor dropping a quarter of an inch a year with the tread of feet and trolley wheels, and the smog filling this old ruin with hacking coughs, and the outpatients shuffling in and out. Men like Cameron keep this old heap going. And if you want to know how, go and ask him to roll up the legs of his operating pajamas, and look at his varicose veins. He got those standing nine hours a day, six and even seven days a week, cutting and mending for nothing more than his pay packet. He has a lot to grumble about, and he does, I don't doubt. But only with his staff. I've yet to hear him make an unkind remark to a patient, and that must be a record before and since the National Health Service."

"As far as that's concerned, he hasn't changed," said Maclean. Delving into an inside pocket, he produced a wallet as thick as a boxing glove and flipped through its leaves until he unearthed a snap, which he showed to Sainsbury. Twenty-eight years had laid a dull patina over it and pulped the border; still, Sainsbury could make out Cameron, in khaki drill shorts and shirt, with half a dozen R.A.M.C. officers around him.

"Who's that?" Jean asked, peering over her husband's shoulder and pointing at a skinny, bony figure with a serious face under a peaked cap, who sat at the end of the front row.

"That is Captain Alexander Gregor Maclean, whose knees are still pale at that time, but he considers himself

40

the pride of the Nile Delta and a dab hand with hypo needle and mask."

"And I thought you were born plump as a tire ad," Jean exclaimed.

"That happened only when I was taken off K rations and worked myself into the high-calorie bracket. Outside every thin man there's a fat man trying to get in."

"It suits you," she said, meaning it. "I don't care much for paper-clip men."

"Another wodge of cake?" Maclean said, holding out his plate. Both she and Joe were comfortable people who had heard his story, yet could pour themselves a dram without acting furtive.

They studied the snap together. It looked like some school group. Banked behind the doctors sat a good hundred and fifty men. Some leaned on crutches; others wore head bandages and eye patches; a dozen or so occupied wheel chairs or reclined on stretchers.

"Ismailia—isn't it?"

"Right. Most of those men came out of Alamein badly wounded. I only gave the gas, but Cameron lost more than a stone in weight during the fortnight he operated on them. Before they left, they clubbed together and presented him with a silver scalpel they'd had made in Cairo."

"It's still in his desk drawer," Joe said.

Jean broke in. "Gregor, you're staying to dinner. If Joe's still acting the Boy Scout, I'll have to tell you what you want to know myself."

"That's the trouble with living over the shop. They learn as much as we do. What did you want to know, anyway?"

"The answer to three questions. Who took part in the operation on Mrs. Fowler?"

"Easy." Sainsbury listed the members of Cameron's firm.

"Who might have had access to the path reports?"

"Almost everybody—but we might find out who was snooping around without any real interest in the case."

"Who wants to destroy Cameron?"

Sainsbury made a supplicating gesture. "You name them. There are perhaps a dozen in the hospital—though most of them wouldn't booby-trap him in this way."

"All right, let's go back to the operating table that day," Maclean said.

Sainsbury thought for a couple of minutes. "It's not that I don't trust you, but this is all Hippocratic-oath stuff. It mustn't go farther." Maclean nodded, and the medical superintendent continued. "You can rule out most of them right away. The senior theater sister, Miss Donovan, has been with Cameron most of his career and dotes on him. If he cut somebody's throat, she'd explain it away. The house surgeon? He'd never know if he was punched or drilled, and that type of operation would mean nothing. You can forget the technicians."

"So that leaves us Wilkinson, who's Cameron's senior registrar, and the younger theater sister, Holroyd."

"And Rothwell," Sainsbury put in. "He would like to see Cameron topple, even though the old man gave him his chance."

Sainsbury explained that the surgeon had spotted Philip Rothwell as a young houseman; his skill at finding a vein with a hypo needle and his touch with the Magill anesthetic tube had impressed the professor, who made room for him in his firm. In any other branch of medicine, Rothwell would have become a drug addict, but giving gas probably accelerated the process. Like many anesthetists, he had started by sniffing the mask to ensure the cylinders were functioning; then he began to crave the cloudy, euphoric feeling that ether produces. From there it was a step to cocaine and heroin, and, at times, the staff had to conceal that the young anesthetist had as much idea of what was going on as the patient. Cameron had discovered the addiction, sent him for a cure and took a personal interest. However, he soon relapsed.

"Yet he's still on the firm," Maclean said.

"That's one of the old man's troubles—once you're part of his team, you can almost get away with every one of the five A's—Advertising, Alcohol, Addiction, Abortion and Adultery—which are taboo among us." Sainsbury grinned. "Rothwell has managed two so far."

"Which is the other?"

"Adultery. He got friendly with one of Fiegler's psychiatric registrars, a chap called Thornton. He picked up the case notes on a woman who had consulted Thornton —you know, one of those failures-to-consummate. Of course, he realized he was carrying medical treatment a bit far, but he's a bit of a chaser—so he went and knocked on the door and did for this woman what her husband couldn't. What he didn't realize was that she had a guilt complex into the bargain, and when he broke things off, this developed into foaming hysteria. She raved the place down and would have taken the affair to the General Medical Council had Cameron not talked her out of it."

"And he forgave Rothwell again?"

"Oh, he bawled him out and threatened to give him the final heave if he fell out of step another time."

"So, what's his grudge? Why is he biting Cameron's hand? I suppose it's what Fiegler would call 'inverted self-reproach.' "

"Who knows? He's so bent he could have written those letters just for fun."

Maclean spent a few minutes jotting down Rothwell's story. It did not carry him much further, but having treated hundreds of addicts, having been one himself, he appreciated how unpredictable and vulnerable junkies were.

"You can forget Wilkinson, the registrar. He would do time for Cameron—in fact, he's already done more than ten years, and this last year he's taken a lot of stick from the old man and hasn't complained. He could have made consultant somewhere else and he had some offer from the States, but he's stuck it here. God knows why. Maybe he thinks Cameron will relent and offer him a consultancy or a readership."

"Why doesn't he?"

"You ask him. Maybe he's just old-fashioned; maybe he wants to keep Wilkinson with him rather than see him more independent; maybe he knows he needs him. . . ."

"Maybe he wants to hang on to his daughter," Jean interjected. "He dotes on Stroma, who works here as an almoner, as you know. Well, David Wilkinson and she were very keen on each other, and I thought they'd get married. Then they had some quarrel over Cameron and haven't made up. Now, why don't you help them sort that out?"

"I'm not taking on the whole of the Cameron clan— just the tribal chief," Maclean replied with a smile.

"I just didn't want to see that little bitch Holroyd get her claws into him, that's all."

"Where does she come in?"

"She caught David as he fell," Jean said.

"I wouldn't mind breaking my fall on somebody like that." Joe grinned and ducked as his wife lunged playfully at him.

"Joe likes them painted and held together with elastic."

"So does Wilkinson, it seems," Joe shot back.

44

"She's hooked him only because she wants herself a consultant who has a nice private practice."

"In that case," Maclean said, "she might see Cameron as an obstacle."

"She's probably right," Jean replied. "I don't know if she hates Cameron enough to do any plotting, but she's tricky."

"Can we think of any others?" the psychiatrist asked.

"Offhand, only two," said Joe, "though you can imagine he's made quite a few casual enemies through jealousy and his prickly temperament. You know of Sir Kenneth Fairchild, the Professor of Medicine here—well, he's probably his biggest professional rival. That feud began ten years ago when Cameron stampeded the board into backing his research unit. Since then they've drawn blood over kidney machines, heart machines and no organ transplantation. It's the oak and the ivy. But can you think that Sir Kenneth, with all his eminence and authority, would try a trick like this—especially at his age?"

"Yes." Maclean grinned and brought a smile from the others.

"The last name I can give you is Conway-Smith."

Even Maclean raised an eyebrow at the name of one of the most successful surgeons in the country. Ralph Conway-Smith, pillar of the Royal College of Surgeons, shareholder in several private clinics, consultant surgeon to St. Vincent's and other hospitals, had built a reputation as surgeon, medical politician and after-dinner wit. Campaigns for heart and cancer research, this and that medical charity, vied for his services. It did his immense and profitable practice no harm at all when his name appeared prominently in the press, bracketed with some injunction about preventive medicine, an after-dinner quip or an appeal for medical-research funds; he seemed inoculated

45

against the ethical rules that proscribed any form of direct or indirect advertisement. Who would dare strike him off?

"Conway-Smith! How did he and Cameron quarrel?"

"They had a blazing up-and-downer in front of several consultants and lecturers at a clinical meeting. Cameron accused him of never having done a single unpaid operation since the Health Service started—and I believe there's some truth in it. Anyway, they say Conway-Smith, for once, was at a loss for words. He disliked the rebuke and hated being beaten in argument. So he would gun for Cameron."

Joe made several other points. Cameron spent too much time in the hospital, five or six days a week in that small flat. Day and night he handled emergencies that any junior registrar might have done. His holidays he mortgaged to institutions in Britain and abroad, at which he gave lectures or surgical demonstrations. Nobody could survive the sort of schedule he set for himself.

Maclean pocketed his notebook. It seemed that Cameron had made some powerful enemies in and out of the hospital, and they were closing in like hyenas. Not one of the people Joe and Jean had mentioned would have dared challenge him at the height of his skill. Some person—maybe more than one—now believed Cameron so weak as to be vulnerable. Even then they had chosen poison, the coward's weapon. The psychiatrist had to consider, too, the ethical question. If Cameron were a sick man, if he faltered or blundered during operations, he had no right to jeopardize the lives of patients; his mind backtracked to the discussion Joe had held about Blatchford. To a superstitious Highlander like Maclean it almost appeared that fate as well as this hospital clique had lined up against the surgeon.

"Tell us, Gregor, who you think he is—the poison-pen

maniac," Jean said. "Joe and I have racked our minds silly."

"It could be any of them, even some you didn't mention. What about Cameron himself, putting out a disguised shout for help? Stroma, doing the same thing? But I'm not really interested."

"Not interested!" they both said.

"No. As I said at the beginning, Cameron's the problem. I shall leave the poison pen with his own problem, which may be as serious as Cameron's. Anyway, I'm just an old headshrinker with no pretensions to detective work."

6

? ?
?

Maclean arrived early at the Shaldon Theater the following afternoon. The program posted outside the gallery stated that Professor M. F. Cameron would demonstrate an operation for atrial septal defect and pulmonary stenosis, using profound hypothermia on a patient of fifty-eight. The psychiatrist had never witnessed this type of surgery to repair a hole in the wall between the upper heart chambers and relieve a blocked valve; nor had he seen the heart arrested with the aid of an artificial heart-lung machine and blood cooling. If he learned nothing about Cameron during the surgery, at least he would not have wasted his day.

Several groups had already taken their seats in the gallery when the psychiatrist entered; he chose a tier near the front and to the side on which the surgeon would work so that only a couple of yards and the glass dome separated him from the operating table; without declaring himself or fearing detection, he could study Cameron's technique closely and watch his movements. The rows of benches quickly filled until Maclean's corpulent shape became wedged between a middle-aged American, dressed in a sports jacket made from something like artificial coconut fiber, and an intense girl with scrawny frame and sharp elbows.

An old anesthetist himself, Maclean noticed that the patient had an unhealthy blue complexion as they wheeled him in and placed him on the operating table. Under the glass screen, the operating area began to move with figures in green smocks and masks, who looked like scene shifters having a final check on the props. The preliminaries began. Rothwell passed a Magill tube into the patient's windpipe, through which he would feed nitrous oxide and ether; Wilkinson supervised the placing of temperature probes in various parts of the body to keep the surgeon informed about the rate of cooling and rewarming; the junior registrar and the house surgeon were attaching the terminals of the electrocardiogram and the electroencephalogram, which would monitor heart and brain signals; Donovan and Holroyd were checking and counting the instruments and swabs. All of them worked as Maclean would have expected a team trained under Cameron: with telepathic precision. In their green garb they flitted like so many shadows against the pale-green walls. Cameron, the psychiatrist remembered, had painted everything quartermaster green in the Middle East. "White's for lavatories and abattoirs. Green is restful on the mind and eyes when you have to cut and stitch for days on end." This was the team which had also done the operation on Fowler's wife, so Maclean started to sketch what he could of their faces and figures, to scribble his impressions on the margin of his jotter.

48

At two thirty on the dot a rustle ran through the gallery as the swing doors opened and Cameron made his entrance; those at the back craned forward to follow him as he padded in green rubber boots to have a word with Wilkinson. Maclean noticed that his tall figure had a slight stoop, from long hours of bending over operating tables; he could see little under the mask and skullcap but could still complete the face, with its high cheekbones, long nose and aggressive chin. Cameron had the fair, vellum skin of the West Highlandman, reddish hair and eyelashes so white that they conferred a naked, staring look on his curious blue eyes. Downy, fair hair sprouted in tufts over his cheekbones; long ago Maclean had noticed it growing profusely on his wrists and fingers. He wore a white band around his forehead to keep the perspiration out of his eyes, for he sweated freely.

"Ladies and gentlemen." The surgical mask thickened his voice slightly as it issued from the gallery loudspeaker, but it had a clear, lilting resonance. "Some of you will be on textbook terms with the technique of profound hypothermia—what the press has dubbed deep-freeze surgery, as though we were a branch of the meat trade." The audience relaxed, and one or two people chuckled. "This afternoon we are using the Drew machine and internal blood cooling. In the old days—maybe six years ago—we used to give the patients gas, stick them in an ice-water bath and drop their temperature about ten degrees Fahrenheit, which allowed us to isolate and stop the heart. But we kept losing more surgeons and theater sisters through pneumonia than patients through surgery. The instinct of self-preservation—very strong in our profession—has produced this handy machine, which means that now only the patient is at risk." Like every good performer, he changed stride to catch each burst of laughter.

Sitting in that cramped, tense circle of students, Maclean could almost imagine Cameron as a fire-and-brimstone preacher with his Covenanting face and fiery eyes. He had heard him deliver such sermons before; this time, however, he was striving to capture the overtones, to unravel the mental counterpoint.

"Nowadays, with this operation, mortality is one in fifty. In the not-so-old days you could reverse the odds, and many a surgeon who had no more Christian solace carried a rabbit's foot and did only appendectomies on the thirteenth day of any month. They felt they were martyrs in the cause of surgery. They were wrong, of course —their patients were the martyrs." At this the gallery roared, and Cameron waited for quiet before continuing. "You may laugh, but it was no joke, and I can bet that most of the noise comes from those of you who have chosen to practice your medicine across a desk or a laboratory bench. Surgeons are not amused. They know that just as martyrs make the faith and not faith the martyrs, so the patients can make the surgeon." His voice bent upward in a high arc. "Why, I can tell you of one such surgeon who lives not more than ten minutes from here— by Bentley, it goes without saying. This nondescript joined the right societies and ate his dinners in the right clubs—no one of us could fillet a sole like him. By and by, a companion, who happened to be a noble duke, developed a pain in his right side. Acute, in the lower abdomen and causing him to vomit. Appendix, did I hear somebody say? Our hero wasn't sure. He left it for a week, until his friend was raving with peritonitis. No one could have made more Herculean but vain efforts to save his life than our surgeon friend. Since then he has never once looked back. A death cert from a duke means more than a handful of fellowships from the best colleges. Our hero now has hundreds of such certificates and a thriving upper-crust practice without the embarrassing poor."

While Cameron was spellbinding his audience, Wilkinson had made a cut-down into the patient's groin and had inserted one of the plastic tubes from the heart-lung machine.

"I've merely been spinning out time while my staff have been getting on with it," Cameron said. "Now this patient—he's a bad risk and should have been done elsewhere years ago. They were, however, waiting until their mortality statistics had declined to face-saving proportions. X rays and pressure readings tell us he has a couple of holes, and the blood is shunting, without being replenished with oxygen from the lung circuit. You don't need all these readings; just a look at him after he's climbed a flight of stairs will prove how badly he needs surgery. I'll explain the steps as we proceed."

As Cameron positioned himself at the operating table, his staff dropped into place around him, taking their cues like good stage performers. He picked up a scalpel, and Maclean heard the American on his right mutter, "I thought I'd heard everything about this man, but nobody told me he was a southpaw." Even the psychiatrist had almost forgotten that the surgeon cut with his left hand, though he had drilled himself painstakingly to use the right as well.

He drew the surgical knife in a long sweep down the center of the ribs on the breastbone line. "To get into the upper chambers we are going to split the breastbone," he commented into the microphone above his head. In the incision he passed a pliant saw as thin as a knitting needle and worked it behind the breastbone; as he severed the bone, he kept up his commentary about the progress of the operation, the type of anesthesia, the monitoring of the heart and brain. "When we make the heart repair, this man will be clinically a corpse—no heartbeat, no brain activity, no sign of life."

The house surgeon had positioned the rib retractors and was holding them apart to allow Cameron to pare away the flesh surrounding the heart. "All right, sonny, they're not chest expanders," he shouted. "You can always pick the physician from the surgeon by the way they hold a set of retractors, by the respect they have for the flesh." Then, as though unable to resist it, he added, "You can also tell by the way they cut their toenails or darn a sock. I hope some of you up there will be fortunate enough to discover the gift in your hands to become surgeons."

The heart now lay bare, still beating, its veined walls slippery. With great deftness, Cameron tied several stitches into the upper left chamber, drawing them tight and nicking a hole between them, into which he pushed the nozzle of a plastic tube from the machine. "We have completed one circuit now," he said. "We can pump blood from the heart through the cooling system and back into the main artery." He gave the order to start the pumps, then incised the right heart chamber and tied the other pump lead into this. The machine would now cope with the main blood circulation and the flow through the lungs.

The whole theater fell silent as the gallery watched the twin pump motors revolving, their whir punctuated now and again by the voice of the junior registrar intoning the temperature readings as the blood was cooled. From its original rate of seventy-four beats a minute, the heart was slowing visibly. Gradually the peaked curves on the tracing paper recording heartbeats flattened; the four needles scrawling the untidy signature of brain signals had all but stopped quivering.

Even the staff seemed to hold their breath for a moment. No matter how often they had seen the heart halted in its stride, the moment always seemed awesome. Now the organ struggled spasmodically. "Sixty-two degrees," the man on the pump sang out. The heart gave one final convulsion and fell flaccid and still into its chest cavity; moreover, it appeared to diminish in size.

The pumps stopped; Cameron glanced at the clock, knowing he had an hour or less to make good the heart defects before the cooled brain cells might suffer damage. Wilkinson clamped off the great vessels leading to the heart, and the organ then sagged like a burst balloon.

Now they could see how Cameron had drilled his firm to operate with subconscious understanding and faultless precision; the solid thud of the scalpel or forceps into his rubber gloves came over the relay system; the wordless communication produced the right surgical needle, swab and sucker at the right moment. As he and they toiled, Cameron annotated each stage of the surgery with rapid commentary, throwing in from time to time the bizarre irrelevancy, and sometimes showing flashes of his temperament with the staff.

He was talking again, jabbing the point of his scalpel toward the inert heart to emphasize some detail. "Wilkinson, how the devil can I teach and how can they see when your big head's in the way?" The registrar moved smartly away, and Cameron went on. "There you are—perhaps the greatest battleground of all between the physician and the surgeon. I think we can say that we won this one. Didn't we prove to them, the physicians, the poets, the priests, that it wasn't the great spiritual center, the seat of the emotions, the vital force? Don't believe them, that it has a soul. I've witnessed a lot of knife work in the past thirty years, and I've yet to see one scalpel blunted on a soul. Now, the physicians have moved on to the brain and what we can't do about that. We'll see, in a few years, we'll see. Oh, there were some God-fearing surgeons, too, who thought the heart would beat us. But you can see what's happened to this heart. Even with a tear in it and one blocked valve it has still carried a man through for fifty-eight years. Work that out at seventy times a minute."

He ran the point of his knife down the right chamber, opening a long wound, and pulled back the thick muscle to expose the right upper chamber; he slipped his gloved index finger inside to explore the defects.

"We have two holes, each about the size of a shilling," he announced. "The pulmonary valve is nearly closed. So we shall first close the holes and then relieve the valve."

His big hands had a couple of square inches in which to handle the forceps holding the tiny, curved needles; each stitch had to be double-tied and cut close to the knot without damaging the delicate tissue of the inner heart wall. Yet, within five minutes, Cameron had knotted the final stitch and raised his head to call for the dilating forceps he would use to open the sealed lung valve.

Perhaps no one else in the gallery noticed; the whole incident could have lasted no more than twenty seconds. Maclean himself would have thought no more about it had he not had a copy of that letter in his pocket, had he not come to the hospital questing after some sign of its truth.

Cameron reached for the scissor handles of the forceps which Donovan pushed toward him; his stretched thumb and middle finger missed the holes; they slipped and landed on the patient's chest before the surgeon retrieved them with his right hand. "Clumsy idiot," he muttered, though it was not clear whom he was admonishing. Maclean observed Wilkinson and Holroyd glance at each other and the registrar give a slight shake of his head.

Brusquely Cameron swung around on the registrar and passed him the forceps. Then he turned to face the gallery. "I've kept this little surprise for my registrar. It's some time since he's had the chance of showing off his

54

skill in front of an audience. He's as good as I am—almost. And, of course, if he does anything wrong, I take the rap. That's the great thing about surgery—the patient never knows." His voice dropped, and he seemed suddenly weary. "I shouldn't really put these ideas into your heads, ladies and gentlemen, but one of my colleagues lost his touch years ago, though he kept the confidence of his patients. So nowadays they see him in the consulting room—they see him by the operating table before they pass out and he disappears round the side screens like some magician's assistant—they see him in the recovery room when they're just able to read his bill and sign a check."

He turned to Wilkinson, who had inserted the forceps into the heart valve. "Take it steady until you feel the valve leaves giving." Thereafter, he allowed Wilkinson to complete the surgery inside the heart and close the various wounds, contenting himself with explaining the procedures and the rewarming and revival of the patient.

When the registrar had finished, someone pressed a buzzer in the gallery, indicating that he wanted to ask a question. He looked like an Indian postgraduate student. He said, "Would the professor be good enough to be making us aware of the postoperative complications? I am considering the consequences of surgical lesions of the atrioventricular node with resultant Stokes-Adams syndrome, ventricular fibrillation or other cardiac arrhythmias."

"I am sure," said Cameron caustically, "that some of us would welcome an English translation of that and every other bit of dog Latin in medicine. We do, certainly, damage the timing mechanism of the heart once in a while, and in this and other cases of heart failure we can drive the organ with a pacemaker until the scars have healed. Any more questions?"

No one else dared put another question. With a nod to the gallery, the surgeon strode out of the theater, pulling down his mask and reaching behind him to undo the tapes of his smock. Although Wilkinson might spent another hour finishing the operating drill, the gallery began to spill downstairs, leaving Maclean and a dozen others on the benches. They had come to watch Cameron, and the psychiatrist listened to the murmurs of disappointment that the surgeon had not undertaken the whole of the operation himself.

When Maclean looked back on the whole affair, he realized that he could have read almost everything into that piece of surgery and Cameron's behavior; he had missed none of the clues—the mixture of phobia and contempt for physicians, the flight of ideas and the zigzagging thought process, the irritability and, above all, the way in which the surgeon froze at the crucial moment in the operation. Later he would chide himself for missing nothing and yet missing everything. However, at this moment, sitting in the gallery reflecting on what he had just witnessed, he felt that Cameron was suffering from some form of mental illness. But he had watched too many patients fool their psychiatrists to put a label on it—manic depressive, hysteric or whatever. It did seem, though, the the poison-pen writer was not far wrong, that he had also spotted the weakness and was going to exploit it.

7

? ?
?

Following his chief's abrupt departure, David Wilkinson toiled through the afternoon; now, as he waited for Donovan to carry out the counting of the instruments and swabs, he realized how exhausted the effort had left him. The surgery itself had presented no problems—a simple hernia and a partial gastrectomy. The incident during the teaching session had, however, unnerved him, heightened his concern about Cameron and forced him to question his own relationship with the professor. Unless he was misreading the situation, Cameron was showing every sign of cracking up. Frozen hand, they called it. "You'll likely have to take over the professor's list tomorrow," Donovan said, as he dragged himself out of the theater. He nodded, cursing himself for his acquiescence. He should pack up and clear out of this dump while he had the chance.

In the shower room he kicked off his rubber boots, tugged off his pajamas and underclothing and focused the needle spray on his head and body; the water sluicing over him did little to blunt the edge of his tension and bleak mood. Yes, he had said. He would act as Cameron's stand-in, his stooge for the next week, the next year, the next decade, until the great professor picked a younger, keener and—he had to be honest—smarter registrar. Then he would finish up in some scrubby hospital, whipping out stomachs and repairing hernias and doing the broken-leg list. Thirty-two years gone and he was earning just about enough to pay his board and lodgings here, run a car and buy his girl dinner now and then. His mood switched ambivalently from reproaching Cameron to excusing him. Couldn't the old man at least have offered him one of the teaching jobs within his gift or put him up for a consultant post here or somewhere else? Instead he was treated like some soppy-eared house surgeon in front of a student gallery. Even when he handed him the knife at the moment of truth, he did it with that bloody-minded condescension, that master-and-gillie touch. But could he really blame Cameron? His bosses had ridden him hard, had abused his talent; he had been forced to take it much longer than registrars did today. Even now he was earning little more than double the wages of a senior registrar, and no one ever caught him cribbing about money. If he had chosen to quit this slum, he could have pulled in twenty times more in the open market and probably earned himself a knighthood for services to some Royal or cabinet minister. He had to go and flout authority, parade his principles. Wasn't that why he admired him, because he never compromised with his ideals or his integrity? As a house surgeon and a junior and senior registrar, David had encountered the best and the worst in medicine—the slick and the careless, the incompetent and the negligent. He had witnessed colleagues lie and trick patients or their relatives, seen them take refuge behind medical gobble-dygook in the coroner's court. Whatever had happened to Cameron recently had not impaired his honesty. He remembered that old pauper on whom they had performed surgery to clear an abdominal obstruction. At best, she had a couple of years to go, yet Cameron had risen at three in the morning when his registrar could have coped. The surgical swab they had forgotten was the sister's fault, not his. But he had done the second operation, then confessed to the old woman that *he* had made a mistake and she should demand compensation. She had got it, too. Three hundred pounds.

If he, Wilkinson, found himself acting as Cameron's spare hand or his errand boy, he was learning his profession as nobody else could have taught him. He had been a raw houseman; now he was a competent surgeon. He had once chafed at dissecting other people's mistakes in the post-mortem room. "Post-mortems don't lie the way we do," Cameron had told him. "And they teach you humility." From the surgeon he had learned the techniques of teaching at the operating table and in the lecture room, the method of dealing with difficult or frightened patients, the whole art of medicine.

And he had a closer, more personal relationship with Cameron than anyone else in the hospital, even Donovan. In fact, Cameron treated him more like the son he had never had than as a member of his firm. He had no side; it didn't bother him that David's father had been a farm hand and his mother had to rely on her widow's pension. He did nothing much to put more money his assistant's way, either. At one time the registrar could have sworn that Cameron counted on him to marry Stroma, but if he had heard of their quarrel, if he knew the reasons for it, he never mentioned the subject. Perhaps it was better that way, for he had the same love-hate relationship with the daughter.

He turned the shower to cold and gritted his teeth as the icy water hit his neck. He stepped out, blaming his mood. He would have found fault with anything and anyone after that session. He dressed and strolled to the canteen, where he sat for a quarter of an hour sipping a beer and listening to the complaints from other departments of the hospital. He was crossing the central corridor toward his small flat when he saw Stroma emerge from a side passage. It was too late to avoid the confrontation; she had caught sight of him and called his name. He waited for her, watching her slender legs swinging under the white coat, the high set of her head and the reddish hair.

"If you stand in this corridor, you're bound to meet everybody that matters, they say. Well, they're wrong. You're the exception. Unless you're avoiding me."

"No," he lied. "I was on the way to X ray to have a look at tomorrow's plates," he added, compounding the lie.

"Can I offer you a cup of tea—or a drink?"

"Sorry, I haven't got time," he said stonily.

"I have a book to give you," she said. "My office is on your route, and it'll take only a minute."

He could hardly refuse, so he dropped into step with her. He remembered the first time he had walked along this corridor with her, the young house surgeon showing the prof's teen-age daughter the hospital. As a schoolgirl she had come to tour the new experimental wing, then Cameron's big obsession. Donovan had fitted a white coat over her school uniform, and she had marched around with her father, embarrassing some of the research surgeons with her questions. "Where do you get these animals? Why do you have to kill them? Where do you bury them? How do you know they're never in pain?" And so on. Halfway around, Cameron had to take an emergency call to one of the theaters and turned to his new house surgeon. "You do the rest, Wilkinson, then take my daughter to the canteen and buy her some tea or orange juice. She likes those ginger buns with icing on top."

Her father gone, Stroma darted back to the animal wing, where she halted before a cage with a solitary guinea pig inside, its pink nose vibrating against the wire mesh. "I can't leave him here; he looks so dejected. I'm sure they guess what's happening to them."

"It's either them or the patients," David remarked.

"But you can tell the patients," Stroma replied. "Do you think I could smuggle him out without my father seeing him?"

"You'll get us all shot."

She paid no heed to his objections but rounded on the technician who hovered in the background. "Can you get a box big enough for him and open the cage?"

"But we're using him as a control in an important experiment to test reactions to a new anesthetic," the man stammered, appealing to David for support; he only nodded to signify that he must carry out Miss Cameron's instructions. So they marched to the canteen bearing the wooden box with breathing holes for the animal, which Stroma had bedded down in cotton wool and surgical swabs. She reveled in the fact that she had beaten the system, especially with the criminal collusion of a young doctor.

"What's your name?"

"Wilkinson."

"Your first name?"

"David."

"I shall call him Dauvit—that's the Scots version of your name." She thrust a crumb of sugared bun through the ventilation holes. "He'll be much happier in the country than doing research in anesthetics."

No one would have called her pretty, he thought. However, when some bright idea lit up her face, it assumed a quality that intrigued and pleased him, a look of beatitude which lent it great attraction for him.

"Why does my father keep calling you Wilkinson?"

"It's the normal thing for professors to do with junior staff."

"Well, I don't care much for it. You know he called me

Stroma for some remote little island in northern Scotland because he said nobody else would have the name, and it would make me feel more individual. He's not very consistent, is he?"

A few days later David was scrubbing up when Cameron joined him; the surgeon flipped over his antique egg timer, which gave him four minutes to ply his hands with the stiff bristle brush while the sand ran through. Only during this ritual would he discuss subjects other than the impending operation.

"Wilkinson, did you connive at or condone the theft of an experimental animal from the new wing?"

"Yes, sir."

"I've a good mind to give you three months' solitary in the dissection room. Why did you let her talk you into it?"

"Your daughter's a very forceful person, sir."

"Don't I know it. She buttonholes every surgeon I bring home, whether they're Arab, Jew or Gentile—and some of them are gods in their own countries—and d'you know what she does? Duns them for a contribution to the antivivisectionists. Some of them cough up as though they were buying a wreath for themselves. I thought you'd know better."

David was eying the sand and waiting for the second that Cameron would finish scrubbing up and he would escape further interrogation. As the surgeon shook the water off his hands—he performed this maneuver as though he were tossing the tension out of his wrists and fingers—he muttered gruffly to the house surgeon, "She got at me as well. Said you had a name, it was David and I should address you by it in future. Don't be surprised if I forget from time to time." Forget he did when anything went amiss in the theater or outside it.

Stroma had often visited the hospital during her period at Oxford and invariably met David with her father.

62

Then Cameron invited him down several times to their cottage near Dorking, sending them tramping over the downs or bullying them into helping him weed his rose beds or shrubs. David often wondered how he had managed to fall in love with Stroma and not realize it. He had met many more attractive women; he had seduced some and been seduced by others; many a nurse he had dated could have given her points in social grace and light conversation. But in her he found the sorts of qualities that had kept him at the old man's elbow all those years. She had his directness, his integrity, his intelligence, even his nose, with its kinked bridge. They had strength, these Camerons. The surgeon, he knew, had beggared himself to put her through finishing school and then Oxford; for her part, Stroma would have made any sacrifice for her father.

It had flattered David when she came down from Oxford with a good degree to take a poorly paid job at Vincent's; he assumed she had chosen the hospital because of him, but then she hadn't told him that she thought Cameron was "losing the place." In some ways it was the best time of his life. They met almost every day and spent many of their evenings together. One of these days, he thought, I'll pull reader or consultant, then we can set up a home. It never entered his head that she would refuse him, just as he had never thought of making love to her until they were married. It might have been better if he had, boss's daughter or not. He had assumed too much, but not that a stupid quarrel would split them, and their pride and obstinacy keep them apart.

It had all begun the day, two months before, that Dr. Harvey M. Judson, well-known American Professor of Clinical Surgery, was passing through London and had dropped in to see Cameron and watch one of his operating sessions.

"Murdo," he had said afterward, "I won't chew the fat with you about it, but I like the style of your young associate—cool, good hands and good eye. He'd make a good associate professor you-know-where if he had a mind to."

Cameron had laughed. "He's over thirty and open to offers." That had hurt, too, the idea that Cameron could dismiss ten years in a phrase.

"What's he getting?" Judson had asked.

The surgeon translated it into American money. "Just over a hundred dollars a week, out of which he has to pay his hospital flat and board. That way we keep them single here and keep their minds on surgery."

When Judson had approached him, David had expressed his reluctance to leave St. Vincent's but agreed to consider any proposition which came from him. He had received the offer from Judson in writing—five times his present salary, with a flat thrown in. "And we do not share Professor Cameron's views about the celibacy of our associate professors," Judson had scrawled as a postscript. It was too good to reject.

He had run straight to Stroma in her office, flourishing the letter. "It's great news, isn't it?"

"Yes, it is, David," she had said quietly.

"Read the last bit."

"I've read it."

"Don't you see what it means? We've got enough to get married on, we have a flat and I have a big job." He noted her change of expression, then smiled. "I'm sorry, darling, I was forgetting the time-honored touch." He took her in his arms and kissed her. "Will you marry me and come with me to America a month from now?"

"Do we have to make up our minds now—right this minute?"

"Of course not. I can accept tomorrow."

She looked at him very seriously. "Yes, I think probably you should go," she said.

"What does that mean?"

She pulled clear of him, walked to the window and gazed out at the surgical block. "What will happen to him?" she murmured.

For a moment he did not understand the import of the question; then it dawned on him. "You mean, your father?" She nodded. "But he doesn't depend all that much on me. He told Judson as much, and you should hear him when I drop a stitch."

"You know what he is; he'd never admit it. But he needs both of us."

Finally he had grasped what she was trying to say. "You mean that you don't want to leave him. That's it, isn't it?"

Stroma nodded. "It's not that I don't want to—I can't. Maybe you haven't noticed it, but he's getting old all of a sudden."

"I hadn't noticed it that much."

"Well, I have. He's clumsy when he used to be so precise in everything, and he forgets things that he shouldn't. I don't know what he's like in the operating theater, but there are whispers. David, I'm frightened."

"You needn't be. I've heard the gossip and know about the complaints. I work with him, and he can still cut the print off a page and take out a stomach by touch if you blindfolded him. Maybe he's got a touch of the jitters, but he'll get over that. Anyway, we'll be—what?—only ten hours from here if he needs us."

"But he needs us now—every day," Stroma replied. "I'd never forgive myself if I left him now. Don't you see that?"

"No, I don't, Stroma. I think you've got to make up

your mind to live your own life, even if your father's as bad as you think."

"Don't say that, David. You make it sound like some sort of choice between you and him."

"And if it were?"

"It's an unfair question. You know I love you both."

"But obviously him more than me."

"It's not true—it's just that he depends on me more than you do. You know what he's like. He's never asked anything from anybody in his life. He's not the asking kind." She faltered, then went on. "If I said I was going, he would give us both his blessing. He might be crying inside, he might think I was deserting him, but he wouldn't try to stop us. But there's nothing to stop you."

"That's another way of saying you don't give a damn whether I go or stay."

"It's your own decision."

"And you wouldn't try to persuade me to stay?"

"No."

"You talk about him—you're both cut from the same strip of tartan. I suppose you think I'm deserting him as well, though, of course, you would never say so. Whatever you think and whatever he thinks, I'm going." And he banged the office door shut, walked to the canteen, bought a bottle of whisky and got drunk in his flat. When he sobered up, he began to write his letter of acceptance to Judson, but he never got beyond the first paragraph. Something halted him. Was it his debt to Cameron or the fear of confronting him with news of his defection? Was it because he might carry a sense of disloyalty with him or the fact that he might lose Stroma for good if he went? His enthusiasm had volatilized. He knew he would feel lost working with anyone else. He had worked so long and so closely with Cameron that it seemed to him he had absorbed not only his technique and his teaching but his moral conscience as well. Finally, he did finish the letter, but it asked Judson for time to ponder the move. They had replied that they would hold the job open for him.

Since the day of their quarrel, he had avoided meeting Stroma, refusing her father's invitations to the country and staying away from the hospital corridors. She had rung him several times, but he had made his excuses—he was too busy. Now he was cursing himself for bumping into her.

They had reached her office. Once there she turned and said simply, "David, I'm glad you didn't go."

Yes, she had got her way; she had kept him where she wanted him. "I'm still giving it a lot of thought," he replied. "You said you had some book."

Stroma opened a filing cabinet and produced an old tome, rather like a family Bible, with leather binding and tooled gold lettering. "Remember how hard you searched for this?" She smiled and handed it to him. "I had the librarian advertise for a copy six weeks ago, and it came this week."

David took the book, an early edition of an eighteenth-century textbook on brain surgery, which he had vainly tried to buy in London. She was trying to bribe him, he thought. For a moment he hesitated between the desire to hurt her by denying all interest in the book, and the pleasure of possessing it. He could hardly insult her by rejecting it.

"They made me pay through the nose for it," she said.

"How much?"

"For an almoner, half a week's pay."

"I'll have to owe you the money in that case. I'm just about smashed."

"Look at the flyleaf," she urged.

It read, "From Stroma to David."

"All you've got to do is say thank you and make sure my father doesn't spot it or he'll steal it from you."

"No, I can't accept it as a gift. I'll pay you for it," he said curtly. He wanted no more condescension. "How much did you say?"

"If you want to know, nine pounds. And in case you hadn't guessed, it's a bribe."

"Oh!"

"They're doing Prokofiev's *Romeo and Juliet* with the Leningrad Ballet at Covent Garden, and I wondered if you wouldn't like to take me. I shall feed you at my flat if you buy the tickets."

He would have enjoyed the ballet and the night out with her. But he, too, had his pride. "Sorry," he muttered. "I'm at the end of a perpetual queue of surgical cases and can't see a free night for weeks. Anyway, I don't feel like watching the Romeo of Omsk and the Juliet from Nizhni Novgorod with snow on their pumps. Thank you all the same."

Stroma did not recognize the slight. She noticed the sag of his shoulders, the tired gray eyes, the slow response. For a moment her imagination dwelled on an assembly line of patients inching their way through the operating theaters, each making this or that defect a mute but compelling demand on David's energy, each taking his toll. It had happened to her father. This great vocation they talked about had worn him down; it was doing the same to David.

"They're working you too hard," she cried. "Shall I speak to my father about getting somebody to relieve you?"

"No, damn you," he shouted, surprised by his own vehemence. Even in his present overwrought state, Cameron would listen and comply. David could not admit to Stroma that the past two months had convinced him that

Cameron's grip was loosening; he might have divulged what had happened only four hours ago during the teaching session.

"Couldn't you at least arrange to swop with someone else for one evening?" she pleaded.

He thought for a moment. "All right, I'll try, and let you know." He turned to quit the office, but some instinct made him pause, look at her and say, "Do you think you could persuade your father to go away for a month or two? He needs a rest, much more than I do."

She shook her head sadly. "I've tried, but he won't listen."

8

? ?
?

In his flat David threw himself on the divan, splaying his feet out in an attempt to relax. His mind, however, still reeled out the afternoon drama like a film playback; his encounter with Stroma had also unsettled him. He glanced at the textbook she had bought him, but his concentration lapsed, and his thoughts hopped about like a hunted flea. His eyes fixed for a moment on the bedside telephone, flickered away, then returned. He could call the nurses' wing; she would have dressed by now and would have forgotten he had told her he was too flaked to see her tonight. He needed her, or something to blunt his obsession with Cameron and his daughter. If he had followed his heart, if he had gagged his perversity, he would have accepted Stroma's offering and her invitation with good grace instead of compelling her to beg. His eyes rested once more on the phone. Why, when he met Cameron's daughter or thought about her, did his baser emotions always rise to the surface? Why did it always stir his lust for another girl, for Patricia Holroyd? On an impulse he grabbed the phone and dialed the call box in the nurses' wing. Of course, she whispered breathlessly, she could come straightway.

Her scent washed away the moist, hot odor of antiseptic, the cloying tang of anesthetic and the memory of his own spent breath behind the surgical mask; her dress, a flimsy print sheath, fitted tightly around her breasts and thighs, which he felt pressing against him; the dreamy, erotic light in her eyes reminded him of the first night when they had returned, fuddled, to this flat and made love. She slipped out of his arms and pulled the curtains to, then squirmed expertly out of her dress and undergarments. Pat Holroyd had long ago dispensed with the verbiage, the preliminaries, the finesse, the hypocrisy of love-making; for her, only the simple, pleasurable act mattered. Like a good meal or a warm verbena bath. She knew how to handle David; she was sure of him, though at this moment the ferocity of his passion surprised her. What had upset him? Only two things that she could imagine. As he lay slack and spent beside her, she said, "I saw what happened in theater this afternoon. The old man forgot where he was for a minute. I thought the show wasn't going to go on."

"He gave me a scare, too—I admit it," David grunted.

"Well, don't let it worry you, darling," she murmured. The textbook still lay on the table; she picked it up, thumbed it open at the flyleaf and peered at the inscription in the half-light. "You saw the Lady Bountiful today, then?"

"For a minute, but we can forget that as well, I hope."

That suited Pat Holroyd, who in any case hardly reckoned Stroma a rival. What could David or anybody else see in that virginal bluestocking? In Sister Holroyd's book, culture amounted to no more than a smear of polish over the primitive flesh, something that could be removed by hot breath and friction. She smiled at her analogy. David was too much of a man to turn silly over some sexless Puritan, even if she was Cameron's daughter.

But the professor. Now he struck her as a more dangerous rival. In the months she had known David intimately, she discovered that she could predict almost exactly how he would react to any situation. It had been fairly easy to seduce him, to establish the sort of possession over him that was better than love. But marriage was something else. Had he worked for anybody other than that clansman with his tribal ideas, they would have been well and truly married by now. Why did he feel he must have his boss's permission, like some army subaltern seeking the commanding officer's sanction? And why didn't he face Cameron with the facts? His absurd devotion to that crude Scotsman, who seemed to have mortgaged his mind and body, she completely failed to comprehend; she wondered at times what part of David she could claim. Their only quarrel had arisen when David had left her standing alone at a party because Cameron had summoned him for some phony emergency, and she had accused the surgeon of trying to break up their relationship.

She admitted Cameron's brilliant gifts as a surgeon and teacher; she did not object to sharing her boy friend with medicine and surgery. Not, however, with some professional idol. His own talents would lift him to consultant, with her assistance. As talented as Cameron and affluent as Conway-Smith—that was the picture her imagination painted. To achieve it, David must quit this rat race of a Health Service hospital, spend a year in America and return as a consultant with a Harley Street address.

"I've got news for you," she said. "Just before I left the theater tonight, Donovan asked me to do her a favor and join Frankland's team in neurosurgery."

"She might have mentioned it to me," David replied. "Did she say why they wanted you?"

"They've lost somebody over there, and I'm filling the vacancy for two months. Those twelve-hour operations!"

"You needn't go. I'll have a word with Donovan and cancel the transfer."

"No, don't do that," she said quickly.

"I'd like to know why, anyway. They're overstaffed in neurosurgery."

"Well, that old bitch won't tell you the real reason. If you want to know, I think she's just a frigid old hag who hates having pretty nurses around her beloved boss."

"I've never seen Cameron look beyond their yashmaks."

He must not suspect anything. She had disclosed as little as she dared and hoped that if David approached her, Donovan would not reveal that she had sacked her for tittle-tattling and spreading the rumor that Cameron was finished as a surgeon. She could settle that score along with the others. However, she noticed that David seemed perturbed by the changes in the firm.

"Why don't we take the car and drive out to that dockland pub and get away from this barrack for a couple of hours?"

David nodded abstractedly.

The pub had filled up and overflowed into the garden, which ran down to the Thames. Pat seated herself with careless grace, which hoisted her dress a few inches and showed half her thighs. She liked watching men pause, their beer halfway to their lips, and glance covertly, running their eyes from her sandals upward; she enjoyed reading the sensations imprinting themselves on their faces; it tickled her vanity especially to see the hard, reproachful stares their girls threw at them. David arrived with the drinks. For good measure she kissed him; very lightly and tenderly, she fancied.

"You're still worried about this afternoon," she said.

"I just wonder how many people noticed, that's all."

"Everybody, I should think. It was so obvious. I thought he looked drunk, or drugged. So did some of the others, except Rothwell, of course."

David shook his head. "Alcohol doesn't worry him—it's for pickling specimens. And pills are for people with weak wills."

"We're kidding ourselves, David. Remember that woman he did the vagotomy on? He lost the place there, too. I know. I pushed that scalpel into his hand, and it felt as though there were no fingers in his glove. It was weird."

"It could have happened to anybody."

"But today was the second time. And remember the woman died, and now they say there's a third letter gone to the Board of Governors about him."

David looked at her incredulously. "That's a bad joke, Pat." She shook her head. "Then where did you hear this?"

She hesitated. To reveal the truth would start him asking questions, arouse his suspicions. "It was only gossip," she said.

"No, people don't invent stories like that. Who told you?"

"Nancy Millard," she lied.

"You mean the one who does private work in the King Square Clinic—the nurse Rothwell was sweet on?"

"Him and a few others. Nancy's an open-minded girl who doesn't remember names too well. She was probably mistaken about the letter."

David fell silent. If a third patient were involved, even the cautious Prior couldn't shrug it aside as another academic trifle. Fairchild and a few others might demand an official inquiry, which could end in Cameron's humiliation and perhaps finish him as Professor of Surgery. Of course, he would resign if they brought enough pressure to bear, and that would cause some gloating in the top dining room at Vincent's. In all his years of collaboration with Cameron he had never once penetrated the opaque shield the surgeon had constructed around his personality; but he knew his Highland character would never allow him to accede to any such inquiry. David felt powerless; he, too, had read the post-mortem report and realized that a case might be made for negligence.

"They can't prove it," he muttered, as though trying to convince himself. "It's a smear campaign. But some of the muck is sticking, and it's having an effect on him. He seems almost afraid to cut these days."

The girl at his side was already several moves ahead of him in her reasoning. If Cameron foundered—and she could imagine no other outcome—he would drag David down with him. She had met this kind of scandal before; hospitals always risked them, and many doctors became adept at concealing their mistakes. But nobody would welcome a young surgeon, however talented, who had allowed himself to get involved in some inquiry into professional negligence. No matter what the verdict. As she sipped her gin and tonic, she was envisaging one way David could escape. Hadn't she advised him to keep Judson's offer open? The moment had arrived to remind him of that offer. Sometimes bright young men with tunnel vision, like David, needed a nudge in the right direction.

"Darling, it's a crumby old hospital, and the doctors and surgeons will go on fighting while you do the real work. You know what I think? You should find that letter from Professor Judson and wire him to say you've now considered the offer and will come."

"I'll think about it," he said.

She squeezed his arm and gave a winsome smile. "Let's go back and listen to that old Sinatra record," she whispered. Even when enticing him to make love, she had to guard against offending his sense of honor. They would hear the first two or three numbers before she had coaxed him once more onto the divan; at least she could obliterate the image of Cameron that way. Sister Holroyd had enough experience to appreciate that passion and love shared the same bed for most people, though she herself never confused the two feelings; love would never interfere with her calculations. As they drove back, she was praying that Fowler's husband was acting on that letter and Professor Murdo Frazer Cameron would soon cease to matter in her scheme of things.

9

On his way to the Department of Psychological Medicine, Maclean found himself confronted by Cameron. Before he could dart into a branch of the main corridor, the surgeon had bawled his name and come striding toward him, hand outstretched. The emergency light clipped on his pocket glowed red, and he was obviously making tracks for a telephone or his office in the east wing to answer a summons.

"What the blazes are you doing here, Alec? Don't tell me. I understand you're sitting in on some quack experiment with that fellow Fiegler." He drew the psychiatrist confidentially, almost furtively, toward the glazed brickwork flanking the corridor, out of the traffic stream. "You haven't joined *them*, have you? No, you'd be the last person in the world. That chap attracts all the queers and pimps in the country to Vincent's with his psychodrama séances. They're no more than sex clubs, and he's the kinkiest member. You're staying at the hospital for lunch? Right then, come along just before one to my office, and I'll introduce you to some really interesting types. Sorry, I've got to rush now, find a phone and ask who's lighting up this infernal gadget that's burning a hole in my pocket."

On he marched, and to his amazement the psychiatrist noticed a cat drop into a running step behind him, its tail oscillating like a pennant, its head and eyes fixed on the tall figure who swept doctors, nurses and trolleys aside as he beelined down the middle of the corridor. No connoisseur of cats, Maclean nevertheless could admire this one —a tawny, velvety Siamese with jade legs, head and neck, around which it sported a tartan collar. He guessed that Cameron and his cat must have become one of the everyday sights of the hospital, since no one even turned his head at the incident.

He mentioned the cat to Fiegler. "Oh, yes, it goes everywhere with him, even into the operating theaters at times. It's a sort of—how do you say?—talisman." Cameron, it seemed, had rescued the cat from his own Experimental Surgery Department; someone had bought it from a cat thief, and a research worker had intended to sacrifice it in some experiment to assess the value of certain forms of leucotomy. The professor happened to visit the department that morning and got into the lift with a technician and the animal; between the first and fourth floors it had chafed its lissome body against his legs, then leaped impudently into his arms and licked his eyebrows. "They can't kill an animal like this," Cameron said to the technician, and the astonished man saw the professor about-turn and transport the cat toward his own office. Although he had fought hard for the grant to build his research wing, Cameron detested animal experimentation and, had he not realized its value in saving human life, would have come down emotionally on the side of the antivivisectionists.

"I sometimes speculate quietly about that relationship," Fiegler said, dialing like mad. "It's a common thing —cat fetishism."

"You must be joking," Maclean replied, containing himself. "Cameron a cat fetishist?"

Fiegler nodded. "You know how it is—his mother probably wore a velvet dress—he felt it on his body—it became an object of veneration, then sexuality. No, I can understand it quite well—it's not all that rare."

No wonder his trade kept the music halls and TV comics in business, Maclean thought. The pure Freudians would have him if he didn't watch out. Shortly before one o'clock, he broke loose and strolled over to Cameron's office. The secretary, a woman of fifty-odd, sat him down and announced that the professor would arrive in several minutes. Barely had Maclean settled himself than he heard the door handle click; before he could swivel his head, the cat had sprung onto his lap. It must have opened the door by standing on its hind legs and turning the knob with its paws. The animal sat staring up at him with those astonishing blue eyes, which squinted slightly;

he watched warily for the first sign of tail threshing, but instead the creature clawed over his lapels, put out a tongue as rough as sandpaper and licked his thick jowls. At that moment Cameron entered.

"I see you've made a friend," he said. "You know, Napoleon used to pick his marshals by holding a wet finger in the air, measuring the length of their noses and having their palms read. I have evolved a much more foolproof method—those that Chula here doesn't like are obviously potential failures. The fact that many failed candidates for jobs at Vincent's are now consultants and professors in famous hospitals does not, in our view, speak very highly for the selection procedures at those establishments. Here we never make mistakes, do we, Chula?"

He dropped into his revolving armchair behind the large desk. For several minutes he remained silent, squeezing his eyes shut as though the sunlight bothered him. Maclean detected a look of weariness as the surgeon flipped open an arabesque cigarette box and took a cigarette. Was Maclean imagining things, or did Cameron look at the flame of his lighter as though guiding it toward the end of the cigarette? The hand itself appeared steady enough, and his other movements betrayed no tension. He was probably reading too much into the simple action. Maclean's concentration switched direction as the cat jumped from his lap to dart lightly onto the desk and prowl carefully over to Cameron's IN tray, where it squatted to gaze at its master.

"Chula, give us a song." Cameron struck a high note, and the Siamese arched her neck, flattened her black ears and uttered a hideous squawk, which ranged from a husky rumble through a couple of octaves to a high-pitched whoop; the surgeon silenced his cat by lifting a finger. Maclean laughed.

"She has other little ploys—ripping my curtains apart,

carrying my lecture notes and letting my secretary know where I am in the hospital a damned sight better than these electronic buzzers." As he spoke, Cameron was toying with a pair of forceps, dexterously picking up pins, one by one, from a tray on his desk and laying them out, with great deftness, in regular patterns. He used the right hand, Maclean noticed.

"Still as good as ever with both hands," the psychiatrist remarked, and caught Cameron glancing curiously at him.

"I suppose so. The younger men handle them like pliers. I like to think I have a slight edge on them still."

"I gave up competing long ago. I leave the younger generation to its own problems."

"Nonsense, Alec"—he used the old name—"you're one of the few psychiatrists I'd trust, and I have no time at all for the general run of mind benders. That chap Fiegler, for instance—he has a ward full of people who are fit and strong enough to dig salt in Russia, and they tie up valuable surgical and medical beds, wallowing in self-pity and playing about with woolen rugs, dog leads and jigsaw puzzles. He's even held an exhibition of their schizoid paintings, can you credit it?"

"There are walking wounded, too, Murdo," he said, wondering if Cameron had begun to believe that everyone outside the surgical ward were hardly worth bothering about.

Cameron did not appear to be listening; he passed a hand over Chula's head and fixed Maclean with his aquamarine eyes. "Do you mind if I'm a wee bit personal— you're not having treatment from that fellow yourself?"

The irony of the question nearly floored Maclean. The surgeon, like so many others in the medical profession, was familiar with his story. Cameron obviously assumed that he was relapsing into alcohol addiction and had

79

called in Fiegler to treat him well away from Harley Street.

"No, nothing like that. I'm just interested in one of his group experiments for a paper I want to write."

"I'm glad to hear it."

"What about you and Stroma?"

"She's fine," Cameron said. "She's working here, you know." He hesitated for a fraction and added, "And I get along. I often tell my patients who complain, 'Nobody over thirty is free from pain.' It's no exaggeration, for us as well as for them."

"You seem to have shed a few pounds, Murdo."

"So would you if you worked here. I'm now a minority of one—the only Scotsman in the place, and we used to run their medicine for them. The rest? They're all turnip-headed Anglo-Saxons, more fitted for animal husbandry and ax work than for the practice of medicine or surgery. I don't trust them and I tell them nothing; they don't trust me and they tell me nothing. So we get along fine, Alec. Just fine."

"Isn't it a bit depressing for you—the atmosphere, I mean?"

"I don't allow anything to get me down—either them or the bad days. You ought to know that the depressives are people who remember only the bad days, and I've had too many good ones."

"You can't be talking about the old student days in Edinburgh. They were hell. I caught everything between the pages of every medical textbook."

"We all had a touch of hypochondria. It's one of the hazards of the trade."

"A touch! Mine developed into bibliophobia. I almost had paralysis of the hands when I picked up any kind of book. I think that's what chased me into psychiatry. No-

80

body ever sees himself in a handbook of mental illness. They see other people's symptoms—especially their wives'."

"I must try it on the people here sometime," Cameron grunted. He had refused to be drawn. Whether he guessed where Maclean was leading the talk, or felt they had sat long enough, he stubbed out his cigarette, levered himself up and opened the door for Maclean. "Your shadow grows no shorter, I see. Hope you don't gag over our cuisine. I've told the dean umpteen times that Vincent's has discovered a new slimming secret—food. Look for a plump patient round here. They'd as soon starve as eat from our kitchens. We seem to think that meals are like medicine, not to be enjoyed."

Chula led them through a maze of corridors and across a courtyard. Now and again she would fetch a twig or a stone and drop it at Cameron's feet; with a chuckle he would bend down to pick it up and toss it for the cat as if he practiced this ritual every day. He seemed in a good humor—until he spied a figure climbing out of a maroon Rolls in the yard. Maclean had no need to refer to the name plate on the parking space. It was Ralph Conway-Smith, tanned face, gray sideburns, Savile Row bedside suit and all.

"Morning, Murdo," he hailed.

"Morning," Cameron intoned, marching toward him. "You've met Alec Maclean?"

"Had the pleasure many times, never too many. Often admired his work."

Cameron cut short the small talk. "What are you operating on Harry Brooke for?"

"Harry Brooke? You mean, Bernard."

"I said Harry and I meant Harry," Cameron snapped.

"Well, for once, Murdo, you're wrong. It's Bernard,

the son, and he has a septal hole and a blocked lung valve." Conway-Smith grinned with satisfaction at catching the old man out.

"So I'm wrong," Cameron barked. "I say it's Harry, the father, and he may not have a septal hole, but he has got three thousand pounds—or did you manage to screw him up a bit further?"

Conway-Smith flushed at falling for the trap in front of another doctor. "I didn't know you were interested in the case."

"I am, because the boy's in a private room in D Block, and I shall remain interested until you get him out of it—that is, if you're going to do the surgery here."

"Who's to stop me? I'm within my rights to operate on him here," Conway-Smith replied.

"You have some rights, I admit. But not to use my staff and my theater to help you earn your extortionate fees, or to nurse your patients. Either you get him into a private clinic, or I shall charge you for every needle and every ounce of blood. I shall also take care to mention the fee to your staff. You can drive him back in your Rolls."

The surgeon walked on; Maclean nodded to Conway-Smith and followed. Was this just the uncompromising Cameron? Or the gentle art of committing hara-kiri? Or a touch of hysteria? Cameron's mouth had a grim set, and he threw no more sticks before they reached the main building. Maclean began to feel queasy about the lunch before he had smelled the food. They passed through the cafeteria, where the staff now sat in scores, then climbed the stairway to the small room and bar reserved for the most exalted members of the teaching and consultant staff.

Several people whom Maclean recognized were chatting at the bar; he had the impression that their voices dropped as Cameron and he entered. Standing apart from the main group were a small man and a tallish woman, both in white coats. The psychiatrist had listened to Sir Kenneth Fairchild lecture, though he had never met him. His height—no more than five feet four inches—surprised him.

"Fairchild and his wife," Cameron whispered. "She's the one on the left. When they departed on their honeymoon, somebody—and they can't blame me—said it was the Night of the Long Wives. They did well to pick each other. Two fewer unhappy people in the world."

Maclean sipped his tonic water, privately feeling apprehensive about sharing a table with the Fairchilds if the surgeon remained in this mood. The malice and venom in the remarks troubled him, for he had never known Cameron to show such spite. He consoled himself by thinking they would probably talk shop, that verbal smoke screen which spared people from asking or answering awkward questions.

Fairchild he knew by repute; he had made several classic contributions to physiology. Wartime troops threw away their sola topees and spine pads when he and others had researched the relationship between salt depletion, heat exhaustion and heatstroke. More recently he had studied the dynamics of blood flow and anticoagulant drugs, work that had helped the surgeons using heart-lung machines. Sir Kenneth had, however, gained more of a name as a committee man on whom the politicians running the Health Service could count. Any medical problem, from drug safety to hospital design, they handed to him, well aware they would receive a neat report which would shock neither the Ministry of Health nor the Treasury. In this manner he had gained his knighthood. They said he had created the committee system at Vincent's by appointing five professors to his department so that they could outvote anyone else. Cynics sneered at his weekly clinical-research conference: "Fairchild has his break-through agenda all written out in advance. He tells his staff what discoveries would please him, and lo! they appear in the British journals of physiology, rheumatology, pharmacology and endocrinology," they quipped. He lectured so quietly that students often thought they were eavesdropping on him as he read from yellowing notes; but they filled his lecture room more often than not and sat quietly.

Maclean knew less about Lady Fairchild, only that she ran the new microbiology wing, that physicians and surgeons complained that the money spent on this Palace of Cultures would have been better deployed in the wards and treatment rooms. Lady Barbara ignored them and communed with her electron microscope and her Petri dishes, in which she cultured bacteria and viruses.

The Fairchilds had taken their places at the long dining table, which appeared to be reserved for the senior staff. The surgeon and the psychiatrist moved over and sat facing them, Cameron making the introductions to them and to the consultant obstetrician, who had half finished his meal.

"Dr. Maclean was one of the best gasmen I ever had during the war," the surgeon said to Fairchild. "I tried to persuade him to go for his surgical fellowship, but he landed up by the side of a couch in Harley Street."

"A very honorable discipline," Sir Kenneth commented.

"Aye," retorted Cameron. "If only it conceded that one or two of us were right in the head. Nothing personal, Alec, but do you have to search so hard to find the normal man?"

"I didn't know they'd come up with a normal psychiatrist, yet," Maclean replied. The Fairchilds laughed politely.

A waitress pushed some tepid pea soup in front of them, and though it revolted the gourmet instinct in Maclean, he welcomed the lull it caused in the conversation; it also gave him the opportunity to study the Fairchilds. Sir Kenneth must have passed sixty, and his wife would be twenty or more years younger. Gray was the word for the physician; he looked pallid, and when he made some comment, everyone had to strain to catch the cultured but monotonous whisper. Several things about him intrigued Maclean: the dandruff on his coat and the unbelievable sign of dirt under his fingernails. When you dealt with patients who could hardly articulate their symptoms, you noticed such things, though you didn't expect them in a Professor of Medicine. He had his notions about Sir Kenneth, but the man did not interest him as a subject for diagnosis, merely as a potential threat to Cameron.

He found Lady Fairchild charming. Cameron had murmured to him that she had studied under her husband at the University of London, had fallen under the spell of his eminence and had married him when his first wife died. "Lady Bug's deeper than she appears on the surface. And tough." He made no mention of her obvious intelligence and spirit.

"Of course, Dr. Maclean, I know your name from the Archer case," she remarked. "I followed the trial and read your annotation in the *Journal of Psychiatry*. I agreed that if the defense had produced your evidence, he'd never have been hanged." She induced Maclean to give the background of the trial, and from the comments she made, in a low, vibrant voice, she had certainly garnered every detail of the crime.

Interesting personality, Maclean thought. She had a brittle attractiveness, fine-boned features, large green eyes and a thin mouth. Her morning's work in the Microbiology Department had rubbed none of the transparent coating off her fingernails or dislodged a single well-disciplined hair. From time to time she glanced warily at Cameron, who was feeding Chula scraps of tasteless lamb; she ate her food fairly rapidly, in contrast with her husband, who picked at random and left as much as he ate. Had someone asked for a personality rating on her, Maclean would have summed her up as the type who might wonder if she had turned off the gas and water but, unlike the compulsive neurotic, would never have allowed the doubt to spoil her hiking holiday in the Dolomites or her shopping along the Rue de Rivoli. No couch for her.

They were engrossed in their chat when they heard Cameron exclaim loudly to her husband, "Well, what's the Department of Medicine going to discover next week?"

"Something, my dear Cameron, which I hope will obviate still another surgical procedure."

The consultant obstetrician ran his napkin around his face and mouth and rose precipitantly from the table, gave a nod and walked away. Perhaps he had refereed one of these contests before.

"You mean, Fairchild, some other completely unnecessary medical practice? It used to be said—didn't it, Maclean?—that physicians practiced medicine while they waited to discover the art. Thalidomide and all that. There's nothing more fertile, in my opinion, than the mind of a doctor on the make inventing new ailments for the pills he has in his box. You've got to keep that one jump ahead of the heavenly posse."

Maclean wanted no part of the argument. He was watching for Sir Kenneth's reaction to the calculated insult. Would he show anger or indifference, reply with sarcasm or a reasoned argument? The physician turned to Maclean.

86

"As you may know, Professor Cameron is our great character. But sometimes understanding him defies even our powers of invention."

Fairchild had executed something between a sidestep and a retreat, as Maclean would have expected from his gray personality. Cameron, however, came back with a frontal attack; his voice boomed across the dining room, though no one at the other tables so much as stirred.

"You know as well as I do that the surgeons have dragged the reluctant physicians into almost every major advance in clinical medicine in the past fifteen years—the heart, the brain, the lungs, the liver, the lot. While you ply your pills and keep your hypo needles busy and air your bedside charm, we take courage in our hands and get on with it."

"Your courage—you mean the patients' courage— those of them who have still survived." It was Lady Fairchild who spoke, her voice just as loud as Cameron's. Her husband had now lowered his head in embarrassment.

"When your husband finally releases them from his Department of Medicine, they are good only for the Registrar General's mortality tables," Cameron retorted, smiling grimly.

"That we shall never know, worse luck," she countered, and the psychiatrist had to admire her spunk. Cameron's face had flushed a bright scarlet at this remark; a vein or a tic throbbed in his right temple. He had, Maclean noted, spilled soup down the front of his white coat.

"No," he shouted. "That's untrue. The surgeon's statistics are always produced as damning evidence, even in his experimental work. We're not as fortunate as the physicians—how can they ever tell if their medicine has worked? Get them to take their pills *before* they get well —isn't that what the old hands say?"

"It's preferable to experimenting on people with a

knife," Lady Fairchild said heatedly. "If every surgeon had his hand cut off or had to pay half the value of every life he destroyed, as they did in the old days, he would think twice about butchering patients. The quickest road to surgical success is through the cemetery. Isn't that what the old hands say?"

The argument might have continued, much to the discomfort of the senior staff, had Chula not decided that she had to stick up for her master. She padded around to the empty chair beside Lady Fairchild and leaped onto it; then she let out a howl which made that lady jump.

"Get your evil creature out of here," she screamed.

"Give us a song, Chula," Cameron roared, and the cat obliged while everyone looked on at this piece of black comedy. It proved too much for Barbara Fairchild. Throwing her napkin at Chula's upraised face, she stalked out of the dining room, followed slowly by her husband. "On your way, Judas," the surgeon bellowed after him. A sigh ran around the dining room, and the staff went back to its apple crumble or cheese.

"You were a little hard on them, Murdo," Maclean murmured.

"Now don't you start. That little man with his little memos to the minister and his pals on the Medical Research Council is guilty of more medical betrayals than twenty chariots full of Iscariots. Come and listen to him in a couple of days when we're debating the moral and medical issues of heart and kidney transplants, and you'll see what I mean. What did you think of her—Lady Bug?"

"Seems an intelligent woman," Maclean replied noncommittally.

"Intelligent, eh!" Cameron's voice carried over the silent room. "I'll tell you this for nothing—she's a whore—no, maybe she's not a whore; they do it for fun—she's a prostitute, that's what she is."

Maclean was shocked; at least half a dozen senior medical men must have caught the slander. He quickly folded his napkin, made an excuse that he had to return to Fiegler's department and was relieved to see that the surgeon was following his example. With a heavy heart he watched Cameron stride off toward the operating theaters.

He had little time to reflect on the precise form of mental illness that his friend had, or how he could persuade him to have treatment. He had just reached the main corridor when he heard the summons on the tannoy. "Dr. Gregor Maclean to the medical superintendent, please."

Sainsbury was sitting in a cloud of smoke, dictating to a secretary and scribbling his signature on letters. He got rid of the girl and closed the door. "We're in trouble. Your friend Barcroft has just phoned the dean and fired half a dozen questions at him about Fowler's wife. Of course, old Prior doesn't know whether it's Yom Kippur or Boat Race Week, and he referred him to me. I just pleaded ignorance."

"What did you get out of him?"

"He had a call from somebody who works here—wouldn't say who. I informed him there was no suspicion of negligence or incompetence, and if he suggested this, the hospital would sue if Cameron didn't."

"I'd better get down and see the Fowlers. Have you got a car handy?"

Sainsbury shook his head, then grinned. "Tell you what I'll do. Bert's just come in. He's got the fastest ambulance in the business, and you can travel in comfort. What are you going to tell them?"

"Just to shut up." He looked at Sainsbury. "But I can't help feeling that we won't be able to shut everybody up for much longer."

10

? ?
?

Cameron paused for a moment, as though searching for a word, and his secretary flicked through her notebook to transcribe some of the more difficult shorthand outlines. She was beginning to worry about the professor she had served for nearly ten years. As she worked, she peeped at him, noting the faraway eyes and the habit he had acquired of kneading the muscle between the thumb and forefinger of the left hand, as if attempting to strengthen it or afraid it had lost its power. Any minute now he would have to report to the North Block Theater and start his afternoon operating list, and he still had a pile of letters to answer.

Cameron acted as though she did not exist. Oblivious of the drama surrounding him in the hospital, he nevertheless realized he was not himself; the feeling scared him, and it heightened this fear to face his staff over the operating table or to teach a class of students. He might do something desperate one of these days, he felt. But this doubt he admitted to no one, not even to his daughter. Before lunch he had been tempted to confide in Alec Maclean but had decided against it. Nor did he complain to anyone of the pain that now throbbed in his temple. It would pass, like everything else, he told himself. Most people ran through an asteroid belt at some period of their lives and had to accept it. He could pride himself on the fact that only a couple of surgeons in the whole country could match him in technique and skill. He could still give the Conway-Smiths and that Harley Street elite the length and breadth of a cemetery and leave them standing. They might salt away a bit of their £70,000 a year, but he could take comfort in the fact that he had never accepted a penny besides the £5,000 a year his professorship brought him. Perhaps he was letting too many of these pinprick incidents prey on his mind; such as the actions for negligence his rivals were trying to stir up, or the negativistic attitude of Fairchild, the ministry sneak with the almost psychotic habit of saying no to everything. He would keep fighting for what he believed —if only he could rely on his mental and physical stamina.

"We'll leave the letters, Cathie," he said. Instead he looked over the case histories of his afternoon patients, mentally bracing himself for the task. His experience would carry him through. What did they say about Ysaÿe, the great fiddler? He had forgotten a chunk of the Kreutzer, and his fingers took him right through it without his even trying to remember. His would, he was sure. After all, John Vallance, his doctor, had given him a clean bill of health seven months ago when he consulted him about headaches and weakness in his limbs.

"Nothing wrong with the pump, Murdo. Blood pressure a bit up, but well within limits for somebody your age who drives as hard at the job. Reflexes all right. No sugar or albumin. And the neurologist has found nothing." Vallance had hinted, discreetly, that he take a couple of months off and just laze. How could he when his department was starving for funds and those vultures from the Department of Medicine were waiting to line their pockets?

He lit a cigarette and idly picked up a piece of silk thread, which he passed through a buttonhole in his white coat; he began to tie one-handed knots, flicking one end of the thread through the loop he had made and pulling it until he felt the tension. He still had the touch. His telephone rang. Miss Fletcher picked it up and passed it to him. "Mr. Wilkinson—they're ready for you."

He took the handset. "Any complication with the gall bladder? . . . In that case, you carry on and tell me when you've set up the little girl with the spleen." The second operation might prove too complicated for Wilkinson; they were removing the spleen to treat a blood disorder.

"Would you like to take Chula for a walk, Cathie? Shove her in my flat, tell them I'll take the emergency calls tonight, then you can go home."

When she had gone, he drew the curtains, stretched himself on the couch in his office and closed his eyes, though he did not sleep; his head ached, and he listened to his heart thudding against his chest wall. He cast his mind back to the best school holiday he had ever had, staying with his uncle in a shieling near Inveraray. He could still see the checkered blur of the collies flushing the sheep out of the heather, which glowed purple; still smell the pease brose and butter his aunt gave them for midday dinner; still feel the burn water lapping over his hand as he lay motionless, waiting to guddle for trout; he caught the screech of whops and the skinkle of sunlight from Loch Fyne. At night they had fresh salmon and griddle scones; his uncle would light the oil lamp, with its warm, pungent odor, then read them several verses out of his Bible. Didn't they say the older you grew the more poignant such recollections stood out, like gold or silver veins in a mass of gray rock? They were all dead now, and he had never gone back; he had fooled himself by arguing that no one can ever go back. But he had been afraid— yes, afraid that his cicatrices might not have healed. Funny, he could think about them now without trauma;

92

somehow they helped to untie the knot in his stomach and quiet his mind. He lay inert until Wilkinson rang to say they were making the first incision in the girl.

At least in the North Block he had no students to bother him; the tight circle of staff around the table unfolded as he approached. Donovan moved toward him and whispered, "This is Sister Tremayne, who has taken Sister Holroyd's place."

Cameron found a pair of eyes staring at him with something like awe. He realized that the skin between her cowl and face mask was brown, a light sienna color. Even at the moment of meeting, she irritated him by continuing to gaze at his face instead of taking her place by Donovan's side and watching his movements and his hands like a good theater sister. He nodded curtly to her and began the intricate and hazardous excision of the spleen. He worked quickly, exploring the organ lying awkwardly behind the stomach, probing for the blood vessels; still distracted by the encounter, he snipped the ligament attaching the organ to the stomach without remembering to call first for a clamp to seal off the stomach end of the blood vessel. She had it there though, without his asking; her greenish-brown eyes were now following his fingers as he began to draw the spleen into the cavity to sever the end joining it to the kidney. For no motive, her very efficiency aroused his wrath; it angered him, moreover, to admit that she could leave Holroyd, whom he had trained, seconds behind when it came to slapping a knife into his hand or passing him the suture needle he required. Once, she went to mop the sweat beading on his brow, but he repulsed her with a grunt and a shake of his head. For Sister Tremayne's part, she had the odd impression that the surgeon's fingers were behaving independently of his mind, acting on some more basic reflex. Gradually he incised the plum-colored organ and hoisted it from its bed. Only an hour and a half had it taken him, and yet he felt exhausted, drained of his strength.

"You take over, David," he muttered as he skinned off his gloves. He rounded on Donovan. "I want a word with you—outside."

She trailed him into the anesthetic room, where he sat down and she helped him off with his boots. "Where was Holroyd today? She's not ill, is she?"

"No. I should have told you. I transferred her to Mr. Frankland's firm in neurosurgery. Matron and I thought she could do with the experience, and he needed somebody."

"Donovan, we've known each other since langsyne, and every time you tell me a lie a red band appears round your neck."

The theater sister flushed; her hand went involuntarily to her white collar before she noticed he was smiling.

"What's the real reason?"

"If you want to know, Professor, she was wishy-washying."

"But, Donovan, you surprise me . . . you're the last person in the hospital I'd have believed has anything to hide."

"You know exactly what I mean," she said determinedly. "She was telling tales about what went on in theater, and I couldn't trust her."

"All right, we'll leave it. Now about this new girl—where did she come from?"

"Leeds—and I may tell you, Professor, that she could have picked her place in any of the teaching hospitals. She worked her way through university in Barbados and knows more medicine than twenty Holroyds. And she doesn't tangle, as you saw—we made up ten minutes on that cholecystectomy before you arrived."

"I'll take your word for her, but do you think she'll stand up to tomorrow's teaching session? Replacing heart valves can be tricky with a new member on the firm."

"She's done it before, with Mr. Carter at Leeds."

Cameron shrugged his shoulders. His character never permitted him to judge people by the tint of their skin or their social background; he liked to give newcomers the benefit of the doubt. Nonetheless, this girl, or the circumstances of their meeting, had irked him in a way he could not define. Maybe he was feeling abrasive; tomorrow his annoyance would have passed.

He was scrubbing up the next day, preparing for the heart operation, when the consultant anesthetist wandered through from the operating room in the Shaldon Theater. "She's a good color, and they've started cooling," he said. He bent down to whisper confidentially, "You can certainly pick them, Murdo. She's a real beauty. That cinnamon skin really gets me; they can say what they like." Cameron grunted and fiercely attacked the backs of his hands and fingernails with the stiff brush.

When he made his entrance, the noise did not subside as it normally did but continued to filter through the plexiglass dome. He had the impression that the whole gallery was watching and commenting on Miss Tremayne, who was moving around counting the scores of curved needles and swabs they would use; Rothwell, the anesthetic registrar, was ogling her frankly. Cameron could understand their interest; this girl had the sort of anatomy that even those shapeless green smocks could not disguise. God! Was she wearing nothing under those flimsy garments? Her breasts and hips seemed to strain under the smock, as though she had tied the tapes in the most provocative way. It embarrassed him.

He glanced at the cavity and went over the steps

which Wilkinson had already finished; he checked with the technicians that he had the right readings; he had a final word with Donovan to ensure everything was ready. He then turned to face the gallery.

"Gentlemen," he said, "you are about to witness one of the most complex operations in the surgeon's repertoire, more so than the grafting of a heart or a kidney. . . ." The drone of voices still penetrated the glass cupola, and for a moment he had the wild notion of stripping off his gloves and walking out. He controlled himself with an effort.

"Gentlemen"—his voice had risen in pitch and volume —"let me tell you something about this patient. . . ." Still the hubbub reached him, and he stopped, peeling off his mask to reveal a livid face. He ordered an attendant to switch off the gallery lights, which silenced the chatter; he took up a hand microphone, and his voice boomed through the theater and the gallery. "My friends in the wider theater tell me there is no more critical and discourteous audience than first-nighters they've issued with complimentary tickets. They should come and see you lot, with your free tickets paid for by the state, by ordinary people who haven't had your chance in life. I don't expect I can teach you to value your privileges, and I don't expect I can teach you good manners or a little reverence, let alone some surgery. But if you don't keep quiet, I shall clear the gallery and let this poor lady on the table have privacy as well as the best chance that we can give her." He turned and began the operation, confining his comments purely to the surgery he was performing.

Had Maclean watched him operate that day, he might have returned to Harley Street satisfied that Cameron had nothing to fear, from himself or from poison-pen letters. Now chastened, the gallery became hushed and intent, aware that it was watching a surgical tour de force. Each of the surgeon's hands dwarfed the heart on which he was operating, and he had to explore and stitch in three of its four cavities. When Donovan had counted the needles, used once, then discarded, when she had estimated the sutures in the heart, she reckoned that Cameron had placed and double-tied more than three hundred and thirty stitches. And that in four hours, with the precision and professional ease of an expert tailor fashioning buttonholes.

Acting as though inspired, Cameron hardly noticed that Donovan had ceded her place to the West Indian sister. Not a knife, a pair of forceps or a needle went astray, though the threads fanned out in scores like a spider's web, and none must be confused with another. Her job was almost as difficult as his, for he was working flat out, grabbing the needles she handed him on forceps and driving them accurately through the rings of the heart valves, hardly waiting until she had caught the end of the thread and positioned it. Surgeons replacing heart valves with synthetic materials hardly ever trusted themselves to gauge the forty-odd stitches around the valve without first marking in the quadrants. Cameron did it freehand, the stitches dropping into the exact place as though measured with a pair of compasses and protractor.

Normally when the heart had taken up its beat and the tricky phase of the operation was over, he left the closing of the big incisions to Wilkinson. This time, however, he sewed up the heart sac, placed the silver pins in the breastbone and sutured the main wound twice as quickly as his registrar would have. As he tied the last knots and laid down his scalpel, a noise percolated through the dome, then a loud burst of sound; he arched his neck to observe the whole gallery standing to applaud him. He gave a twitch of his head to acknowledge the compliment, then quit the room.

In the surgeons' cubbyhole, he dropped wearily into the one easy chair; the pajama trousers clung to his knees, and he felt the perspiration ooze through his gown and run down his neck onto his mask. Donovan fetched him a mug of sweet tea, which he drank at one gulp. "I've never seen that happen before," she commented. "From those gangrels of medical students, forby." She never concealed her detestation of medical students for their profanity and the cynical arrogance they seemed to acquire with a smattering of human anatomy and physiology.

"What do you think of Sister Tremayne now? She did far better than I could ever have done."

"What havers, Donovan. You're still the best. But she's a good theater sister—for some other firm, not this one."

"But, Professor . . ."

"I don't want to discuss it. Get rid of her tonight."

Sister Donovan stared at him, perplexed. "I don't understand it, sir. It's not because . . . because she's colored?"

He shook his head. "If you really want to know, she's too much of a distraction to young students who have recently discovered sex, and I can't compete with that. There's room for only one star in my operating theater." He caught the surprise in her face. "Oh, I don't mean myself—I mean the patient. I won't have anything that diverts interest from the figure on the table."

"I see, Professor. In that case, perhaps you could tell her yourself. She'll be disappointed."

"All right. Send her along to my office in an hour, and I'll have a word with her. We don't want to lose her, and she can find another firm, which doesn't do teaching sessions."

"Not Conway-Smith," the sister said quickly. "You know how he is about women."

"No, Margaret—not Conway-Smith."

11

? ?
?

She had changed into her white uniform when she appeared in his office an hour later. Cameron reflected that they ought to cut those overalls a shade more lavishly around the chest, though, thank God, they reached below the knee. Her face had a serious set, but she gave him a smile and held out her hand, which he shook too quickly. He was seeing her fullface for the first time and began to discern what had made his gallery so restive. She had the look of a Mediterranean beauty; though her skin had an ocherous sheen, it was hardly darker than a Grecian woman's; she had high cheekbones, not unlike his own, and her lips were perhaps too full and pouted slightly. Every now and then she moistened them with her tongue, and he caught himself staring at this. She had hardly sat down when Chula opened the door, padded into the room, sniffed at her, then jumped into her lap to squat there, purring and licking her hand.

"Put that damned cat down," Cameron snapped. Even Chula seemed to have taken Donovan's side.

"Sorry, Professor Cameron," she said.

Her manner of gazing, almost rudely, at his face was disconcerting; he had the impression she was trying to place something she remembered about his features. "We haven't met before, Miss . . ."

"Tremayne," she put in, shaking her head. "It's just that this is the first time I've seen your face, and I expected somebody much older."

"I don't know why most people do. Some of them think I speak with an och-aye accent, operate in a kilt and plaid and keep a tight watch on the supply of suture thread."

She laughed, ignoring the tinge of sarcasm in his voice. He sensed that the interview might take the wrong turn; he began quizzing her about her experience, then said, "I really asked you here to thank you for the way you assisted today. I've seldom seen a more efficient performance from someone who had not worked with me or rehearsed a difficult piece of surgery like that." Pausing, he picked up one of his sets of forceps and started to arrange his pins on the leather desk top. "However, Sister Donovan was wrong to give you the idea that you would be with us permanently. I'm afraid I can use you only until Sister Holroyd returns in a day or two."

The color spread rapidly across her skin. "I don't think you know what it would mean to me to be part of your firm, Professor Cameron. It's really the only reason I came here." Her voice had a pleasant intonation, with hardly a trace of the clipped consonants or the singsong cadence of the West Indian.

"That's very flattering to hear, Miss Tremayne. But we have some excellent surgeons at Vincent's, and you can pretty well have your pick if you stay."

"Professor, I'd like you to be frank with me. I have my own reasons for wanting to work with you. I get the impression that you don't want to mention why you're getting rid of me."

Cameron spent a few minutes playing with his pins, unconsciously forming them into a heart shape. When he noted the shape, he scattered them across the desk. He tried to soften the sharp edge of his voice. "As you probably know, Miss Tremayne, medical students and even the older postgraduate students are a rough-and-ready bunch. And, as you probably know, you're a very pretty girl, and I'm afraid that you might distract their attention from my brilliant handiwork. There . . . now you have the reason." He hoped the explanation sounded convincing.

He watched the smile spread over her face; he had no call to dislike her, and yet all he wanted to do was slam the door between her and himself. But she sat there, fishing in her handbag and pulling out a large snapshot.

"Now that you've told me, here's why I came to work for you."

He studied the color photograph, taken against a background of hibiscus, azaleas and two palm trees. From the cut of his clothes he would have dated it eight years ago. He was standing with a doctor, whose name he had forgotten; beside them, in a basket chair, sat a small man with gray hair and a wrinkled brown face; he was clasping hands with him. It began to come back to him.

"Bridgetown, wasn't it? About eight years ago. Let me see. He had a rupture of the esophagus, a bad one, on which we did an emergency operation." Curious how he recalled the symptoms but couldn't put a name to the man.

She nodded, pleasure in her face. "That's my father. You were there for the opening of the new operating theater and were walking round the wards when the ambulance brought him in. He would have died. Who would have diagnosed it? And even if they had, they couldn't have carried out the operation like you."

"Rubbish," he muttered, though he admitted to himself it had been something of a triumph. Now he remembered. The man stretched out in Casualty, his agony tempered by morphine, blood-streaked vomit on his lips; left side of the chest and stomach rigid as a board; distention of the neck muscles; tortured by thirst. He had quizzed too many fellowship candidates to mistake those symptoms and had helped to bear the man through to the new operating theater, which he was going to baptize the next day. It had been close for the old man.

"So that was your father. A works foreman—right?"

"You became his hero. Your secretary sent us a picture which you'd signed, and we had it and this one—bigger, of course—on the sideboard. He says a prayer for you every night of his life."

"He's still well, then?"

"He's retired now and takes things easy, but he's fine. When he knew I was coming here, he asked me to give you this." She dragged a gold watch from her handbag and passed it to him. He flipped the back open and read the inscription: "Presented to J. H. Tremayne by his colleagues at the Island Canning Company to commemorate forty years of service."

"It's the thing he values most," she said.

"That's why I cannot possibly accept it."

"But he'd be deeply offended. You see, it's because he thinks it's so precious that he wants you to have it."

He contemplated her for a moment; the mouth did not turn down like Holroyd's; the lips didn't purse into that set expression which marred Donovan's features. By her face he could see that she would be hurt if he rejected her outright. She had come a long way from home just to hand him the right instruments and do the hundred and one chores of a theater sister when her obvious intelligence would have taken her much further.

"Does it mean all that much to you—working for me?"

"I've set my heart on it since I was so high," she replied, holding out a hand at the height of his desk.

"Well, we'll have to do something." He thought for a moment. "What about this? When we're doing a teaching list, we'll have to hide you with Mr. Sewell in thoracic surgery. But most of our work is nonteaching, and you can join us for that. That suit you?"

When she had thanked him and gone, Cameron called Chula, who came running and sprang on his shoulder. Talking softly to the animal, he strode down to the hospital kitchens to scrounge some food; he then crossed the rear courtyard to his flat, with its sitting room and bedroom. Sarah had left it shipshape, except for the pile of papers on his table. He had a huge backlog of work: an article on "Advances in Surgical Techniques" for *The Practitioner;* a paper on the results of a series of goiter operations, which he was writing with Wilkinson; the eternal heap of admin which he never succeeded in demolishing during office hours. He dumped himself in a chair to read over what he had written early that morning, but its import did not seem to penetrate, and his small, precise handwriting wavered and squirmed in front of his eyes. Even when he had pulled the curtains to shut out the evening light, he still found it impossible to concentrate on reading or writing.

After a while, he ferreted in his bureau drawer and pulled out a drawing block and charcoal. Like many surgeons, Cameron had artistic flair; he often astounded his classes by drawing freehand on the blackboard the most complicated anatomical sections, or by inking in expertly on the human body the exact areas along which he was going to cut. He began to doodle with charcoal on the piece of cartridge paper, distractedly filling in the planes of a face, crosshatching around the cheekbones and the eyes, shaping the nose, the line of the hair, then the pouting mouth. Only when he had done this did he realize that the girl he had drawn bore an uncanny likeness to the West Indian sister he had left only half an hour before. Savagely he tore the paper into tiny shreds, thrust it into the cold fireplace and put a match to it.

12

? ?
?

Maclean had never attached himself to any particular school of psychology or psychiatry; he treated each person who consulted him as a unique product of human experience with his own cryptic set of motives, his own pattern of behavior. He never sought confirmation in anyone of the classic picture of psychosis or neurosis, trying instead to read people, searching for the abnormal trait or the too-normal trait, the conformism that went too far, the influences of heredity and environment. His textbooks consisted of half a hundred thick notepads in which he had summarized his own cases, both failures and successes. However, he conceded the contributions of the dog-and-rat school, which followed Pavlov, as well as what he dubbed the dream-and-drivel school, inspired by Freud. At St. Vincent's they had an empirical mixture: Fiegler, the Freudian, and his senior registrar, Michael Thornton, who went in for rats.

"You must see them, Dr. Maclean," Thornton said, in the tone he might have used about home movies of his children. He had thick glasses, which gave his eyes a weird, suspended look, and a neck twitch, which must have worn out his shirt collars. No good looking there for the normal psychiatrist.

Maclean had met the cleverest rats—those that could lose 90 per cent of their cerebral cortex and still puzzle their way through a maze to a food reward; he had run himself ragged in the two previous days to placate the

Fowlers and prevent Deirdre from throwing in her hand. The thought of rats made his spirits sag, but he agreed. He had a couple of hours before the clinical conference; Thornton was a friend of Rothwell, who, his instinct told him, might disentangle the story of the anonymous letters.

"I'm afraid we're over in the microbiology building," the registrar said apologetically. "Psychiatry doesn't rate very highly here, and we've had to find house room wherever we can."

They had done Lady Fairchild proud, Maclean thought. Now he understood why they called it the Palace of Cultures. It had a modular design, the six-story block, enabling the staff to change the shape of labs for various experiments. The two psychiatrists mounted to the second floor, where the animals were kept. Mice swarmed there, too. Like a thousand pairs of unwashed socks, the smell nearly brought tears to Maclean's eyes. He masked it with a quick pinch of snuff and began to look forward to meeting the rats.

Thornton had two colonies caged in wire compounds; in one, the rats had plenty of space and food; in the other, they jostled for living room, fought over scraps or just fought. Maclean required no explanation of the phenomenon, but the younger man was already in full flood. "I'm almost ready to publish," he said. "I started off with the same strain of rats and equal numbers. As the first colony grew, I weeded out the old and some of the young, keeping the population stable. As you can see—beautiful rats; healthy, sleek, intelligent and long-lived." He was almost driveling, Maclean noticed.

"A different story," Thornton continued, turning to the other colony. "I let them breed until they outgrew this compound, and restricted their food. Then the bickering started—over food, over their females. They even started eating one another."

105

"And they began to die for no reason that the pathologist could discover," Maclean put in.

"How did you know? Even when we increased their food, they kept on dying in this odd way. It's obviously stress."

Maclean nodded agreement. "All you've got to do is find whether it operates psychologically or on, say, the hormone system, and urban man will erect a monument to you beside those of Fleming and Pasteur." Thornton's eyes gyrated behind his goggles.

Of course, Maclean saw the parallels between the microcosmic world of rats and the human species. If Thornton had watched the effect of unemployment in the cities of the middle thirties, he might have inverted his thesis, deducing the behavior of rats from a study of the street corners and the dole queues. He might also have observed that the species around him in the hospital bickered and fought as primitively as the rats, that his masters practiced professional cannibalism. He felt almost grateful to Thornton for driving the analogy home to him. St. Vincent's was a closed compound, the classical overstressed society, with physicians and surgeons battling to keep territory, to gain more, to increase their prestige; they suffered the same frustrations, the same insecurity, which created friction and violence in the rat world. Except perhaps that in the human cage, bounded by walls, wards, theaters and lecture rooms, the contest lay beneath the surface; the conflict was more subtle, more devious, though no less savage. Maclean hit on the inference: Find the stressed character at St. Vincent's, and he would solve at least the problem of the poison-pen letters.

Thornton was still communing with his rats. "What happens when you transfer a rat from one cage to another?" Maclean asked.

"If he's not immediately attacked and killed, they ostracize him—even in the healthy colony. Obvious analogy with tribal customs or even the present racial problem and the malaise of city civilization."

Idly the psychiatrist wondered what might occur if anyone here ever discovered that he, Maclean, was the rogue in their midst. "You know, Thornton, we owe the rat a great debt, we psychiatrists. I think the whole discipline would fall into decline without these rare creatures. In a sense he is our symbol."

"It's true, so true," cried the registrar, and for a moment Maclean fancied that his tongue darted in and out and he bared his teeth. Didn't they say there was a personality transference between animals and humans?

"But you must remember that although people quite often behave like rats, the reverse is quite often not the case," Maclean said. Somehow he had to erase his cynical observation and enlighten this young research worker on the fact that you could hardly found a new medical philosophy on two cages of rats.

Thornton was hardly listening. "We've even tried this on several of the rats," he said, handing over a large vial of white crystalline powder, marked "Lysergic acid diethylamide," the potent drug which produced hallucinations. Maclean gazed at it, fascinated; that vial of LSD would, he estimated, fetch more than £10,000 if peddled to addicts.

"And the effect?" He posed the question, but his mind was already on the way to answering it. Why would the wayward Philip Rothwell strike up a friendship with a long-haired psychiatrist? Because, as a research worker, Thornton had supplies of LSD which lay handy on the shelves and were probably stocked in his consulting room. Thornton and his rats would never miss the stuff. He was still absorbed in his thoughts when they heard a voice.

"Absorbing creatures, aren't they?" Lady Fairchild

must have appeared from one of the labs beyond the rat house; she could, Maclean supposed, have seen them enter the building from her office on the fourth floor and made a point of running into them casually. Her eyes fixed for several seconds on the flask of white powder Maclean still held before she swung her gaze to the animal pens.

"I was visiting some mice on which we are conducting experiments with antiviral compounds," she explained. Maclean said nothing, and she went on. "Just plain chemotherapy tests. Not half as complex as Dr. Thornton's work. Have you seen the building before, Dr. Maclean?"

Maclean shook his head. "A nice place. Quite a few patients would be glad of the accommodation the animals have—without the atmosphere."

"Ah, but patients don't have animal lovers and their societies fighting for their rights. Or antivivisectionists inspecting their quarters."

She had the crystalline structure of a diamond. A white one. Capable of cutting almost anything. Different in every light. Indestructible. The hand holding the clipboard and notes looked white and soft; its pointed nails glittered with clear varnish; the white silk foulard lay just right on the throat; her hair, lipstick and make-up must have consumed as much time and trouble as her chemotherapy tests.

"Will you be coming to the clinical conference in about half an hour?" she asked Maclean.

"I wasn't intending to," he replied, lying blandly. "Will it be interesting?"

"The ethics of transplanting," she said. "I should think your friend, Professor Cameron"—she dwelled on the last four words—"might let off a few fireworks. He always puts on a big act in front of these audiences."

"In that case you can sponsor me."

She smiled. "I have a Bunsen burner and a retort full of coffee upstairs. It might help you through the long session."

In her office she lit the gas burner under the two glass coffee spheres, then fastened her green eyes on Maclean.

"What exactly are you doing here?"

"Co-operating in a joint experiment with Fiegler's department."

"I'm sorry, I find that hard to credit. If Fiegler and many other psychiatrists got into personal trouble, they would take it to you, almost undoubtedly. You're known as the psychiatrists' psychiatrist. I can't imagine you lending your time and your ability to some footling little exercise in group therapy."

"Well, let's call it a sort of busman's holiday," said Maclean. She poured the coffee into bone-china cups, handing him one. A strange smile played around her small mouth. In that moment Maclean sensed the aura of suppressed sexuality, which washed over him like the faint whiff of the perfume she wore. Had he been playing a guessing game about her origins, he would have placed her in a vicarage, perhaps as an only child of a High Anglican clergyman, the type in which religious fervor had nurtured strong emotions and stronger repressions. Who knew how they would seek their outlet? He almost felt the conflict and wondered how such a dominant personality had ever allied itself to the arid, withdrawn character of Fairchild. Probably the master-and-pupil relationship, as Cameron had observed.

"I had the strangest idea that you had been called in by someone to have a look at Professor Cameron," she said.

"Cameron!" He laughed. "What's wrong with him, apart from being a bit crabby and, according to Fiegler, acquiring a cat fetish?"

"Come, come, Dr. Maclean. You saw him at lunch. I, for one, wouldn't like to be operated on by someone with such obvious signs of mental illness." Lady Fairchild plainly had no intention of equivocating.

"You know what these surgeons are—an eccentric race," Maclean replied, echoing Joe. "Cameron is probably a degree worse than most. But even if he were ill, he would treat it like everything else—as a private matter. Can you honestly see him climbing onto my couch or anybody else's?"

"With you he might. You're an old friend."

"And he's a very proud man, as you've noticed."

"Haven't I?" she cried. "I've often wondered what it must have been like to be married to him." She quickly amended the thought. "I mean, I wonder what hell his wife went through in the eighteen months they lived together. You knew her. What was she like?"

Maclean paused for a moment to have a dialogue with his conscience. His pictured Nancy Fordyce, the nurse Cameron had married when he came south. Auburn hair, blue eyes and a wide mouth with laugh wrinkles around it. She would have guessed intuitively what this arcane creature meant while he fumbled for its significance. She would have chuckled and dug him in the ribs: Go on, Alec—what's a small lie, if it'll help him?

The psychiatrist shifted his attention to Lady Fairchild. "In a great many ways you remind me of her," he said. "The same hair and eyes, the same poise and grooming—she was a very lovely girl." She preened herself, but behind this reaction to the compliment he noted a gleam of deeper interest in those green eyes. "Of course, she wasn't so intelligent," he added.

"That might have been a drawback," she answered. "She could not have competed with his great love."

"But his wife was a theater sister, as keen as he was on surgery."

Lady Fairchild shot Maclean a look which implied that he might know his textbooks but he was not well up on human nature. "I didn't mean surgery—I meant himself. I don't think that anyone as proud and arrogant as that man could ever fall in love with anyone. He wouldn't know how to sacrifice even a small bit of himself. Am I right?"

"I don't know. He's been a very lonely man since his wife died all those years ago."

"Any sympathy I have for him doesn't alter the fact that he's ill, he's a danger and he should do something about it."

"I'm glad it's not my case," Maclean said, deciding to change the subject. "I'm too easy-osey to go looking for trouble outside my consulting room. Anyway, Cameron wouldn't take advice from me, no more than, say, your own husband would."

"That's different. My husband isn't ill."

"I didn't say he was."

"But you think he may be," she insisted dubiously.

Maclean shrugged. "Nothing that a holiday and a change of surroundings wouldn't put right."

"It's only that he's been a bit off-color lately . . ."

"And gets tired easily, yet he can't sleep beyond about five o'clock."

"Who have you been talking to about him?" she asked accusingly.

"Nobody. Word of honor. As I said, it's presumptuous of me to get involved unless I'm asked."

"And I probably deserved it for interrogating you about Cameron."

Maclean acknowledged the half-apology with a smile

as they rose to leave. He had quoted a few of the signs of nervous depression merely to show that he had weighed up her husband's condition. He might have warned her not to take chances with a stress illness like that, but someone who had made so many correct guesses about Cameron had probably drawn the right inferences. She seemed more interested in Cameron and his dead wife. Why? It was something to exercise his thought as they walked together to the clinical meeting.

13
? ?
?

The lecture hall had already filled with senior and junior members of the staff and several doctors from neighboring hospitals when they took their seats in one of the front tiers. To his surprise Maclean spotted Joe Sainsbury at the back of the audience; he must have reckoned the meeting important to force himself to sit for the best part of two hours without a cigarette. Ralph Conway-Smith, too! Gossiping and smiling as always. What did Cameron call him? The fastest set of teeth in Harley Street. It must have cost him a few hundred guineas in private fees to attend. Why should he waste time and money listening to dry, clinical details of a case of coronary thrombosis in a donor who had given a kidney to save a relative?

Sir Kenneth Fairchild shared the front row with several of his professors. Before Cameron took his seat, a few yards away, the meeting had begun. Carmichael, a Reader in Medicine, took them through the case history. The patient, a man aged forty-four, had agreed to the operation to remove his right kidney after being informed that it might save his sister, who was dying from renal disease. Professor Cameron had performed surgery on both brother and sister; the kidney transplant had taken, and the sister was convalescing; the brother had, however, suffered a heart attack ten days after the operation and died two days later. Carmichael dropped his voice three or four tones and assumed a more lugubrious style to read the pathologist's report. At autopsy they had discovered degenerative changes in the major arteries, gross damage to the coronary arteries, some fluid in the lungs.

During this monologue, Cameron had sat, chin in hand, scribbling notes on a pad balanced on his knee. Carmichael turned to him. "Would you care to comment, Professor Cameron?"

Cameron marched to the rostrum. He stared, not at the audience, but intimidatingly straight into Fairchild's eyes. The Professor of Medicine dropped his head and consulted his notes.

"I don't know whom we have to thank for the choice of this case, but really, ladies and gentlemen, the etiology of the ingrowing toenail or the present state of preventive treatment for glass-blowers' lung would waste our time just as profitably. Here we have a patient who died of a heart attack. True, it followed surgery, but heart attacks have to follow something. They're not unusual. They happen to more than one hundred thousand people in this country every year. One in five of you in this room will almost certainly die from coronary disease—and many people die with very healthy bodies from this type of seizure. As they say in the courts: Next case, please." And he sat down.

Carmichael turned to Sir Kenneth. But before he could get to his feet, Conway-Smith had jumped up to ask a question.

113

"Professor Cameron with his characteristic pithiness has perhaps understated the importance of this case. What many of us would like to examine is the relationship between the loss of the kidney—and the consequent surgical trauma in such a serious operation—and the coronary attack. I also understand that the patient was the father of three small children, and I think it fair to ask ourselves whether the head of this family might not still have been alive if he had not been persuaded to sacrifice a kidney for his sister, who has a doubtful chance of survival. Shouldn't we take this opportunity to study the mortality in kidney and heart transplants and balance this against the risks to donors?"

"No comment," Cameron muttered, without bothering to rise. His face had as much expression as a stone.

It was Fairchild's turn. The brittle, pedantic whisper did not carry to the back of the hall; every now and again he glanced at his notes but normally fixed his gaze on some air molecule a few feet in front of his nose.

"There are two distinct issues here," he said. "A medical and a moral one. So far as the death of the patient is concerned, the chronology and the coincidence are striking enough to warrant a suspicion that the operation, and perhaps the adjustment required by the surgical excision of a kidney, set up the conditions that resulted in the coronary attack. Proof of this would be difficult, if not impossible, to elicit. However, we have to face the ethical dilemma which these homo-transplants present. It is a sound principle in medicine never to interfere with the function of a normal organ, and in this instance we may be in danger of overlooking this canon. Look at the mortality rate of such transplants in this hospital. We have carried out twenty-six such operations, with an average survival rate of four months. The longest any patient has lived is three years. Eighteen of the cases have died within six weeks of surgery. These figures would be alarming even if the patient alone bore the risk. But here we are asking donors to submit to major surgery and spend the rest of their lives with one kidney. If they get over the surgery, can we still say how much their disability shortens their lives or impairs their mental and physical efficiency? We cannot give prospective donors these answers, and I contend that we should not persuade or cajole people into making such sacrifices while these operations are still so experimental and offer so little encouragement to patients. What I have said about kidney transplants applies equally to heart transplants, even though these do not involve a living donor. We should wait until the genetic problems of such surgery are better understood before attempting to practice it clinically."

Delivered in a tired monotone, the words seemed far from momentous; however, to the majority of people in the hall, they amounted to a declaration of open hostility between the two professors. Surgeons experienced enough difficulty winning the co-operation and confidence of patients in risky, experimental operations when they had the collaboration of physicians. If that support were withdrawn, the supply of patients would cease. To Cameron and his surgical colleagues at the meeting, Sir Kenneth's statement spelled virtually the end of kidney and heart transplants at Vincent's; no physician would dare incur his chief's censure by advising such surgery or by referring patients to Cameron. The surgeon's team had devoted more than ten years to overcoming the problems of transplanting organs; they had evolved proven surgical techniques; they had come within sight of developing methods of matching donor and recipient to prevent the rejection of transplants. Fairchild must have appreciated the strangling effect of his strictures on the Department of Surgery; and if the clinical program stopped, many of

Cameron's younger men might move to other hospitals with a broader attitude. And where Sir Kenneth led, the University Grants Committee, the Medical Research Council and the larger, wealthier foundations generally followed. Why, they would ask, spend government or private money on a branch of surgery that had produced such despairing results? The official purse strings would tighten around experimental surgery, choking it and other projects more effectively than Fairchild's vague injunctions.

Cameron rose to his feet. His voice would have filled the small lecture theater many times over. "I came here tonight to do no more than hold a watching brief, since I regarded this subject as one for the cardiologist or the physiologist rather than for the surgeon. I still contend that it lies outside my responsibility, but the whole issue has been obscured and confused by a curious moral emphasis, dubious statistics and broken-backed logic. With his figures, Professor Fairchild reminds me of the air traveler who got the jitters about flying after reading reports about bombs exploding in aircraft. A statistician put him right. 'Pack a small bomb in your cabin baggage,' he said, 'for the odds against getting into a plane with two bombs aboard are several hundred million to one. . . .' The professor's venture into statistics reminds me, too, of the girl who was proudly telling her friend about her triplets. The doctor, she said, told her it was a very rare event which happened only once in fifteen thousand times. With some awe and admiration, her friend gasped, 'But however do you find time to do your housework?' "

The audience, until that moment held fast in the tension, suddenly convulsed, as though relieved at some excuse to laugh. Lady Fairchild did not share the joke. "What's that if it isn't hysteria?" she whispered, tugging at Maclean's sleeve. Cameron was certainly putting on a highly theatrical act, waving his notes and gesturing like an actor or a politician. How many times had people uttered the word "hysterical" to him when describing the surgeon's behavior!

"We can dismiss this statistical nonsense," Cameron was continuing. "We all know that the mortality from the sort of kidney disease we are treating with surgery is one hundred per cent in the hands of the physicians. No one survives their treatment, while five of our twenty-six patients are still alive after a year, and that is a record of which I and many others can be proud. While I have control of the surgical beds in this hospital, we shall continue to try to save patients and leave the moralizing to others."

He sat down. From his choice of words and the manner in which he had delivered them, it was obvious that he had accepted the challenge. Carmichael stilled the hubbub by calling for questions or contributions to the discussion. Several members diffidently put their points of view, but the meeting seemed restive and intent on disbanding to debate not the issue but the row between the two professors. The chairman was about to close the meeting when he spotted someone at the rear of the hall. Heads swiveled to note that a theater sister had risen to speak. It was Sister Tremayne.

Her voice quavered slightly but had emphasis. "I cannot, I don't think, make any contribution to the moral lessons of such cases as these. Maybe it is presumptuous of me to say anything at all. But I feel that this afternoon we may have lost sight of the patient's own privileges. Before this meeting, I took the liberty of finding out if this man had been in any way persuaded to act as a donor. He had, in fact, volunteered and indeed talked Professor Cameron into performing the surgery to save his sister. This point was not brought out in . . ."

The shout from the front row halted her. "Sit down,

Sister, and shut up. I can fight my own battles." Cameron had gone puce as he bawled the order. The chairman banged his gavel for silence and quickly closed the meeting. The crowd was murmuring as it quit the hall. Maclean edged his bulky figure along the tiers to the gangway and descended to meet Cameron, who had lit a cigarette and was dragging deeply on it.

"You came to see the shindig like the others," he said acidly. His movements and his face betrayed agitation.

"Lady Fairchild persuaded me to come," Maclean replied.

"She would," he muttered. As Maclean turned to leave, the surgeon caught him by the arm. "You remember Stroma? She suggested you come down and spend the weekend with us in the cottage. I'm free this weekend if you can make it. Bring your secretary if you want to."

Maclean accepted willingly; it would give him the chance to study the surgeon at close quarters and to see how he behaved away from the hospital environment.

14
? ?
?

No epidemic of hospital staphylococcus could have shaken St. Vincent's like the headline *The World* flaunted across its front page the next day. "MEDICAL CHIEFS IN ROW OVER PATIENT'S DEATH," it proclaimed in daunting type. Somber pictures of Cameron and Fairchild confronted each other over the unsigned article. Every detail of the argument was outlined, some even quoted, although such meetings excluded the press. The story stressed the mortality among transplant patients, named the donor who had died and spared no effort to squeeze sympathy out of the quotes from the widow; it also drew the right conclusions about the feud between the two department heads and its effect on the clinical program. "Professor Cameron lost his temper when Sir Kenneth indicated that the death rate did not justify continuing with this type of surgery. But the meeting seemed to confirm the opinion that surgeons were using patients as guinea pigs in such experimental operations." The journalist had tackled Cameron about the meeting and had extracted a quote from him: "This is a medical and not a press matter." To cap its scoop, the paper had printed bills and posted a couple of vendors at the hospital entrance, so that most of the staff had read the story early that morning. Who had leaked it, and why?

In his house at Ham, Sir Kenneth Fairchild woke shortly after five o'clock and slipped quietly out of bed, leaving his wife slumbering. He realized he would not get back to sleep. He had a dry mouth, a sensation of nausea in his stomach and a feeling of lassitude, symptoms that in other people might have pointed to a hangover; he, however, had not touched more than a glass of wine a day for thirty years. Wrapping a dressing gown around himself, he padded downstairs. Barbara had tidied the papers and reports on which he had worked late the previous night after she had given him his sleeping pill. To open them and pore over the mixture of civil-service jargon and the dog Latin of his profession would have sickened him; instead, he made himself some black coffee and took it into the conservatory. He liked the sour odor exuding from the plants, though the weak rays of sunlight, filtered by the condensation on the glass and fractured by the vine leaves, irritated his eyes. He closed them.

On mornings like these, morbid thoughts assailed his mind, causing him to question his own life. Some of his memories recurred, haunting him like the leitmotiv in a Wagnerian music drama. He remembered, for example, his first wife pleading with him on the only occasion she had ever offered any opposition. "But, Kenneth, it's not the end of the world because the boy has failed his exams. He just doesn't want to be a doctor."

"He could hardly have demonstrated it in a more emphatic manner," he had retorted. "If he wishes to further this juvenile ambition to design and fly airplanes, he can indulge it at his own expense."

Then the wartime call. It had come when he was working at the Medical Research Council laboratories in Hampstead; they had given him a car to take him to East Grinstead. Robert was lying in that hutted plastic-surgery ward in the Queen Victoria Hospital with forty other airmen. They had fished him out of the Medway after his plane had gone down in flames. He could only whisper inarticulately, for the flames had consumed much of his face and burned his lips. It had almost turned Fairchild's stomach to look at the boy. "Nice to see you, Dad. I've had some of my bark knocked off, but McIndoe will put the pieces back, and you'll see, I'll be flying again soon." McIndoe and his staff had accomplished a remarkable job of reparative surgery; when he saw him again, Robert's face had a static, sculpted look, which had even lent him a certain charm. Why, why had he volunteered to fly again when Fairchild had lobbied him into a ground-staff job? With those scarred hands he hardly stood a chance. The second time Robert crashed, not even East Grinstead could do anything with the bits. For the only time in his life Fairchild had felt like weeping—but he did not; he could not. Emotionally—or was it physiologically?—he seemed incapable of showing his feelings and seeking release in the normal way. It had been bad enough to watch the shock slowly killing his wife.

These days his thoughts seemed invariably to whirl around Cameron. When he reflected on the clinical meeting the previous evening, he experienced a moral qualm, which he quickly smothered. How could anyone stop fighting with a man of that ilk, even if events would probably prove him right about kidney transplants? Once concede the smallest thing to him and he would take over the whole hospital with that ridiculous surgical circus which appeared to fascinate the press and television so much. He was just a rude, obsessive clansman. Perhaps there was a quality of brilliance—he had to admit this—but it hardly added up to the genius so many people believed he was.

His mind swung back to that day three years ago when Cameron had convened a meeting of department heads to argue for a bigger share of the research grants for his own wing. Determined to oppose him, Fairchild had mustered his full team of professors, though he went into the dean's room himself with some apprehension. Maybe that awful canteen food had disagreed with him and caused the choking feeling and the slight pain in his chest; maybe he had wrought himself unnecessarily into a state of anxiety. He had listened to Cameron make his plea, then had watched that idiot, Prior, act as his advocate, before he got to his feet.

He had never really known what had happened. As he rose, the room suddenly receded, and he felt a thump in his chest and pain reach into his throat and along his arm and fill the cage behind his breastbone; he could catch stray words and a cataclysmic hammering sound, though he could relate these to no one or no thing in the room; flashes like lightning appeared to him, and a rushing sound filled his ears. Those seconds were a nightmare which he tried to shake off and couldn't. It was like the hypnagogic images which sometimes pervade the mind while entering or emerging from sleep.

When he had opened his eyes, he realized he was lying in a bed in one of Cameron's emergency wards, near the main operating theater; gradually his mind took in the oxygen cylinder, the intravenous drip, the electronic lung. Ten minutes after he had woken, Cameron himself had visited him. "You'll have to relax and stay here for a couple of days, then we'll get you home. You passed out."

What no one divulged then—he learned it piecemeal —was that Cameron had saved his life while his own associates were standing bewildered. The surgeon had performed closed-chest cardiac massage, had injected adrenaline into the heart and was prepared to open his chest had his heart not restarted. Cameron had also given him what was popularly called the kiss of life. For no reason the Biblical fragment from the Second Book of Kings came into his head: "And when Elisha was come into the house, behold, the child was dead, and laid upon his bed. He went in therefore, and shut the door upon them twain, and prayed unto the Lord. And he went up, and lay upon the child, and put his mouth upon his mouth, and his eyes upon his eyes, and his hands upon his hands: and he stretched himself upon the child; and the flesh of the child waxed warm."

When he was convalescing at home, Fairchild wrote to Cameron expressing his gratitude—the hardest struggle he had ever experienced to find words. While he wrote, a verbal refrain ran through his thoughts: "That man's breath saved my life. How many molecules of his breath are circulating in my body?" This thought obsessed him, so that at times he even doubted the clinical picture and the yards of trace paper with the electrical

122

record which clearly indicated a heart attack. He avoided all mention of his coronary, and Cameron for his part never alluded to the board-room incident. Though he disliked the thrusting, imperious nature of the man, he would never have brought his antipathy into the open had it not been for Barbara, who detested the surgeon more than he did. But Cameron attracted enemies. Fairchild told himself that the surgeon was acting like some figure in a Greek tragedy, pursued by gods and Furies. Whom God wishes to destroy He first makes mad. Cameron's destiny was inexorable, inevitable, needing no action from him or anyone else. That thought comforted him and would help him face yet another day at Vincent's.

Hearing the newspapers drop on the doormat, Fairchild rose from his chair. Rarely did he glance at the daily press, dismissing it as so much irrelevant information served up to the public to shock it at its breakfast table and create the illusion that the man in the street could be privy to everything that happened from the Cabinet Room to the football clubhouse. How much history did they contain, the papers? He put on the kettle, made a pot of tea and carried this and the papers to the bedroom.

Barbara Fairchild stirred as he entered, sitting up in bed. She had no need to ask how he had slept when she looked at the drawn, bloodless face, the thin body draped in a dressing gown, which appeared to grow bigger each month. She pitied him, though it might have surprised her, had she sought the real motive, to find that her compassion sprang from disdain for his weakness and dependence on her. For years her marriage had meant no more than a bit of paper, the title which she valued, a shared economy and a mutual interest in medicine, their careers and the hospital. No one began life with a man of sixty expecting virility, and she didn't lack male bedfellows.

However, she perceived her husband failing in other ways, mentally as well as physically. She picked up the papers, her eye falling on the story about the hospital.

"Have you seen this?" she cried.

Sir Kenneth ran his eye down the article, pursing his lips. "No more than cheap sensationalism," he muttered.

"But who could have informed them about the meeting?" She had made her own guess but kept quiet about it. She must act, force him to take a positive step.

"It's of no consequence who informed them."

"Perhaps not. The main thing is that it brings the whole business of Cameron into the open, and now the dean will have to take action."

"What action? There's nothing he can do. Professors are like archbishops and field marshals—they can't be sacked."

"Couldn't old Prior ask Cameron to explain his conduct and, at the same time, ask about his incompetent handling of certain operations? If he had the guts of a butterfly, he would demand his resignation."

Sir Kenneth shook his head. "A man like Cameron would never throw in his hand—and no one could compel him."

"All right, the dean gives him the alternative of resigning or facing an official inquiry. That would make up his mind."

"Can you see Prior doing that?"

"If he's prodded. If you don't go to him this morning, I shall. It's time we stopped this scoundrel."

"Very well, then, I'll go and see him this morning." He agreed reluctantly, for he could envisage her letting her temper override her discretion and revealing things that would make Prior suspicious. Her anger sometimes frightened him; he picked up the tray and went downstairs while she dressed.

124

How many more mornings like this? he asked himself. How much longer would this game go on? For if he were truthful, he had to admit that both he and Barbara were playing a game in which Cameron's head was the prize. He loved her, but perhaps he had been foolish to marry someone more than twenty years younger. Now he needed her, leaned on her, relied on her resilience, her strength. As long as he could draw on it to get him through each day . . .

People had to rationalize their twisted emotions, to invent excuses, to lie to themselves in order to make life bearable. He had to tell himself that he hated Cameron as a professional rival, as a threat to his own position, but where had that ended? In this gray sickness and self-reproach and the desire to escape from everything. It might have been better to acknowledge openly that he detested the surgeon because his wife had fallen in love with him and he had snubbed her. Oh, Cameron had behaved honorably. Fairchild knew that from the stories that had made the rounds of the hospital, from the fact that she had become almost impossible to live with. He almost hated Cameron for his rectitude. What comfort had it brought? Barbara had gone elsewhere for her pleasure, since her husband was beyond providing it.

And Barbara? He had tried to understand what went on in her mind. He felt that Cameron's snub, his scorn, had turned her love to hatred as well as leaving a festering sore which had poisoned her mind. She, too, was pretending to hate the surgeon for what he was doing to her husband. And so the game went on. Where would it end?

Fairchild was too queasy to touch his breakfast; the idea of demanding that the dean should call Cameron to account deepened his despair. But he made the call and sat mute over his untouched breakfast.

*

Dean Charles Prior stared at the headline in *The World,* a paper which seemed to him to bring out the worst side of people. It smelled of scandal, and with two years to fill in to retirement he wanted more than anything else to avoid scandal. Now he waited for the Professor of Medicine, wondering how to take the sting out of this crisis. The dean hated any form of action and people who confused or equated action with movement. Perched like a gray owl between IN and OUT trays, he pushed his quantum of papers across his desk and at five thirty every night sheathed his fountain pen and drove home to the flat he shared with his aged mother in Kensington. The art of medicine, he maintaind, could be pursued without the encumbrance of patients; he had therefore done his general practice and become a lecturer in obstetrics before securing the job as dean of St. Vincent's Medical School. "I bet he was the obstetrician who didn't know he was examining his own wife until she was writing the check for his fee," Cameron had quipped. He viewed his three years in practice as a microcosm out of which he could distill the whole art of medicine. "I had a case like that once," he would murmur to hardened professionals.

He offered Sir Kenneth tea and biscuits, which the professor refused. Running his eye over the wizened, emaciated figure, Prior felt privately that Fairchild might consider retiring soon. From his yellowing complexion, cloudy eyes and weary attitude, the dean guessed something was gnawing at him.

The professor sank into a chair and said bluntly, "Well, Prior, what are we going to do about this article? You're going to challenge it, I trust."

Prior shook his head. "How can we? It's distasteful, but accurate. I think we can treat it as a one-day wonder."

126

"But for how long, Dean? You know what is going on, that Cameron stirred up this whole question. The man is becoming a squalid and dangerous nuisance, and we have to do something about him now or later. Do you know that many of the physicians in this hospital no longer trust their patients to the Department of Surgery? In some cases they even make arrangements to transfer them to other hospitals and private clinics."

"We're talking about one of the most talented surgeons in the country."

"Really, Dean, you're being too kind. We're talking about a man who is past it and who is suffering from hysteria, *folie de grandeur* or both."

Dean Prior munched one of his midmorning biscuits and took a sip of milk. "Just a touch of the Celtic blood, Sir Kenneth." He smiled. "I've seen it so often in my career. A different race, you know. They lack our phlegm, our *sang-froid,* and we can't do much about that."

"So you're going to sit there until something happens that we can't hush up."

"Hush up?"

"What about the three letters? We've had to hush them up, haven't we?"

"Three letters, Sir Kenneth?" Prior noticed that the Professor of Medicine hesitated for the merest second. For the first time in the interview he appeared at a loss.

"I understand—unofficially, of course—that there has been a third complaint about an operation Cameron performed."

"Then you must know more than I do. To be perfectly fair to Cameron, neither of the accusations in the two letters I have seen was ever substantiated. They were malicious, as you know."

"That's what was said. But an official inquiry might have reached other conclusions."

127

"Is that what you want to see—an official inquiry?"

"No," Fairchild replied. "Nobody would like it to come to that and see the good name of the hospital dragged through the press. But I can foresee something like that happening if we sit and do nothing."

"What would you do?"

Fairchild paused. "If I were you, Dean, I would demand that Cameron resign his professorship. Put it to him that you've had complaints, you fear they might hold a ministry inquiry and he would be better to step down."

"Unthinkable," said the dean.

"Oh, I know. You and so many others believe that this place would collapse if that man were to resign or retire," Sir Kenneth exclaimed vehemently.

"I feel we've carried this conversation far enough," the dean said. "Frankly, Sir Kenneth, I'm surprised by your attitude. I would have thought that if what you say about Cameron is correct, you of all people would have offered him medical help instead of hostility."

Stung by the remark, Fairchild got to his feet. Before he left, he rounded on the dean. "I'd like you to know that I have nothing personal against Cameron. I was merely thinking of the good of the hospital. If Cameron wants treatment and cares to put himself in the hands of one of my staff, he shall have the best there is."

The dean gazed at the door which Fairchild had closed. He could imagine Cameron applying to Fairchild for help and getting everything short of assistance; Sir Kenneth's jealousy and his poisonous wife would make sure of that. Prior nibbled his arrowroot biscuit and wondered how long it would take, by devious government corridors, for Fairchild's request to reach him officially. He sighed, thinking of his two more years and the tranquillity of retirement, and resumed dictating letters precisely where he had stopped before the interruption.

Barbara was walking up and down his office impatiently, waiting for his return. "I told you he wouldn't do anything," he said, at her questioning look.

"Well, if he won't, we will," she muttered. She had typed a letter, which she handed him. With apprehension, and some horror, he read it. She had addressed it to Sir Maitland Foulkes, chairman of the governing board of St. Vincent's, outlining the complaints against Cameron, describing his behavior and what it had meant in adverse publicity for the hospital, stressing the fact that physicians had lost confidence in his department. The only thing that would clear the air was an official inquiry, she had written.

"But you can't send this," he objected.

"I didn't intend to," she replied. "You're a friend of his, and there's no reason why you shouldn't write to him in the strictest confidence about a matter as grave as this."

His heart sank, but he accepted the sheet of note paper and sat down to copy the letter in his precise hand. When he had finished, she addressed the envelope, stamped it and placed it in her handbag to post it outside the hospital. It was a game, he thought. A game they both had to play to the end.

15
? ?
?

Patricia Holroyd had worn a dark-green linen costume, her best; the *bouffant* blond hair shimmered with lacquer, brittle and enticing as a meringue; from her green eye shadow to the toenail varnish glowing through her open shoes and her stockings, her appearance suggested she had spent meticulous hours in front of a mirror. Eternal student of women, Conway-Smith missed none of these things, accepting them as hints that she, or any other woman, intended to impress and gratify him; that, in turn, signified that she meant to seduce or be seduced. He kissed her, running a hand over the hollow of her back, one of her sensitive areas, as he had discovered through long practice. She rebuffed him, but gently, without making him feel that the contest was altogether lost. She had more important matters to discuss, which was why she had phoned him from the hospital and come straight to his flat off Harley Street after her stint in the operating theater.

"I could do with a drink," she said. He mixed her a powerful amalgam of gin and vermouth, his formula for unclenching the jaws and dousing the inhibitions. She gulped a mouthful or two and slumped ungracefully into a chair, scissoring her legs with a swish of nylon stockings and silk underwear. "That boiler room was hell today," she muttered. "Thank God, I only do his teaching sessions now. Even the patients were sweating on the table."

"How did he perform? Badly, I hope."

"Sorry—he did brilliantly," she replied, without enthusiasm. "Two cancers—intestinal obstructions—and a lung resection without missing a stitch."

"As well as me?"

Patricia Holroyd studied him for a few moments, wondering if that smirk disguised a serious question. In the three years she had known him, shared his bed, listened to his pillow talk after the act of love, she had never succeeded in piercing that air of bland cynicism which overlaid his real personality. No one had, she guessed. He had worked so long on his bedside and bedroom manner that he took love and sickness, pain and death, in his stride. Even sex. His triumphs he shrugged aside as though the gods owed him those. Even fellow-surgeons envied his nerve and confidence; anyone who could go in with the knife after hopelessly inoperable cancer won their admiration, if not their respect. So did the man who could face the family or relatives waiting in the foyer with their checkbooks and intone with the right confessional words, "There is a thin thread of life. We are doing our best to hang on to it." His suave conviction made it sound like a steel hawser; and even in their bereavement, the next of kin spoke of him with praise and gratitude.

"I doubt if you could have done it as well, in front of all those students and postgraduate types," Patricia Holroyd responded candidly.

"Oh, well, we must accord him his little victories." His lip curled as he said it. "I thought seeing the newspaper might have brought on a touch of frozen hand."

She shook her head. "He didn't seem to be worried, though he must have read the story. Everybody in the hospital was talking about it, and the BBC mentioned it at lunch time." She lit a cigarette. "They say Fairchild saw the dean about the argument this morning, but I don't think he got anywhere."

"I know. He asked for Cameron's head, but old Prior has as much stuffing as a worm. He couldn't run a rabbit farm."

How did Conway-Smith keep his intelligence service going? She worked in the hospital, and he spent no more than half a dozen hours a week there; yet she often got her information from him. He had a policeman's mind; he knew who had killed whom in any one of the major teaching hospitals or clinics, who had left a swab in whom, who had taken a swig too many before scrubbing up, who earned what and from whom.

"I'm worried about one thing," she said. "I heard that Fairchild might press for an official inquiry about the operation on Fowler's wife."

"Why should you worry?"

She described the incident of the dropped scalpel. If they did hold an inquiry, she might be implicated as well as Cameron. And so might David, as his senior registrar. "It would be just Cameron's luck to get away with it," she muttered.

"He does seem to have a friend up there," Conway-Smith said, pointing heavenward.

"I wish I could get out of it," she said miserably.

"You can, you can."

"How?"

Though he did not reveal it, she had just given him an idea. If that spaniel of a senior registrar on whom she was so sweet had not covered up for Cameron, the job of deposing him would have been that much easier. Conway-Smith could hardly wait for the day the Professor of Surgery fell from grace, and it would make his triumph all the sweeter if he did the tripping, however indirectly. At one shot he might settle all those scores. His mind, resilient as it was, boiled at the injuries he had suffered. Everyone knew that consultant surgeons used the facilities of their hospitals to perform private operations. Except that great Gael with his fanatic conscience.

He could hear that peculiar voice, raised in a shout, telling him to take his private work elsewhere. "Other surgeons have the good grace and the moral sense to do at least some free work for the Health Service. Until you do, I'm damned if you're going to use my theaters to sterilize men and women. Any more of it and I'll drop a hint to the governors and let them deal with you." Cameron knew he had him, that male sterilization was frowned on ethically. Then that elderly patient with the hormone-dependent cancer. He was wealthy; he wanted to live. Why shouldn't he have removed his adrenals, then his pituitary? Why shouldn't he have castrated him, even if his physicians had whispered it was better to let him go? But that Highlandman had seized on the case at a clinical meeting, when everyone could guess who was being discussed, and used it to illustrate the ethos of surgery. He could hear him. "We are all licensed to commit grave errors in the name of medicine, to carry out purposeless assaults on the bodies of others, even to kill—but the man who makes his mistakes honestly cannot be called in question. However, the surgeon who operates for money becomes no more than a bloodsucker who lacks dedication or vocation, who practices a trade in flesh." The death of a thousand checks, he had called that case.

He might have fought Cameron in the open, defied his injunction about private work; he might even have won, for hospitals did not like tangling with men of consultant status. One thing stopped him: his fear of Cameron. For no reason that he could imagine, that man terrified him. He had other methods.

"I suppose you're going to the League of Friends' Ball next week?" he asked Holroyd. She nodded. "Wilkinson taking you, the lucky chap?"

"Yes," she replied. "Why do you ask? You're surely not turning up at that hop? I didn't think slumming with nurses and ex-patients was much in your line."

"It might be interesting this year," he said cryptically. In fact, he detested the ball, with its beer-and-sausage atmosphere, its horsy women, the mindless chatter of former inmates of St. Vincent's. "I'd like to see the fun. I might even join you and try to talk some sense into your boy friend."

"What about?"

"Well, for instance, taking that job in the States and letting his master do his own cutting. I think if we could persuade your David to buy his ticket, the great man might even sheath his scalpel without even the governors having to twist his arm."

"This I must see," she said. "I've been trying for months, and he won't listen to me."

"Or me. But there's one man he will listen to—his boss. Cameron himself."

"And, of course, you can easily arrange that!"

"Easier than you think," he murmured. When she had swallowed a few more drinks, had a good meal, when they had returned and quenched their passion, he would tell her how. As always, she would fall in with his wishes. "I've booked a table at Chez Luigi," he said. "We can come back afterward and have a nightcap." Patricia had relaxed and was smiling at him. Once they yielded, they always yielded, he thought. In sex, in everything. But she would come out of it well, with a first-class ticket to America.

16
? ?
?

When he read the newspaper story, Maclean instinctively sensed the hand of Barcroft. But who besides? As the taxi drove him to his consulting rooms that evening, he ran over the characters at the meeting. The Fairchilds he ruled out. Whatever his private doubts about Lady Fairchild, she could not possibly consort with a sleazy, boozy pound-a-liner with no morals and halitosis. As though to suggest an answer to his question, they passed a port-wine Rolls sitting at the curbside in Harley Street with a number plate reading RCS 2. When they asked Ralph Conway-Smith why he hadn't bought RCS 1, he had replied, "The Royal College of Surgeons would have thrown me out for breach of copyright." Yes, he and Barcroft would make an ideal pair, Maclean reflected. They both slit people up for gain; the journalist would damn Cameron or anyone else for a few column inches and an item or two on his expenses sheet.

At his consulting room he had to quell another rebellion by Deirdre, who expressed herself bluntly about the patients she had turned away, including Lady Blye. "We haven't made enough in the last two weeks to change the magazines in the waiting room," she complained.

"Not to worry. I'm learning so much about group psychiatry from Fiegler that we'll be able to fit in another three couches and take the fees at the door like a picture house."

She was not amused; he had to agree that he would spend no more than another week at St. Vincent's.

"There's something I'd like you to do for me," he said. "Pick up the phone, call Conway-Smith's secretary and ask when he has his appointment with Mr. Barcroft of *The World*."

"If this is something underhand, I'm not getting mixed up in it," she said. He had to move carefully with Deirdre; she struck these High Catholic attitudes. When he had assured her she was making a simple inquiry, she dialed the number and put the question while he listened on the extension.

"Who is this speaking?" asked the receptionist.

"Mr. Barcroft's secretary," Deirdre replied, without a tremor or a hint of impiety.

"But I'm sure he was here earlier this morning, and so far as I'm aware, he doesn't have another appointment."

He had guessed right. Conway-Smith had given Barcroft the details of the meeting, probably the contents of Fowler's letter as well. He might even have written those letters. He turned to Deirdre.

"As a reward, I'm taking you out tonight." For a second she forgot the unpaid bills and her scruples; her face beamed, then just as suddenly clouded over. She looked at him suspiciously.

"Where are we going?"

"I was thinking of the Sampan."

"What! That place they raided two months ago and caught all those drug addicts? You'll never get me in there. What would I tell . . ." She stopped, but he completed the sentence in his mind. What would she tell Father Gorman, her confessor?

"There'll be no hanky-panky. And I promise to let you reinstate Lady Blye and turn my appointment book into a supplement for Burke's Peerage."

"No."

"And I shall take you away for the weekend."

"Where to?" She was weakening.

"It's a surprise. But they're very rich people with a big country manor. We might even get them as patients. I said I couldn't possibly accept their invitation unless they extended it to my assistant."

That flattered her, but she was still dubious. "You're up to something," she said. "But I'll come to this place—only till midnight, though."

For such a dingy club in Soho they had imported astonishing talent. The man with the *Flügelhorn,* who sat

136

with his back half turned to the tables, his black face perspiring and his eyes hidden by sunglasses, was splitting chords into upper and lower harmonics like a maestro; the tenor sax player, another Negro, would catch his phrases, remodel them and toss them back while the pianist, drummer and bass player filled in the melody with variations. They took Maclean back to the days when he would stack up records of Hawkins, Ellington, Basie, Parker and Gillespie.

As he sipped tonic water, at five shillings a glass, he wondered how the liquor surcharge and the few bob extra on food could possibly pay such musicians. Was the answer not obvious? For "Sampan," read "Junk." These five jazzmen were touring to recharge their drug stock, which they could procure only at great cost in the States and by staying ahead of the Federal Bureau of Narcotics.

"What are you thinking?" said Deirdre, who looked as incongruous as a nun in a bordello.

"Just that I would like to run a saliva test on those players. They're all looking at the reflection of their own eyeballs."

"Half these beatniks are on drugs, too," she whispered darkly, indicating the contorting figures on the floor who were making contact only through their fingertips. "They're bound to notice us," she hissed.

"They're too far gone. But the waiter has got us both sized up."

"What do you mean?" she asked apprehensively.

"He thinks I'm a rich West End abortionist just running a reconnaissance eye over a potential source of profitable custom."

"And what does that make me?"

"Oh, you're my nurse. But you could be somebody doing the social rounds for the VD department at St. Vincent's, checking on known contacts and delivering little sermons to them on sexual hygiene."

Deirdre sawed off a piece of her steak with great gentility. "It's nearly midnight," she observed. "It doesn't look as though he's coming."

"He'll be here, don't worry." Rothwell invariably made the rounds of several clubs on his day off, and Sainsbury had listed this Soho basement as his favorite.

Just before one o'clock, Rothwell appeared. Maclean eyed his thin chest and stooped shoulders, the angular face with sagging cheeks and premature lines. "Poor goon. He'll do a lifetime of penance to heroin, cocaine or whatever. There but for the grace of God and Deirdre . . ." Rothwell sat at his usual table, a yard or two from where they sat, though half hidden by a pillar. He seemed to have friends everywhere in the club; and few of these who came to greet him left without taking one of the cigarettes he offered.

"Hashish?" Deirdre asked, giving the words a sinister ring, as though it signified the last thing in addiction.

"Amphetamine, I would think. Rolled into the cigarettes."

He watched Rothwell's face and hands. The anesthetist was inspecting his glass of liquor with a fixed look through his dark glasses, as though carrying out a census of the carbon-dioxide bubbles. He kept his back to the stage but every now and then took up the rhythm with his palm and fingers. The sounds might have been far away from the way he acted; a curious expression, dreamy, trancelike, lay over his face; his legs stuck out at a grotesque angle.

Maclean led Deirdre onto the floor, where they shuffled around among the twisting, pirouetting couples with Deirdre shuddering at the slightest touch, probably believing their addiction to be infectious. As they returned to their places, Maclean collided with the corner of Rothwell's table, spilling the glass of liquor over the anesthetist. "Sorry," he muttered, mopping up the mess with his handkerchief. Rothwell just stared through him.

"You must let me buy you another drink," the psychiatrist said, beckoning a waiter. "What is it?"

"He knows," Rothwell murmured. "He knows."

Maclean sat down. "My name's Glencoe—Malcolm Glencoe. And this is my friend, Peggy Kiernan." Rothwell swung his eyes on Deirdre, making a clicking noise with his tongue to acknowledge her attractiveness. Maclean could see that his secretary was wondering how she would square this acquiescence in a lie with Father Gorman, but she resolved her doubts and took the seat that Rothwell indicated. She looked like a canary watching a cat.

The anesthetist was staring silently at her hands. Finally he said, "Remarkable hands—translucent skin—blood ebbing and flowing through your wrists—systole, diastole—upbeat, downbeat—pulsing in the chitin of your fingernails." Deirdre fidgeted, as though he were X-raying her. He had switched his fixed stare to her eyes. "It's there, too—red arteries and black veins—pretty pictures on the retina." He leaned over to gaze into her eyes, and Deirdre sat, wide-eyed, as if she were submitting to her oculist. Then, suddenly, he kissed her on the mouth, and Maclean almost felt her shudder of disgust.

He realized that Rothwell was high on LSD. That bottle of Thornton's would be a bit depleted. He could imagine the anesthetist sitting at the hub of his own private cosmos, his skull gyrating with bright lights, his mind hovering between delirium and schizophrenia, all of this on a few pennies' worth of a chemical compound.

"You seem to know a lot about medicine," the psychiatrist remarked. "You a doctor?"

"At one of the country's renowned scientific abattoirs —graveyard over the road—funeral kilns half a mile away —need them both, man—I tell you, we need them both."

"Sounds a bit grim. What's it called?"

"St. Vincent's-in-the-Slums. If you're ever lying in the gutter and hear them utter that name, make your peace, man, make your peace. That way lies the coroner's office."

"And they told me it was a good hospital." Maclean grinned. "Who's the professor who did so much for the blue babies—Cameron, isn't it?"

Rothwell held up his hand, like someone taking an oath. "The great man—great surgeon—great humanitarian—piss-poor psychologist. My old man, he thought he was—didn't know nobody could sit in for my old man. For that he needed to be a swollen-headed, small-minded, sententious, swinish, scurrilous sadomasochist. How's that?" He lifted his head, as though to acknowledge his brilliant series of expletives, but Maclean noticed that his eyes were brimming with tears. He stretched out his left hand. "See that?" The little finger was mangled and permanently bent onto the palm. "A punishment. I was twelve and played hooky to go and hear Beecham conduct the Philharmonic. I was mad to play the clarinet. He smashed it. I was a doctor or nothing."

"And he broke your finger?"

"He hadn't the physical guts. No, he prayed and God heard him. Always there on the end of the line. I caught this on a bicycle chain. Funny, it didn't hurt—except between the ears. Even I thought the sign came from on high. Wish old Cameron could've met him."

"He seems just as bad, this professor of yours?"

Rothwell shook his head. "To hate him I've got to try."

Maclean had only sympathy for him. His casebooks grew fat on such stories—people crippled by parental misunderstanding or cruelty. Rothwell's conflict would

140

have split him down the middle without his resorting to drugs like LSD; he was rebelling against medicine, and what better way than to use medicine to ruin his career and his life? Cameron just happened to be there. Even if he had thought Rothwell deeply involved in the plot against the surgeon, Maclean could not, as a psychiatrist, leave the wretched character sitting in a place like this with his pill peddling, his fixes, listening to music he could never play and hating just for hating's sake.

"You must know the Fairchilds," Maclean said.

"Only one of them—Dame Barbara—she's my favorite character—after Cleopatra and Lady Macbeth."

"She's not that bad," Deirdre said, picking up her cue from Maclean.

"Give her a chance," Rothwell replied. He made to elaborate, but a shadow fell across the table; it was the *Flügelhorn* player. "Hiya, Phil," he said, nodding to Maclean and Deirdre.

"Sit, Charlie, sit. Meet these characters. He's a professional pie eater, and believe it or not, she's with him. Charlie Kerr's from Kansas City. He drops in here three, four times a year, and they don't pay him enough to buy lip salve."

Kerr's hand dropped limply into Maclean's, as if he were scared for his fingers. Behind his glasses he was watching the psychiatrist warily; he fingered the tuft of hair that sprouted just under his lower lip. "Interested in jazz?" he drawled.

"He's no croaker, Charlie," said Rothwell, slapping him on the back. He turned to Maclean. "Charlie's the best in the business. Better than Dizzy or Miles. Man, that obbligato the number before last—those harmonics, the passing notes, the inverted chords. Genius, real genius."

"Just good old gut-bucket jazz from way down there." Kerr smiled, pointing to his navel. "I'm still using the same sheet o' music I started out with." He looked hard at Rothwell. "Feel like takin' the air?" Rothwell gave a nod and followed him over the dance floor toward the exit leading to the toilets.

"What's a croaker?" Deirdre asked.

"A doctor who supplies junkies with their drugs. What Rothwell is doing now."

"He'll remember all those false names," she hissed.

"He's too high. He'll think he met us in some bad dream."

While he talked, Maclean was fishing in an inside pocket and brought out something like a packet of headache powder. He leaned over and tipped the contents into Rothwell's drink. "Just a couple of grains of something to make him really forget," he explained to the wondering girl. "When he has drunk it, you slip out and phone Dr. Sainsbury at Vincent's, and I'll find a cab."

After a quarter of an hour, Rothwell and the Negro returned. Kerr flapped a hand toward them and climbed back onto the stand to take a solo, which seemed to have no beginning or end. Rothwell sipped the drink slowly while they watched and waited. It took half an hour for the cigarette to drop from his hand and his head to loll forward. Deirdre went to the phone booth, and Maclean signed to the waiter.

He helped Rothwell across the floor. When he picked him up to carry him up the narrow stairs, he realized the young man was no more than skin and bone; he laid him out on the back seat of the cab.

On the way he emptied Rothwell's pockets, ignoring the pills and ampoules that filled them, but seizing the wallet and ferreting through it. "Not a thing," he muttered, stuffing it back. But he pocketed Rothwell's key ring.

Sainsbury waited for them at the hospital gate. Jump-

142

ing into the cab, he instructed the driver to circle the courtyard and make for the rear buildings. "We've arranged to put him in a private room in the geriatric wing. Donovan will look after him until you've finished. How long?"

"An hour at the most, then you can give him some chlorpromazine and his keys. And, Joe . . . make sure he has a couple of weeks away from here, and when he comes back, send him to see me in Harley Street. No gas machines until he does."

"You're on a loser with this one."

"No—he hasn't got a bent mind. Just a bent finger. I think I can straighten it out."

In the short walk from the hospital to the block of flats, Maclean had to rationalize what he had done in the club. He also had a pang of conscience about ransacking Rothwell's flat.

His living room stank of stale liquor and smoke; cigarettes and matches stippled the floor and carpet; newspapers and magazines littered the place. A pair of trousers and a shirt hung from the knob of the bedroom door. Maclean picked up the bottle that stood on the small piano. Two hundred of the most potent amphetamine capsules! The chaos and filth reminded Maclean of another flat that had the signs of a hapless, shiftless character—his own flat, before he had broken his drink addiction. The props of Rothwell's purposeless existence had more impact on him than half a hundred hours of free association.

But Rothwell's personal problem could wait a fortnight. First, the letters, which he would find there if he had guessed correctly. The writing-table drawers bulged with paper, drug samples, bric-a-brac. As he sorted through them, several photographs spilled from a paper wallet. That girl lying in the bows of a punt like a bra ad

—yes, it was Holroyd, that gregarious nymph. He recognized none of the others, and he was about to push the snaps into the folder when he stopped and cast through them again. The towel, the smile, the fact that he did not expect her in this company—all had fooled him. The face of Lady Fairchild stared at him. A few years younger. When did she marry Fairchild? She stood on one leg, draped in an outsize bath towel, holding aloft the costume she had wriggled out of, giving the photographer—Rothwell, he supposed—a triumphant grin. A curious liaison!

Back to the bedroom drawers, the bedside table, the wardrobe and the piled cases. They yielded nothing. Where would an addict hide documents? With his most precious material. The bathroom caught his eye, and its small, locked cupboard. One key fitted. And there, behind the bottles, the vials, the hypos, lay a package with two of the three letters he had been seeking. He hurried back.

"So it was that bent-head after all," Sainsbury growled.

"Maybe, but I don't think so. Addicts don't have that sort of follow-through. We'll probably find copies elsewhere." He spread the letters and ran a magnifying glass over them. "From the alignment and pressure, I'd say an electric machine." He halted the glass. "Both on the same machine." He handed the lens to Sainsbury. "Have a look at the colon in the address. You'll see a small spline of metal between the points. Now if we got samples . . ."

"We don't need to. There are—what?—nine of those machines." Sainsbury went to a filing cabinet, pulled out several sheaves of correspondence and weeded a couple of dozen letters from them. They sieved through the letters, but none of them contained the same flaw.

"Does Cameron's secretary work on an electric machine?"

"Miss Fletcher! You can't be serious."

144

"Let's have a look." When they found some of the letters and peered at them, there it was—the same thin line.

"It's got to be somebody else," Sainsbury exclaimed.

"I didn't say it was Miss Fletcher. I just thought it might be Cameron sending out some sort of SOS."

"But anybody could borrow that typewriter."

"Not anybody—it would have to be somebody who knew more than a little about psychology and wanted to make it appear that Cameron might have written those letters himself."

"You're the expert," Joe said. "But why would Cameron try this roundabout way instead of going to the dean or myself?"

"If he's mentally ill, which I believe, he's quite capable of an irrational act which would focus attention on his illness without admitting it. Think of the people who go to the brink, attempting suicide, to alert their friends or even their doctors."

"So what do I do?"

"You make sure that Cameron never operates alone. Wilkinson is nearly always with him, isn't he?"

"Unless Cameron's on emergency call. He spends his nights here and often turns out when something is happening in Casualty. I'll have to pass the word on quietly that he's not to be called until further notice."

"I wasn't so worried about Casualty. Blatchford is due in soon?"

"This weekend the ballyhoo starts. Cameron will have to do that one. He'll want to, and his Lordship will insist."

"Just make sure that young Wilkinson is at his elbow and well briefed," Maclean said.

They quickly photocopied the letters, and Maclean marched back to the flat to replace them in the cupboard. As he did, he was grappling with the many possible solutions to the puzzle. Holroyd, Lady Fairchild, Conway-

Smith, Rothwell—and now Cameron himself. He wished it were an ordinary problem in human behavior with nice, rounded motives like greed, jealousy, lust, revenge, instead of a conundrum with its answer lying in the bottom layer of somebody's mind. He must forget the others and their motives. Cameron was his priority. Could he, consciously or unconsciously, have rung the bell himself with those letters? Running over the surgeon's actions since their first encounter, Maclean could not rule out the possibility that he had chosen this way. Hysterics and depressives often employed every form of trick to warn people that they were ill, that they might do something desperate. And Cameron had many of the signs of hysteria. As he had just hinted to Sainsbury, such actions came from one group in particular: those who intended to commit suicide. It might explain Cameron's act if he had formed the idea of killing himself, even though he might not have admitted the possibility to himself. How much longer did he have to solve the problem of Cameron? The Fowler brothers would not wait forever; Blatchford's operation would have to be done within a week or so. Above all, he had to prevent Cameron from doing anything desperate. He quickened his stride.

17
? ?
?

Early that morning, before Sainsbury could pass his instruction on to Casualty, they brought a young man in for an emergency appendix operation. Since Cameron had left orders that he was acting as duty surgeon, they summoned him and Sister Tremayne, who was standing in for Donovan. Cameron arrived in the nurses' room at the Casualty theater, a sports coat thrown over his pajama jacket, his old flannels bagging at the knees; his red hair was disheveled, and a curious light sparked in his eyes. As Sister Tremayne held his gloves for him to don them, she was sure she smelled whisky on his breath.

"Where's Donovan?" he said brusquely, without looking at her or so much as greeting her.

"She's having tonight and tomorrow off," the sister replied. "She asked me to take over her duties." Donovan had made no mention of Rothwell to her or to anyone else.

"So I've got only you," he barked. "All right, let's get on with it."

He glanced at the patient, swathed everywhere except the lower abdomen with green cloths; then his gaze traveled to the nervous house surgeon, who sat near the anesthetist's trolley, monitoring the instruments and glancing warily at both the surgeon and the patient.

"Now, what the hell has happened to Rothwell? I know for a fact that he was on duty this morning."

"They said he has fallen sick, Professor," Sister Tremayne answered.

She was beginning to grow concerned because of the distrait attitude of Cameron. His hand movements seemed awkward as he kneaded the appendix area with his gloved fingers prior to making the incision. When he finally made the oblique cut, she noticed with surprise that it ran a good inch and a half too long; but she retracted the tissue around the wound, handing him a pack so that he could prize out the appendix. Even that simple action appeared to give him great trouble. She began to wonder if he were ill or drunk.

The organ was small. To clamp off the upper end and

sever it should have presented no difficulty to a surgeon of Cameron's skill and experience; however, he fumbled with the forceps, his hands working against each other, seemingly incapable of co-ordination. Sister Tremayne reached forward and grasped the forceps, thinking this would allow him to cut the appendix more easily. Roughly he thrust her hand aside. "I'm here to do whatever surgery is necessary, Sister," he snapped.

"Professor Cameron," she said quietly. "May I have a word with you outside for a minute?"

"No."

She released her hold on the retractors, which made it almost impossible for him to carry out the surgery. "All right, Sister," he said, shooting her a grim stare, then following her into the changing room.

"Professor, perhaps I shouldn't say this, but I think that we need some more help. Shall I call Mr. Wilkinson?"

"What are you suggesting, woman? That I can't do an appendix without my registrar?"

"It's not that, but it seems to be a difficult case, sir."

"Difficult!" He snorted. "I could do it with a razor blade and a piece of twine. Now you keep your head and your place, and do what you're told, and we'll finish what we started."

She stood where she was, shaking her head. "No, sir. If you want the truth, I think you're ill or . . ."

"Or what?"

"Drunk."

His face went white, then a flush spread over his high cheekbones above the mask; his eyes narrowed, and his hand rose in an arc. For a moment she was convinced that he was going to strike her. Then the crisis passed as quickly as it had arisen; he seemed to remember where they were. He smiled and took her arm. "Sister Tremayne,

I'm neither drunk nor ill. I give you my word. Perhaps I was a bit sleepy. We'll get this boy to give us a hand to see the patient through, what d'you say?"

Although his hand had steadied and he did the cutting and sewing without faltering or further incident, she still had misgivings about the operation. She kept them to herself, however. In half an hour they had finished and gone their ways.

Cameron returned to his flat. He still had a couple of hours before the tea was brought. He rolled into bed and closed his eyes. But sleep did not come; between him and oblivion appeared the face of the girl he had just left. He was no longer angry about the reproach in those curious, greenish-brown eyes. He could see, too, the fluid curve of her breasts and hips, the full, sensuous lips. He conjured up the sweep of her supple hands as she went through the drill with instruments and swabs. He tried to erase the images from his mind but failed. Had he come all the way for this—to fall prey to lust—or was it love? Not that, for God's sake! Involuntarily he let out a long groan; perspiration burst from him as it might had he climbed out of a hot bath or risen after a night of hard drinking. Jumping up, he quickly threw on some clothes and walked out into the first long rays of sunlight. The fetid night air of the East End had been laid by the dew, and he caught the sweet, damp incense from the yellow candles of the linden trees in the courtyard leading to the maternity wing.

The dew spangled on the quartet of lime trees like the sweat on his eyelashes. Under them the roses glowed yellow and red within the border of pinks around the small garden; the lawn flashed with a million tiny light points. Why had he never found time to pause and look at such things before? For some time he just stood, marking the slow procession of the sun, which shone without warmth, throwing a fleshy sheen onto the concrete buildings. The morning breeze eddied around his bare throat. Above him he heard the racket of a jet, and he glanced aloft at the frayed string of its contrail. Up there it was cool, pure, sterile. Suddenly he felt utterly, helplessly, miserably alone; his life seemed to have lost point and continuity. Surgery had been his all, his existence, his obsession. Even there his touch was deserting him. That he could not face. His mind turned in on itself, his night thoughts prowling again. He found that he had wandered, without awareness, to the nurses' wing, where Donovan lived. Where Tremayne had her room. Welling up within him came the outrageous desire to barge in, to face her, to lay his contrition before her, to plead her forgiveness for his insults, to confide his thoughts and fears in her. His conscience checked him. No, you old, dishonest Highland fool, that is cant and hypocrisy, it said. You want to say sorry, though you don't mean it. You would beg her pardon, for which you wouldn't give a damn. Be true to yourself. You really want her body. Her lips. Her tawny skin. Her acquiescent flesh. That's what you want.

He discovered that he had picked a yellow rose from the courtyard garden. He crushed it in his fingers, tossed it away from him and wandered with dragging feet back to the solitude of his own rooms.

18
? ?
?

She had never set out to seduce anybody before; but she had to do something desperate if she did not want to lose him altogether. Most of her savings had gone on the right sort of black dress, which showed off her figure without actually flaunting it. There, at least, she scored over Holroyd; thank God she needed no structural engineering, no geodetic bra to support and emphasize the shape of her breasts, no three-way stretch girdle to contain her hips. But how would David react to it? He was a bit like her father, and he would have damned the dress as being too vulgar. So, too, her new perfume, which its makers called À en Mourir, and which she translated loosely as "One Sniff and He's Stone-Dead." Sylvester had toiled for three hours, back-combing and lacquering her hair, until it sat on her head like some candy-floss turban. She found no fault with that. It was the nose, the Cameron nose, that caused her to grimace in the mirror. Half an hour of plastic surgery would have turned that bead into a tiptilt and buffed away the prominent blade of the bridge. However, it would have outraged her father's professional and Presbyterian conscience to have resorted to "one of those beauty merchants." She was stuck with it.

She glanced finally around the tiny flat to which she had invited David for supper after the ballet. Had she overprepared the event? She checked the fridge for the umpteenth time—truffled *pâté de foie gras,* cold chicken breasts, ice cream. Hardly a banquet, but there was champagne and white wine to soften the atmosphere. She had laid out the records he admired: on top, *L'Après-midi d'un faune.* She hoped that wouldn't make her appear like a female faun, whatever that was, hungering for its *après-midi.* Did it look too obviously like a seduction supper? And could she bring it off? She had inherited too much of her father's character to make it easy: his taboos on sex, his tight control on emotions, his honesty. With that sort of genetic equipment you did not have holes in your chastity belt. It would be a tussle between her instinct and her Scots scruples. But she had to compete with the Holroyds of this world.

How had Holroyd managed it? Of course, David and she had a common bond: They could talk about appendectomies, mitral valvotomies, all the jargon of their job. They strove together to ease pain and sickness. They also slept together, which all the jargon in the world, had she learned it, would not have counterbalanced.

When he arrived, David seemed weary and preoccupied. He was also half tight, the first time she had ever seen him with so much drink. She guessed it might have some connection with the clinical meeting, the newspaper reports and her father's reactions. At all costs she must keep the hospital and his name out of the conversation. She hid her disappointment that he had not even glanced at her dress, her hair, her make-up. And who could smell À en Mourir through all that drink?

"Have we time for a quick one?" he asked, pointing to the drink cabinet. She nodded and poured him a whisky, which he gulped neat. "Can I help myself?" he queried, slopping a larger one into the glass and downing that just as quickly. "I feel like getting drunk tonight," he said.

"Any particular celebration?" she asked, thinking he was getting his tenses mixed up.

"No, nothing—just a decision I've made, an important personal decision." He caught her quizzical look. "I'll tell you later," he went on, eying the clock. "We've got to hurry."

He's leaving the hospital, Stroma thought as they got into the car. She had never met this side of him before. He seemed bitter and hard. He drove too fast and too recklessly through the evening traffic between Kensington and Covent Garden, slaloming around cars and racing through the narrow, crowded Soho streets without regard for cars or pedestrians. She uttered a word of caution, which he ignored.

If she had expected any help from *Romeo and Juliet,*

she was disappointed. He dozed through the first act, and she sat on tenterhooks wondering whether he would snore in the middle of the balcony scene. Between the second and third acts they descended to the bar behind the foyer, where he pummeled through the mob and came back clutching a Martini for her and two large whiskies for himself. "To sustain me through the death agonies in the final act," he said.

"Don't you like the performance?"

"Not bad." He shrugged. "I suppose they're putting the right norm of proletarian sweat into it. But Slavs trying to play Shakespearian Italians is a bit of a strain on the imagination."

She let his cynicism go. They were finishing their drinks when someone elbowed through the crowd to confront them. "Professor Cameron's daughter, isn't it? How is he? I'm one of his old patients." He introduced himself as an official of the Royal Opera House and went on effusively about Cameron as a man and as a surgeon, describing his stay in St. Vincent's and his health before and after.

"Get him to take off his soup-and-fish and show us his scar," David whispered loudly. She pretended not to hear, and he nudged her. "Go on, dare him. It'll make the evening."

Fortunately the man pretended not to have heard. As he was going, he said suddenly, "I've just thought—we're giving a small party for the Russian *corps de ballet* after the show and have invited a few guests. If you and your friend would like to come and meet them and have a drink, you're more than welcome."

"We'd love to, wouldn't we, David?" Stroma said. From the set of David's face, she realized she had made the wrong response. That "we" splintered what had remained of their fragile understanding.

"Miss Cameron will come, but count me out," he said. "I'm on duty at the hospital from midnight on and have to get back."

"If you can make it, well and good," the official said as he departed.

"You didn't tell me you had to get back," she said.

"Sorry, I'm on call."

"But I thought you said . . ."

"That's the trouble with some people—they take too much for granted. They think—and everything must follow."

"You're not being very fair, David. You did agree, but if you don't want to come back for supper, I'm not going to plead with you." For a moment her face reminded him of her father's when someone had interrupted his rhythm or misread a diagnosis. His temper flashed.

"No, the Camerons never plead. They snap a finger. Well, I'm fed up with this divine-right attitude. I spend my days taking stick from your old man like some Oriental slave. I even cover up for him when his hand shakes or slips. That's fine in the operating theater, but not outside it. Not outside it." He repeated the words savagely.

"So you're another," she said. "And I thought that you at least were loyal. You know that he's never in his life asked anyone to cover up for him. He may be hard, but he's just, and he's given you and others their credit. No . . . why should I have to make his excuses or defend him, to you or to anybody? And I don't have to stand here and listen to insults about him."

She pushed her way quickly through the bar crowd and up the steps, through the foyer and into Covent Garden. She hailed a cab. She heard him call her name and saw him running toward the cab; she hesitated for a moment before ordering the driver to take her home. She found herself trembling, not with anger but with reproach

154

at having lost her temper. She had probably finished herself with him for good. But on those terms did she want him? The trouble was, she did. In her flat she gazed wistfully at the table, with its candles growing out of sprigs of leaves, and thought of the meal they might have had. She could not face that recollection the next morning, so she slipped into a negligee and began to clear the things away. The flat bell rang, and she switched on the intercom.

"It's me—David," the voice said. "I must see you. Open the door."

"No. It's too late, David. Anyway, you've got to get back to the hospital."

"Damn the hospital. Open the door. I've come to apologize."

"David, stop shouting. Everybody will hear you."

"All right, if you don't open up, I'll ring every bell in the block until somebody comes down and lets me in." She pressed the button to unlock the front door and heard him bounding upstairs, tripping over the lopsided top step. She held the flat door open. He was breathless, and his voice was slurred. "I had to see you, to say I was sorry," he got out.

"You didn't drive here?" she asked, and he nodded. "In that state! You might have killed somebody. You'd better leave the car and take a cab to the hospital—I'll call one."

He grabbed her by the arm. "No cab—no hospital."

"But you said . . ."

"I know, I was on duty. It was a lie, and don't ask me why, or I'll get all mixed up about the whole Cameron clan again."

"Well, if you're determined to drive back, you'd better have some coffee and something to eat." She shuddered at the thought of his bobbing and weaving halfway across

155

London in thick traffic when he could hardly walk straight.

"No eats," he said. "You said you had some champagne."

"Think of tomorrow."

"The night before is always worth the morning after."

"On your head, then," she said, handing him the champagne bottle and stepping out of the line of the cork, which he was pointing at her, while his fingers groped at the wire binding it. The liquid bubbled and frothed over the rims of the two glasses; he handed one to Stroma and raised the other.

"I'm sorry about tonight, Stroma," he muttered, swallowing the champagne in one go. "Am I forgiven?" She nodded. He refilled the glass and trinked hers again. "Here's to the huge decision that I've just unmade."

"So now you can tell me what it was."

"No, impossible. You'd slap my teeth out."

"You're teasing, David. I know what it was. You were going to leave the hospital."

"It wasn't that. Well, maybe it was. I mean, I suppose I might have had to. Anyway, I wouldn't have wanted to stay around and watch the tragedy."

"What tragedy?"

"Oh, nothing. I've shipped a bit too much." She needed no telling; he was drinking so fast that she wondered how long the combination of drinks would take to knock him over. She asked herself why he was so resolved to get drunk. He was grasping the end of the bottle with both hands, as though squeezing the final drops into his glass. "I forgot," he said thickly. "I was going to apologize to you."

"For the third time?"

"So you're counting, but you haven't accepted."

"Yes, I have—twice."

156

"Know something? I don't deserve it." He proffered his glass, and she filled it with tonic water, which he gulped without detecting the difference. He spoke slowly, choosing his words. "Did I ever tell you how pretty you were? I mean, how pretty you are . . . good figure . . . and those legs . . . and your face."

"Yes, my face?" she said.

"You know the thing I like most about it . . . it's interesting . . . and you know the thing I think is most interesting?"

"My nose."

"How did you guess? Did you know it has a bead at the end and a kink in the bridge?"

"I had noticed," Stroma said.

"Well, I like it . . . I adore it . . . it's a nose of character . . . great character. Not stuck up like some of those retroussé items the plastiqueurs turn out in Harley Street . . . not dead like Greek snouts . . . something to be proud of . . . like that chap Cyrano de what's-'is-name."

"I know who you mean, and I know exactly how he felt. But it's not as bad as that; it's not a ski run."

"Don't change it for anything . . . it's your trade-mark . . . just like the old man's. Promise?"

"I promise." For a moment she thought he was tantalizing her, but his expression stayed serious. What could she do with him? Drive him back to St. Vincent's or call a cab? What if they saw him in that state or perhaps summoned him to an emergency before he had sobered up? She would have to put him up in the flat.

"David." He raised his head and looked sleepily at her. "I don't think you ought to go back to Vincent's tonight. I can put you up here, on the couch."

"Im-possible. Sleep here and compromise the boss's daughter? What would old Cameron, the Highland chieftain, say about that?"

"He'd probably laugh if I ever told him."

"Yes, I know that laugh . . . before he cuts me down."

She ignored the hand that stuck out the glass; she put his feet up onto the couch, pulled off his shoes, loosened his tie and covered him with a traveling rug. She switched off the main light and went to put out the standard lamp, when he called her over. "I'm sorry, Stroma."

"How many more times?"

"But you can't guess what for. My big night . . . a bit of a giggle now. Know what I was going to do? Bring you home and get you slightly oiled . . . not too much, not enough to spoil things . . . just slightly, that's all. I was going to throw compliments all over you . . . tell you how pretty I thought you are . . . I mean how pretty I think you were. Then I was going to unbutton you . . . all those buttons, one by one . . . then the shoulder straps, a quick pull . . . and snap! the hooks at the back that hold things together . . . then the what's-'is-name . . . I can never remember . . . it's like skinning a banana . . . where was I?"

"Pulling off the girdle that I don't happen to wear."

"I'd never have known. Anyway, then I was going to make love to you . . . no, seduce you."

"And if I hadn't collaborated?"

"I'd figured that out as well . . . collaboration, co-operation, calibration . . . it wouldn't have mattered. I would have violated you, assaulted you . . . yes, even raped you."

"But why, David, why?"

"How am I to know? I don't know . . . honestly, I don't know." His voice trailed off. "If you want to know, there's one person who'd know . . . your old man . . . he would know."

He had talked himself asleep. Stroma switched off the light and went into her bedroom. As she undresssed, she wondered what had stopped him, why he had drunk himself incapable of going through with his plan. His babbled confession had not shocked her. Worried her, perhaps. She almost wished her guess had been right, that he had made up his mind to leave the hospital, to get away from her father's influence for a time at least. While her mind tried to resolve the riddle of David's behavior, she heard him tossing and groaning in the next room, as if he, too, were wrestling with some problem. Finally, she fell asleep. When she rose, just after dawn, he had already gone, without a word or a note.

19
? ?
?

Like most phobias, Maclean's horror of cars was irrational and emotional. Since his own crash, he had given up driving. He made a wretched passenger, too, sitting on the edge of his nerves. Now he had Cameron at the wheel, and knowing his record did not help. In the Canal Zone the surgeon had once cannoned into a derelict Valentine tank he must have passed at least twenty times; he had cracked a wristbone cranking a diesel generator; he had to submit to a series of painful antirabies injections following a bite from a pariah dog. No wonder they had called him accident-prone. Surely, Maclean thought, nothing much can happen between the hospital and the surgeon's home, twenty miles away. The cat worried him. It lay astride the back rest just behind Cameron's shoulders, poking its black snout through the window to catch the breeze on its whiskers, croaking into the surgeon's ear from time to time. Only too vividly did Maclean recall stories of crashes where everything had perished except some cat, which had dusted itself off with its tongue and padded on to its next life as though nothing had happened.

Beyond Dorking, they turned into a drive flanked by sweet chestnuts and rhododendrons, which they followed for a quarter of a mile until Cameron's cottage came into view. "What a charming place," Deirdre cried. It was a stone building, two storys high, with an attic which virtually made a third floor. The surgeon explained that he had bought it from the owner of the estate five years previously and rented a couple of acres of ground. He used it mainly for weekends and holidays. Maclean found it attractive, with its porch giving on to lawns and rose beds among the birches and yews. All the same, he thought of the mansions and the vast estates that other surgeons had acquired and compared them with this modest dwelling, which had probably put Cameron in debt to his bank. But then, he knew money had never interested the surgeon.

Stroma came out to greet them. She had driven down before them and had tea ready. Except for a glimpse of her in the hospital, Maclean had not set eyes on her for several years, not since he had spent part of his drying-out with the surgeon at another house near Hampton Court. Stroma had come there between terms from her boarding school. As a child she had called him Uncle Mac, trotting him around her cages of rabbits, guinea pigs and birds, twisting his arm for some small addition to the zoo. Now she noticed the look he gave the small hut near the end of the garden. "Nothing there," she said. "We had to part with them all when we moved. It was very sad."

"And the jackdaw—what happened to that thief, the one that said, "Turnyourhead . . . totheright . . . and-cough'?"

160

She laughed. "It was a long time before I realized you had perverted him with that little speech from the army-doctors' medical-inspection manual. We lost him. He got very snooty and superior and up and left one day." When Stroma smiled, or when her face reflected some bright thought, she was pretty; but now and again she turned sad, as though some shadow had petrified on her face. They had tea on the porch and chatted. Then Cameron said to Maclean and Deirdre, "What about a stroll before dinner? You can have a look at the estate and the river. The squire gives me the run of his place."

"Sorry, Murdo, I've got a lot to do before dinner, but Deirdre's a country girl. She'd love a ramble through nature with you."

"What are you going to do?" Cameron said suspiciously.

"If you want to know, Father, it's a surprise. Uncle Mac's going to cook us a Scotch dinner."

"What's that?" Cameron grunted. "Finnan haddie and chips?"

"Wait and see," she said.

They watched Cameron and Deirdre follow the path out of the cottage grounds, the Siamese cat loping behind them. Stroma smiled at Maclean. "I suppose I'd better look you out an apron and show you the kitchen if you're still serious about that dinner."

"That can wait. I thought you might want to have a chat about him while he's away."

"About my father?" she answered incredulously.

"You mean," he said, "that you didn't invite me down here to talk about him?"

"I didn't even invite you. He suggested it himself and seemed very pleased when you agreed."

"The old fox," he muttered. "And you? You're not worried about him?"

She fixed her eyes on him for a moment, then gazed after the retreating figures. Camerons still didn't tell, Maclean reflected. Though this time Murdo had made some mute appeal for help, whether he admitted it or not. Stroma was watching his face, asking herself whether she should break her own vow of silence. The psychiatrist made up her mind by rapidly outlining everything about the case, from the letter he had received up to the moment when Cameron had exploded before the clinical meeting. "And don't think this is my first house call," he said.

"I'm glad you came," Stroma said. "I was too scared to say anything to him or to anybody else. And yet I was afraid he'd do something silly."

"As long as he has this clever assistant—Wilkinson, isn't it?—he won't get into much trouble at the hospital."

"I didn't mean that. Perhaps I had better show you." She rose, and Maclean trailed her down to the shed, where, she explained, her father did most of his writing. It had a desk and a chair, a leather couch and a library of books. His eye took in the dust on the medical books, some by Cameron himself, the classics, the piles of medical journals. No one seemed to have used the hut for months. Stroma lifted the lid of the iron stove, which was full of charred paper. "That's what's left of the book he was writing on experimental surgery. I came on him tearing it up and burning it, chapter by chapter, and cursing in a way I had never heard him in my life. It was awful."

"Do you remember when it was?"

"A Saturday afternoon—about eight months ago." She replaced the lid. "After he had started the fire, he lay down on the couch and just sobbed."

"Did he say why he had burned the manuscript?"

"He had lost the place, he said. I remember something

of what he was muttering. He said it was like driving along a road you'd known all your life and suddenly not knowing where you were. The houses, the gardens, the lights, the crossroads—everything seemed strange and terrifying, because he couldn't identify them."

"He hasn't done anything rash since then, and it's a long time ago. Probably just a fit of the blues."

"That was what I thought. I told myself he was letting the hospital get on top of him, and that was why he'd forget important dates or names and fly off the handle at little things—at times he was like a caricature of himself."

"Was there another episode?"

She nodded. "Just two weeks ago we came down here. He was very cheerful—he'd done a successful operation on Sarah's old dog, we'd been to the theater and it was my birthday. On Sunday he disappeared into the attic, where he has piled all his junk over the years. He had a fire there as well. I didn't know until afterward."

"Can I have a look?"

She led him back into the cottage and up the narrow, twisting stairs. The attic was small, with double dormer windows and wainscoting on the walls, which had clean square patches where pictures had obviously hung for years; charred and burned paper filled the tiny, iron grate. "He stripped the pictures off the walls, tore them out of the frames and burned them. The same with the papers and diaries and things he had treasured, like university scrolls and mementos of trips abroad. At times he's quite normal, and then he does something like this. Is he going out of his mind?"

"That's what I came to try to find out."

"I'd have thought," she said, "that somebody at St. Vincent's would have noticed he was ill and done something about it."

"It's like looking for the thief or murderer in the pulpit. They're too busy treating the sickness that's brought to them to go out of their way looking for it."

Stroma took up a position by the window, to alert him if they returned, while he started to ferret in the writing desk. He reflected sourly that he was becoming practiced at snooping. As he opened the drawers, he grew more and more disquieted about Cameron's frenzied action and its obvious purpose. He must have emptied drawers and pigeonholes and burned letters and photograph albums as well. Maclean looked for photographs of his wife but found none. Had he destroyed those along with the others? However, in one small recess, he fell upon a scrapbook of the kind children kept a couple of generations ago, with garish, angelic figures stuck to its pages with flour and water. Several sepia photographs were scattered among the scraps. From the style of dress, Maclean reckoned they dated from the years after the First World War. The curly headed child would be Cameron, aged three or four; the woman holding him in her arms had a wistful look, a beautiful face, even if the mouth seemed too wide, the lips too full. She wore a blouse of Brussels lace, pinned at the neck with a gold clip. She had no marriage ring. Cameron's mother? The other pictures showed an older boy with two grandparents, the man with high Celtic cheekbones and walrus mustache and the woman wearing a hand-knitted shawl and a mutch on her head. Why had these escaped the fire? The room presented Maclean with a peculiar puzzle. Cameron had suffered his bout of pyromania a fortnight ago; if it were part of a process of personal annihilation, why hadn't he followed it with an attempt at suicide?

He turned to Stroma, signifying that he had finished. "It's hard to say what all this means," he muttered.

"I thought he was going to kill himself," she said.

"That's what frightens me. He's never had much patience with people who were less than perfect, and if he thought he was past his best, he wouldn't want to go on."

"I can warn one or two people at the hospital to keep an eye on him. But knowing Murdo, I don't think he'll do himself in." Maclean hoped he sounded sincere, but he had as grave misgivings as the girl. The two fires might have been the same sort of sign to Stroma as the letters—if Cameron had written those himself.

"Your secretary's coming back," Stroma announced. They went downstairs to meet Deirdre, who looked flushed, as though she had run all the way back. She hurried upstairs, saying she would see them at dinner. Minutes later Cameron returned to find them in the kitchen, preparing the meal. "Can I give a hand?" he asked.

"Go and stick your feet up, and we'll be ready to eat in an hour," Maclean replied.

The apron Stroma had given him dangled like a sporran on his massive frame. She was amazed by the speed at which he prepared the soup, set the main course going and organized the table. He had brought wine for the girls and a bottle of rare whisky for Cameron; each plate had a sprig of purple heather beside it, and he had even provided candles in the Scottish colors: blue and white.

From the porch Cameron watched the table taking shape. "What are we celebrating? Burns Night was five months ago."

"Bannockburn," Maclean said with a straight face. "It's the six hundred and fifty-sixth anniversary on Monday, though being a Highlandman, you'd prefer to forget that during that great battle your ancestors were only the gillies that Bruce used for brewing and for making pease brose and bannocks."

Cameron let the gibe pass. "Don't say you've got pease brose and bannocks?"

"The next best thing," Maclean said. He had drafted the menu in French, the only language, according to him, in which Scottish food could be made to sound palatable. He handed it to the surgeon.

"What in Jock Thamson's name is this?" Cameron exclaimed, reading the card. "*Potage cultivateur?*"

"Scotch broth."

"*Andouillette à l'écossaise?*"

"That's haggis, and you can thank my secretary, who had Coopers make it up specially and fly it down, well away from the pilot. And the *navets* and *pommes purées* are mashed tatties and neaps."

"*Crêpes à la mode d'Edimbourg*—'Edinburgh pancakes'? Never heard of them."

"Leatherjackets with apricot jam inside. The only thing I couldn't get was a quaich for your whisky and a piper to pipe in the haggis."

The psychiatrist's sense of fun infected Cameron, and he entered into the spirit of the thing. Only Deirdre seemed subdued when she came downstairs at the start of the banquet. Maclean asked why.

"Probably me," Cameron put in. "I have to confess that I've been attempting to suborn your secretary. Fletcher's getting a bit long-toothed, and I feel that Miss O'Connor would welcome a real job instead of playing handmaiden to people who need their psyches dismantled and reassembled."

Maclean let out a peal of laughter. "You wouldn't last a week with her. She'd take over the department and have everybody clocking in and doing scalpel drill by numbers. And she'd never get used to the gore and finality of surgery. One thing about mental cases: their illnesses don't usually kill them unless . . ." Maclean broke off, aware that he was treading on dangerous ground.

Cameron merely chortled, but Deirdre did not share the joke.

When they had finished the soup, Maclean carried in the steaming haggis and placed it with great ceremony on the table. He filled up the glasses, then turned to Cameron. "Come on, Murdo, you've got to say the right words." Many a time he had listened to the surgeon propose the toast of the Immortal Memory on Burns Night, highly impressed with his ability to recite screeds of "Tam o' Shanter" or "The Cotter's Saturday Night." Rising in the steam from the meal-and-meat pudding, Cameron began to intone the poet's "Ode to a Haggis":

> *"Fair fa' your honest, sonsie face,*
> *Great Chieftain o' the Puddin-race!*
> *Aboon them a' ye take your place,*
> *Painch, tripe or thairm . . ."*

That was as far as he got. A puzzled look crossed his face, and he muttered to Stroma, "Can you believe it, lassie? I've forgotten how it goes, and I must have said it a thousand times." She glanced quickly at Maclean, who had picked up the carving knife and slit the paunch of the pudding. "Och, it's no matter, Murdo. It'll taste just as good, the beast." He dipped a warmed serving spoon into the mash of meal and meat and served them with it, then served the vegetables.

Cameron took a mouthful and swallowed it; a rare light came into his eye. "You're a wizard, Alec. I'd forgotten it tasted like this."

"I didn't make it, Murdo. I just heated it."

"But you knew where to buy it." He spurned the wine, preferring the traditional Scots way of washing the haggis down with sips of neat whisky, masticating each morsel like some schoolboy a choice sweet. Something of a raconteur himself, Maclean was content to prompt the surgeon about their hard times in Edinburgh and their days in the Nile Delta. Cameron capped each story as though delighted that he could pin down names, dates and places without effort of memory.

"I've never seen him so relaxed," Stroma whispered.

"That's what this exercise is all about," Maclean replied.

The summer light ebbed out of the small room, and they lit the candles while Maclean served his hot pancakes, filled with apricot jam. The yellow glow made a circle just big enough to illuminate their faces around the table. The candlelight atmosphere, the food and the alcohol had muted the talk. Cameron's face had a dreamy, faraway look. Watching him, the psychiatrist wondered what memory was flitting through his mind. It had nothing to do with the truth drug, for he had drunk no more than two large whiskies. "A bawbee for what's in your mind, Murdo," he said.

Cameron smiled. "Bawbees and an aul' knife. When I was a bairn and pestering my grannie about the price of this or the next thing, that was always her answer."

"What's a bawbee?" Stroma asked.

"It's a Scots ha'penny—worth about a shilling of English money in a Scotswoman's hands," her father grunted.

"Two bawbees—that's what we used to pay to get in to hear those latter-day minstrels who would come round the towns in their plaids and kilts and sing Scotch ballads."

"Don't talk about it, Alec. Often when I'm cutting and stitching I'll see and hear them in my mind's eye. J. M. Hamilton and Nellie Wallace singing 'Bonnie Mary of Argyll' or that other song . . . it goes, 'Aft, aft ha'e I pondered, On scenes of my childhood, The days ance sae happy, Are come back again . . .' And so on."

" 'Memories Dear,' it was called."

"Aye, that's it." And Cameron began to croon the words, his voice cracking a little and his eyes not far from tears.

Maclean switched the conversation away from Scotland to Cameron's pet hobby: rose growing. He had done enough psychodrama for one evening, had struck enough old chords. Cameron would return to the subject tomorrow, he was sure. Stroma and Deirdre disappeared into the kitchen to make coffee. By the time he had finished his, the surgeon's head was drooping, and his daughter suggested he go to bed while they did the washing up.

When they were alone, Maclean turned to Deirdre. "You were very quiet at dinner. Something happen this afternoon?"

"I know you'll laugh at this, but that man scares me. While we were walking through the woods, I thought he was going to take advantage of me once or twice. He had that look in his eye."

"Pure imagination," he said. Deirdre had a surplus of common sense in everything except sex; she believed that every man but Maclean had designs on her.

"But he put his arm round me and started paying me compliments."

"All right, you're very pretty—I hope you thanked him."

"I told him in no uncertain terms to behave himself and act his age. Then I ran straight back."

Maclean had often counseled younger psychiatrists to weigh every word from their patients. "Somewhere in what the patient is telling you, and in his reactions, lies your diagnosis. So listen as though your own life depended on it." Now he was ignoring his own advice, smirking at Deirdre's account of her walk in the woods, believing her petty obsession with sex to have distorted her judgment. He would regret not having heard part of Cameron's tragedy in her words; he would reproach himself for ignoring the fact that Deirdre had watched mental patients come and go through his consulting rooms and probably had as much insight as he himself when it came to abnormal behavior.

20

? ?
?

Next morning the sun lay so hot on the porch that the two girls and Maclean ate breakfast there. Deirdre then announced she wished to go to church, presumably to purge the memory of her narrow escape the previous evening. Stroma offered to drive her into Dorking and attend the Roman Catholic service with her. "But don't, for heaven's sake, let on I've gone to a papish kirk," she said to Maclean.

"I thought he hated all kirks equally."

"But you know what Presbyterians are. Theirs is the true path to redemption. Everybody else has gone astray, and nobody more than the papist."

Shortly after they had departed, Cameron stumped down the stairs and tossed a sheaf of Sunday papers on the table. "I see one of our pundits is calling for the abolition of the Health Service or a charge of ten bob on each patient to reduce the queues. We both know him, and he couldn't treat a pimple on his own backside. We lose respect when we behave like this."

Maclean picked up the paper and began to read the article. He knew the surgeon's views about the Health

Service too well to be drawn into the argument. No market in medicine. Money contaminated the relationship between doctor and patient. The sick must always have the benefit of the doubt. Such a discussion might get personal, with the psychiatrist having to defend his Harley Street practice.

"Why are we so mealy-minded? We should declare openly that we're in the business for the cash and the kudos instead of blaming patients for wasting our time. It's the only business I know in which the customer is attacked by the person who's supposed to give him service. And he's often too sick to complain. We need more doctors, they say. I say we need better medicine. They talk about going on strike. They'd be like the Dublin dustmen who downed tools for a fortnight. Nobody saw any dirt and rubbish during that time, so they drifted back without complaint. The same with us. If we stopped writing useless scripts for pills, the country would be a damned sight healthier, and people would forget or ignore the phony ailments we help to promote."

And so he ranted on, berating doctors for their hypocrisy. "And have you seen the ranks close when there's the slightest breath of a scandal? No murderer ever covers up better. At least I've always admitted my mistakes."

"By the way," Maclean put in, "Stroma has driven Deirdre in to confess her mistakes for the week."

"From what I've seen that won't put a strain on the priest's ears."

"Oh, she has a rare imagination. I tell her that she ought to confess that the sins she's confessing don't exist. But it's like credit in the bank to her, against the day when she breaks out in all directions. You let the weekly sermon go by?"

"I haven't been in a church since I was fifteen."

"Like me, you were probably vaccinated as a boy.

Two Sunday schools, the morning service, evening Bible meeting—that was me."

Cameron picked up a piece of stick from the porch and heaved it into the garden for Chula to run after and retrieve.

"It wasn't any worse than our town. The only folk allowed to do a Sunday shift were the bell ringers. You know, my grandmother and grandfather banked the fire with peat on Saturday night to prevent them from sinning on the Sabbath day by soiling their hands with work. We froze in winter to keep the faith. They refused to read Sunday papers until Monday. The word of God from the old Ha' Bible was news enough for them. So much humbug and cant. I can remember couples reeling out of the evening service with damnation ringing in their ears, and their nostrils full of fire and brimstone, and then going courting. Religion never seemed to quench the fire in their loins."

"Your grandfather was a crofter, wasn't he?"

"No, he worked most of his life in a sawmill. He was a grand old chap—fond of a dram with his cronies. But every hour he spent in the pub he'd have to pay for with an hour on his knees praying. He kept a diary, full of remorseful phrases. 'On the high road to hell again last night with Rob Strachan, Jock Logie and Bob Menzies.' But he was back at the bar again the next payday."

"I suppose your father compensated by being a teetotaler."

"That's a laugh. From what I gathered of that reprobate he had everything associated with too much drink—cirrhosis, DT's, deficiency of the nerve endings and of cash. I'm sorry, Alec, I shouldn't have been so thoughtless."

"Go on—I'd like to hear about him."

"You'll be the first outside my family. I couldn't even

bring myself to tell Stroma." He paused for a second or two and lit a cigarette.

"I'm a bastard, Alec—in the real sense of the word. I can remember very vividly the day I found out. As a wee boy, I was at the corn thrashing, more of a hindrance than a help, and one of the men shouted, 'Get that bastard callant out of the road.' When I got home that evening, I said innocently to my grandmother, 'What's a bastard?' She blushed and wouldn't tell me. It was my grandfather who explained it. 'It just means, laddie, that your father didna marry your mother. That's the long and short of it,' he said. I went up to bed and cried the whole of that night until my heart nearly burst. I was different, and you know what bairns are when they find there's something not normal about them. School was the worst. They discovered it, and they gave me hell. I just had to take it— the insults and the beatings, the malice and the sadism. I thought that I had been branded by God, that I would die young, and I had a horror of that. My fear of death hit me hardest when I was on holiday from school. Somehow the beatings and insults toughened me, made me feel I'd survive. My blackest day was when one of the more rotten older boys ran to me with a Bible in his hand. 'There you are, Sunday-school boy—read all about yourself. He had marked that second verse in Deuteronomy Twenty-three, the one that says, 'A bastard shall not enter into the congregation of the Lord; even to his tenth generation shall he not enter into the congregation of the Lord'!"

"But somebody should have enlightened you about the value of the Old Testament."

Cameron's eyes were filling with tears. He blew his nose and gazed out over the garden for a moment.

"I couldn't forget those words. They burned like a branding iron into my brain. It was the Bible. Indisputable truth. As far as I was concerned, they had shut the doors on me. Why go to hear about hell-fire when I knew I'd get there soon enough? You know, Alec, I could smell the blast and reek of the sulphur that these Scots ministers were so obsessed with. To me, hell was real—it was descending into something. like Vesuvius in a miners' cage. And even at that age I could imagine eternity—the Scots Sabbath with a recurring decimal behind it."

"You never met your father?"

"No. He ran off and died in some Australian flophouse. I had the story from my grandfather. He was the second son of a laird who lived outside Oban, and my mother went there as a young serving lass. You can fill in the rest for yourself. My mother died when I was nine. 'God's will,' they whispered in the town."

Maclean sensed the unwisdom of pressing Cameron too far; those reminiscences had been dragged painfully from the part of his mind that corresponded with that attic above them. They explained much of Cameron's conduct in his student days: his obsession to outdo everyone in his studies; the way he shunned student life outside the university; his desire to quit Scotland as soon as he had qualified. Maclean had often wondered why Cameron led such a Puritan life, why he had never once seen him out with a girl. It must have cost him a great deal to repress his sexual drive, to play the part of a reluctant and miscast atheist.

As though to punctuate his thoughts, a church bell boomed across the valley. He could imagine how this sensitive boy had suffered in that hypocritical, dog-collar society. That would have bred in him the desire to shine in a profession that those Presbyterian elders esteemed as highly as the ministry. He had got out; he had obliterated all but a faint ring of his West Highland accent. At what price? the psychiatrist would like to know.

The day burned like a sapphire. The sun was drawing

174

perfume out of the flowers and trees, and a breeze was bending the tip of the golden cypress beyond the garden and playing among the birch and lime leaves, so that they vibrated in the stark sunlight. Among the shrubs the tawny body of Chula prowled, presumably stalking some unwary bird. From behind the house drifted the odor of wood smoke.

"That takes me back," Maclean remarked.

"What?"

"The smell. Remember the scouting patrols? Rain every day until our flint stones were wet through. And I was the fire lighter."

Cameron gave him a puzzled glance, twisting his head one way, then the other, until he spotted the blue streamer of smoke. Hadn't he smelled it?

"The squire lets a few campers in on weekends." He paused. "I remember you were the worst hand at making porridge in the troop."

"You're mixing me up with Chalmers—the Aberdonian who was left an annuity by his father as long as he kept at his studies. He's still up there swithering how he can fail the next exam, I should think."

"A big chap, with a face like a dumpling?" Cameron queried.

"Yes," Maclean lied. Cameron had no recollection of Chalmers. Who else could he try? Lachlan Donaldson, the piper.

"I wonder at times what's happened to Lachie Donaldson?" he said. Lachie had gone to school with Cameron, who had a great affection for him. Poverty had driven him into the army, and he had become a pipe major in the Cameron Highlanders. Maclean could recall the day Lachie turned up with shrapnel in his left lung at Ismailia. As Cameron worked to remove the splinters, he told Maclean how he had done Lachie's homework and

Lachie, in turn, had done some of the fighting for him in the playground. When Lachie recovered, he would take his pipes, walk up and down the mess hut and play Cameron and his staff into breakfast with strathspeys, reels, an occasional pibroch and even a lament; invariably he finished with Cameron's favorite, "Laddie with the Plaidie." One morning he ended with a new tune, which had a quick, martial lilt. Cameron stopped him. "That's good, Lachie. What is it?"

"It's a wee tune called 'Murdo Pibroch,'" said the piper.

No gift had ever pleased Cameron more.

"Aye," Cameron said. "I've mind fine o' Lachie, but we've lost touch."

Maclean began to whistle the pibroch Lachie had composed for the surgeon. He played the chanter a little himself, had a good ear and made a passable job of the melody. Cameron listened intently. "Lachie used to play that?" he asked.

"Something like it," Maclean remarked. "I'm no' such a grand wheepler as Lachie was a piper."

For several minutes they sat saying nothing. Then the surgeon rose. "This light's giving me a bit of a headache. I think I'll go and lie down for a wee while."

Maclean remained on the terrace. His thought was a ball in a pin-ball machine, hitting and illuminating the numbers at random, making no score to speak of. The wood smoke—hadn't he smelled it? He should have identified Chalmers; he should never have forgotten Lachie and his pibroch. The psychiatrist's first thoughts on the case didn't seem so brilliant now. Hysteria was bad enough, but the impairment of faculties, with partial paralysis, mood changes and the flashes of temper—this could point to something graver. He trembled on the sunlit porch.

21

? ?
?

Trying to resolve the riddle ruined his Sunday dinner. He was a sapper, given the job of defusing a new type of booby trap. Only, he was working in total darkness, relying on touch and good luck. He could hear the timing device ticking. How long had it been ticking? And how much longer would it allow him? He chided himself for growing fatalistic about Cameron and his problem. We were not all set to run for so long, to consume so much time and then stop. He would have liked to know if the surgeon was reacting to his prompting or offering his reminiscences to help Maclean diagnose his illness, if he was confiding in him as a friend or as a psychiatrist. Such knowledge would have helped, though with the human mind how could you tell? It had self-delusion built into it, and he had long ago renounced attempts to pin motives exactly, his own or anyone else's. He pushed his chair away from the table and drank the dregs of his coffee. The human brain doesn't answer unposed problems. But inject the facts, let it scan them several times and meditate a while, and it will come up with the answer. But maybe only after that ominous second when the clock stopped ticking and the whole mechanism blew up in his face.

Stroma leaned over the table and put a halfpenny in his hand. "A bawbee for them, Uncle Mac." He smiled at her.

"He spends too much time in that complaints' box in

Charley Street. You need more fresh air, Alec. I'll walk you round the garden."

They made a curious pair, the gaunt figure of Cameron contrasting with Maclean's floppy contours. They stopped by the beds of roses, drawn up like a regiment in dress uniform.

"All our own work," Cameron remarked. "We grew the briars, and I budded them." He caught Maclean's surprised look. "It's easy. Even an old headshrinker like you could learn in time." From a pocket he fished out a knife with a stubby blade, its bone haft spatulated. Cutting a shoot from one of the bushes, he flicked off the thorns and ran the blade of his knife under the skin and through the point at which a small branch entered the stalk; he gouged out the remnant of wood, trimmed off the branch and shaped the bud, holding it up for Maclean to see the nodule which would draw nutrition from the briar. He cast around, spotted a stalk with a double root, bared it and made a T-shaped cut; he prized the wound open with the haft of his knife to slot in the bud. With great deftness he wrapped some thin twine from the bottom to the top of the slit, embalming all but the tiny shoot. "We should use raffia so that it can burst through as it grows . . . and, of course, it's the wrong time of the year. But it'll probably take." He spat on his index finger and anointed the bud. "For luck."

"And all that with the wrong hand," Maclean observed, pointing to the surgeon's right hand.

"My nonprofessional hand," Cameron replied. "I built those garden walls and the new kitchen extension. When I retire, I shall landscape the whole place and build a summerhouse."

"Retire? I've heard that one before. You'll still be operating when Fairchild is on the fifth volume of his memoirs."

Cameron shook his head. "I may be listening to my fingernails growing sooner than people think."

They walked through an avenue of lime trees, skirted a maze of beech hedge and finally arrived at a spot by the stream where the light was filtered and checkered by willows and alders which overhung the water. Cameron picked up a piece of wood and began to whittle it with his budding knife, very artistically, into the shape of a human figure. When he had finished it, he tossed it into the stream. "I often ask myself why I ever went into surgery. The challenge, I suppose. When I was a boy, I could hardly stand the sight of a cut finger, and my neurosis showed through my skin. But I chose surgery, even though those Grand Guignol illustrations—they choose the worst cases on purpose—gave me nightmares. How did the human body survive? And mine in particular? I should have gone in for the sort of medicine Fairchild and you practice—always at one remove from death. Or even research, which would have put some barrier between me and death. Long live pure medicine, and may it never do anybody any harm!"

"But look what you've done. Who has done half as much?"

"Oh, I nearly gave up," Cameron continued. "You know who I worked for, and he was as jealous as hell. I was knife-happy in the post-mortem room. Maybe that's why I'm so hard on my own staff. Anyway, it taught me more than I could have learned watching his ham hands making the mistakes I was dissecting down there. Alec, the surgeon who can't follow his patients into the morgue should give up, and with him the man who relies on his juniors or palms off his terminal cases on some clergyman."

"Those are impossible standards, Murdo. Even for you."

"I wouldn't do chiropody if I had doubts about myself." He threw a glance around the glade, as though somebody might be eavesdropping on them. "I'm not half as good as I was, Alec. And, if you want to know, that's why I invited you down here. It was under false pretenses, but *I* asked you. Not Stroma."

"Oh," Maclean said, feigning surprise. Now he would get Cameron's confession about his illness.

"I was worried," Cameron said quietly. "About Stroma. If anything happened to me, she'd be left alone. I wanted to make sure she was settled. You know what I mean."

Again he had caught the psychiatrist off balance. Maclean thought of saying straight out, Murdo, you're not thinking of retiring. You think you're dying, and you know why. Come on, you fey old Gaelic goat, out with it. Just a bit of the truth. Instead he said, "What did you want me to do?"

"Talk to her. She's got some daft notion I need her when she should be finding some decent young fellow and getting herself married. I'd tell her myself—but you know how Scotsmen are."

"Have you got anybody in mind for her?"

"What do you take me for—some Highland patriarch?"

"Now, how would such a thought have entered my head?"

"She's always been free to make her own choice," Cameron exclaimed with some heat. "Though I did think once that she and Wilkinson, my registrar, were fond of each other. I don't know what happened. Nobody up there ever tells me anything. . . ."

"Except that Donovan just mentioned in passing they'd had a row over his offer to go to America."

Cameron stared at him. "I knew it. That's why you've

made a name at this business—your mother was a spae-wife, who put you through Edinburgh reading teacups and palms. I'm glad you'll talk to her."

"I didn't say I would." Cameron shot him a furious look. "Oh, I would, Murdo, but it wouldn't do much good. Funny thing about psychiatrists—normal people don't want them or their advice."

"But you're a friend."

"And you're her father. I could give you some advice, but you wouldn't take it."

"Try me."

"Go to her, and tell her what you've told me about your childhood. Get it off your chest. Young people these days look at such things in a different light. You can solve the marriage problem very simply—just put this chap up for a readership in clinical surgery, which you should have done years ago."

To Maclean's surprise Cameron thought for a moment and then nodded his head. "It might not be such a bad idea," he said, rising to return to the cottage.

"There's one more thing, Murdo. Stop all this blarney about retiring, throwing down your scalpel for a budding knife. This is a thin patch, and it'll pass."

"Oh, a lot of people at the hospital would breathe easier if I chucked my hand in." He confessed to Maclean about the letters, the whispering campaign and the move to make him give up his chair.

"You're big enough to ignore them. Have a holiday, and let them get on with it at Vincent's."

A smile lit up the surgeon's sunken face, and he cuffed Maclean between the shoulder blades. "I know," he said with a flash of his old fire. "You'd like to get my mind into your hands—hitch me up to the mains and fire a few hundred volts through my gray matter."

"Nothing like that—but maybe a few tests, such as . . ."

"Forget it. I'll get my occupational therapy down here soon enough. A few more operations, a bit of clearing up at the hospital and I'll ask the dean for my cards. But, Alec, not a word to anybody. Not even Stroma."

"You've done wonders for him," Stroma commented as they walked through the garden before calling it a day. The surgeon had retired after supper to his room.

"Anybody who can teach a jackdaw medicine shouldn't have any trouble with a curmudgeon of a surgeon. Has he talked to you?"

"What about?"

"Something that has been worrying him. He'll tell you himself."

They walked around the back of the house. A light burned behind the curtains in Cameron's room. "Does he still read a lot?" Maclean asked.

"No, he's probably gone to sleep."

"With his light on?"

"He keeps it on now. He came down one morning with a gash on his head. I think he must have fallen during the night."

Maclean said nothing to Stroma; but it was another factor to inject into his mind. Could Cameron have some sort of brain lesion? The surgeon would hardly be aware of his own gross personality changes. And if the brain damage had been caused by, say, syphilis, this would explain why he had resisted attempts to investigate his condition. What had Stroma said? He seemed to be a caricature of himself at times. She might have borrowed the phrase from a textbook. It was imperative to run those tests. But how?

22

? ?
?

At St. Vincent's the senior staff went about their tasks without betraying the smallest concern for the Professor of Surgery. The committees argued through their sessions, and if members noticed Cameron's odd behavior, they ignored it. The queues of outpatients arrived and departed; the Casualty officers dealt with their quota of home and road accidents, of coronaries, of failed suicides; the operating teams toiled to whittle down the perpetual waiting list of surgical cases; the kitchens managed to abstract most of the taste and quality from the meat, the mash and the vegetables. Life had not changed. Maclean marveled that Cameron could manifest such alarming symptoms without provoking some physician to comment on them to the man himself. It amazed him, too, that the Professor of Medicine could drag himself around in such an aura of depression that it would have been spotted and treated in 50 per cent of patients. But Maclean was an outsider and could do nothing. Had anyone asked his opinion about the relative health of the two department chiefs, he would have unhesitatingly named Fairchild the worse casualty. Depression was a dangerous state.

"You know, Joe," he observed to Sainsbury, "I have reached the intriguing conclusion that if you transferred this—or many another hospital—into the business of making matches, nuts, bolts or plastic teaspoons, not many of the staff would spot the change."

"You're an old cynic," Joe replied. "Though I sometimes wish we ran as efficiently as the typical factory. We have good doctors, but they're not organization men."

Maclean was sitting in Sainsbury's office, having a break before returning to Fiegler's clinic. He had honored his promise to Cameron to repeat nothing of their conversation by the stream, but he had outlined his observations during that weekend to Joe. "I wish we could run those tests," he said.

"Can you see Cameron putting himself in the hands of Fairchild's department?" Joe replied. "If it were only Fairchild, he might forget the past, but he hates Lady Bug so much that he would never sink his pride and give her the satisfaction of helping him."

"Why has he got it in for her?"

"I don't know the whole story. Only Cameron could tell you that, and he wouldn't. I can give you the versions which spread round the hospital at the time."

Their feud, Joe explained, dated from seven years ago, not long after Lady Fairchild came to St. Vincent's and a year after she married Sir Kenneth. She had reported to Cameron at the Department of Surgery with symptoms indicating an ulcer. However, the barium meal and X rays had revealed nothing, and Cameron suggested that she consult one of her husband's staff. For some reason she seemed unwilling to see a physician. She again made several appointments with Cameron and would wait for him in his office until he had finished his list for the day. According to Sainsbury, it caused talk in the nurses' wing and the doctors' club; the whisper went that the lady was in love with the Professor of Surgery. "Even to me," Joe went on, "it appeared there might be some truth to the story. I know Miss Fletcher walked about as though she'd been caught trying to smuggle a box of liqueur chocolates through customs, and Donovan snubbed her Ladyship in every corner of the hospital."

184

Nor did the story end there. Lady Fairchild persisted in reporting to the Department of Surgery with every abdominal symptom in the book, mostly those that required detailed investigation. "They might have been cribbed from an army manual of malingering," Joe said. "She even got to the stage of asking Cameron to carry out an exploratory operation on her."

"How did he react to that?"

"He sent her packing. Barred her from coming near him or his staff and advised her bluntly to consult a psychiatrist."

"You know what he thinks of us—he must have been desperate."

"He's a wily old cove, for he made sure she took his advice. He phoned Fiegler and made an appointment." Sainsbury smiled. "She wasn't the first crank he pointed in Fiegler's direction. The principle of fighting fire with fire. What Fiegler did with her I don't know, but it cured her passion for Cameron."

"You mean it transformed her love into hate."

Sainsbury nodded. He doused another cigarette in the grounds of his coffee and grinned at Maclean. "Thank God I have only simple problems. The prem-baby unit is closed with some mysterious creepy-crawly, an atheist in one of the life-and-death wards is bawling his head off because the two chaplains are trying to convert him and the pressure in number-two boiler room is hardly high enough to soft-boil an egg."

Maclean ambled back to Fiegler's office in time to have a word with the psychiatrist before he resumed his session. He would have to exercise all his tact in quizzing him about Lady Fairchild or the little man would imagine he was trying to pirate one of his patients.

"You'll soon be able to send them out into the world to fend for themselves," he said as he sat down.

"I'm glad you think so," Fiegler retorted, his voice carrying no gladness but almost a hint that he would regret losing them. Psychiatrists sometimes got this way about their patients, Maclean thought to himself; they felt personally involved, or they disliked the idea of leaving case notes unfinished, even though the treatment had succeeded.

"You won't mind my saying so, but it's struck me that you don't get much help from the Department of Medicine here. Doesn't Fairchild look in or refer any patients to you for treatment?"

The little Austrian looked glum. He selected a paper clip from a file on his desk and meticulously began to straighten it out and array it with half a hundred others; he hardly needed to draw such a symbolic picture of his problems at St. Vincent's. Maclean would not have posed the question had he not known of the cat-and-mouse relationship with Fairchild's department.

"Professor Fairchild is one of those people who believe there is no illness that you cannot see or touch. So far as he is concerned, we are all quacks or sorcerers."

"I'm astonished," Maclean said. "I thought he once sent his own wife to you."

"You are mistaken, Gregor. She did consult me, but she was referred by someone else."

"Well, there's your answer. He found out, he was bitter about it and that's why he has put psychiatry in solitary confinement."

Fiegler shook his head. "He never knew about her visits—at least, I would have been very surprised if he had found out. Indeed, I asked Lady Fairchild if I should see her husband, and she expressly forbade me to mention that she had consulted me." Fiegler was talking volubly now, apparently oblivious of the fact that he was discussing one of his patients; his pride must have taken a knock. "Of course, there was a good reason why she didn't want him to know. I was even relieved myself to be spared interviewing him. How can you ask the Professor of Medicine who controls your own department about his sexual deficiencies? From what I gathered, he was not far from being completely impotent, and he must have known there was little he or I could do about that."

"Poor lady," Maclean muttered, with the picture in his mind of someone who could scratch glass. "She had a hard time?"

"She was a psychiatric problem herself," Fiegler said. "A very difficult childhood, with her parents battling over her. You must have met the type yourself. Their emotions are bleached. You know the cause, and yet you feel difficulty in sympathizing with them. Her father was authoritarian to the point of sadism and gave her mother hell. Yet she respected him. He was also—how do you say it? —a Bible puncher. So God and love and pain were all mixed up in her mind—what I have christened, in a recent paper, the Abelard Syndrome. She could easily, in other circumstances, have been a nymphomaniac."

She hadn't done too badly, Maclean thought. "Did you take any case notes or free association?" he interjected, in case Fiegler wandered off onto his favorite theme—sex and the Bible, Héloïse and Abelard.

"Oh, yes, whole pages. I remember how difficult those sessions were and the trauma those early recollections produced. Wait, I still have them." He chose a key from his ring, opened an oak filing cabinet and rummaged through it. "That's very curious. I could have sworn I put them here—though she did come several times to Harley Street." Picking up the phone, he dialed his consulting rooms and asked the secretary to search his records; after a few minutes, he shook his head. "I can't understand that —I'm sure those notes were here. Nobody else has a key to this cabinet." His eyes blinked behind his pebble lenses, and he tugged at his beard.

"Perhaps Fairchild himself asked for the notes," Maclean prompted.

"Never." Fiegler gave an emphatic shake. "She said some very harsh things about him, and I would never have released those notes."

That piece also fitted into the general puzzle, Maclean reflected as they wandered toward the session room. Either Fairchild or his wife would prove more devious than he had suspected. It required no great criminal aptitude to purloin a file from Fiegler's office, but small offenses often led to larger ones. He began to weigh what he knew of the characters of both Fairchilds in relation to that theft. He might have uncovered some interesting details had he felt inclined. But his patient was Cameron. Sir Kenneth and his lady concerned him only as aspects of the surgeon's problem.

23
? ?
?

The high spot of the year at St. Vincent's was the League of Friends' Ball, which helped to swell the hospital funds and promote good will in the community. The ladies of the league commandeered the huge staff restaurant and transformed it into a ballroom for the evening. The din of the decorators and the electricians for a whole week before the event gave the doctors and nurses something to discuss and distracted their palates from the unappetizing menu. This year the league had excelled previous efforts;

from the restaurant roof hung yards of green silk, which conferred on the room the appearance of something between a marquee and a Turkish harem; three vast chandeliers swung from the apex of this indoor tent, and streamers and colored bulbs floated between them.

The hospital always turned out in strength. For the senior staff the ball had the force of a command performance at which they should meet and chat to various benefactors and mingle with their junior staff. Housemen and nurses seized the opportunity it gave to get better acquainted. On that night physicians, surgeons and other rival factions proclaimed some sort of truce. Only the Casualty Department disliked the annual revel, since it made vast inroads into their supply of aspirin and antacids and kept their stomach pumps busy into the next day. Impoverished housemen concocted their own Vincent's cocktail by spiking their own and their companions' beer with ethyl alcohol hijacked from one of the research labs. It often landed them in the recovery ward for a couple of days. "It's a good thing this stramash takes place only once a year, or we'd have half the hospital running around with their optic nerves on their cheeks and rocks in their livers," Joe said to Maclean as he handed him a ticket.

The ball was getting into its stride when the psychiatrist arrived and pushed his bulk with difficulty through the throng around the dance floor to the table where Joe and Jean were sitting. "This'll make your evening, this little titbit," Joe whispered. "The governing board has asked for the post-mortem on Mrs. Fowler. Nothing more —but I'd say that somebody had tipped them off."

"It won't prove anything," Maclean said.

"No, but they'll raise a stink if they try."

He would cross that bridge when he came to it. Cameron had not yet arrived. He looked around for Stroma, who had said she would join them, but she had not made an appearance, either. He spotted Wilkinson and another man at a table ten yards away with two girls, one of them Sister Holroyd. At that moment Conway-Smith crossed the floor and asked her to dance. As they maneuvered into the crush, Maclean noticed that even this early she was leaning heavily on her partner; every now and then she would toss her head back and laugh at some crack he was making. "That one for the stomach pump later on," he thought.

Had he guessed what they were plotting, he might have stood her a few drinks himself and ensured she became one of the ambulant wounded who visited Casualty. They left the floor, and Conway-Smith escorted her rather unsteadily to her table. As he returned, he spied Maclean and halted.

"You're spending a lot of time here these days," he said with a grin, flashing his teeth. "Don't tell me it's because they're still delousing your Harley Street place. Priceless story about Lady Blye—earned me quite a few drinks, that one." He slapped Maclean on the shoulder. "But seriously, what does bring you here?"

"I have friends here." Maclean kept his voice neutral.

"Ah, of course. Cameron. How is the old firebrand? I hear he's thinking of retiring. I hope it's true."

"Just a story put round by people who find him and his principles a nuisance."

The band had paused between numbers. Conway-Smith leaned confidentially toward Maclean and whispered in his ear, "I don't need to tell you the old man's losing the place. You'll do him and his patients a favor if you persuade him to quit before he does any real damage. I wouldn't like to be Lord Blatchford—you know he's going to do him—pardon the Freudian slip."

"I'll tell him you said so, Ralph, and he might call you in to give him a hand. Of course, you'd have to do it on the Health Service."

Conway-Smith grinned, but his amusement went no deeper than his white teeth. He nodded, disengaged himself and headed toward the bar.

Maclean let his gaze travel around the room. Most of the tables were occupied, and the bar was dealing with a huge queue. Dean Prior, the chairman of the League of Friends and the Board of Governors had quit their duty as reception committee and had taken their seats, indicating that almost everyone of note had arrived. Still no sign of Murdo, but he would come; he had promised.

At the dean's table, but on her own, sat Lady Fairchild. She smiled across at him, and he rose to go and greet her. "I'm no great shakes at this modern dancing, Lady Fairchild, and if you'll allow me, I'll prove it."

She fixed those remarkable green eyes on him, questioning, wondering, then gave that quick smile and nod. "The name is Barbara, don't you remember?" Still trying to charm him.

"Are you alone?" he said.

"Yes. Kenneth is working on some papers and didn't feel up to standing the racket of this sort of function."

On a dance floor Maclean considered himself as no more than an efficient biological shield for his partner; he moved himself around with a shuffling step which fitted any rhythm. Yet she adapted herself adroitly to this style and did not shirk contact.

"I'm afraid I must make a confession," Maclean said. "When you asked me about my interest in Cameron's condition, I denied it. That was a half-truth. I did come to help him."

"At his instigation?"

"No. You see, one of my patients had the third letter."

191

"And he brought it to you." She expressed no more than ordinary interest and still followed his steps without faltering.

"I felt I had to look at the matter—from Fowler's viewpoint because he had come to me; from Cameron's because he was a personal friend. Anyway, I'm interested in the poison-pen personality."

"Fowler? Who's he?" She showed an extraordinary aptitude for picking up names against a noisy background.

"He's the man who brought the letter."

"But what if the author of the letter is right—that Cameron should not be allowed to carry on as a surgeon?"

"You know what it said, then?"

"No, not exactly. But it's common talk here."

"Whether he's right or not, he shouldn't have used this method of denouncing Cameron or trying to blackmail him out of his job." Her hand still lay languid in his; she gave no hint of tension.

"Do you have any idea who wrote the letters?"

"Somebody not as clever as he thinks—or someone so clever that he wants to appear stupid."

"Why do you say that?"

"The cases he chose. Had there been an inquiry into Cameron's competence, nothing would ever have been found against him on post-mortem evidence from those three operations." He almost fancied he was keeping step with her private thoughts. She might be thinking, that rules out Conway-Smith and my husband, unless they were bluffing very cleverly. He has more or less admitted that I had no part in it. Which leaves Rothwell, Wilkinson and Holroyd.

"Whom do you suspect?" she asked.

"I think I know who it is."

"But you have no proof."

"I could find proof, but since I don't intend to have the law on them, I don't need it—just the assurance that the letters and the attacks will stop."

"If I happen to bump into this anonymous writer, I'll tell him," she answered lightly. The band had stopped, the floor was clearing and Maclean led her back to her table. Had he written the dialogue for her, she could not have uttered her lines or controlled her feelings more perfectly. When he returned to his table, Stroma had arrived. From the glances she threw toward Wilkinson and Holroyd he guessed that Cameron had still not mentioned anything to her of what they had discussed. He wondered when Cameron would appear.

Scattered chords of music filtered through to Cameron in his flat, reminding him that he should make an appearance at the ball, even though he dreaded the occasion. He had always looked forward to it, but now he felt apprehensive for no motive. Whom did he fear? Neither Fairchild nor his wife nor Conway-Smith. Nameless dread— wasn't that the worst kind? The fugitive images of Donovan, Frances Tremayne and Maclean projected themselves one after another on his mind. He had forgotten that Alec had promised to join them; the thought allayed his anxiety temporarily. He remembered that he had a duty to dance with Margaret Donovan. People would note his absence, and it would give rise to gossip.

Several minutes of relaxation would set him right. Stretching himself on the divan, he tensed each limb in turn and let it go lax. He transposed his thoughts to the valley at Aberloch, where he had spent his boyhood, and allowed his mind to dwell on it until the tight sensation left his head. If you concentrated on anything powerfully enough, you could induce physical and mental oblivion.

Wasn't that the mystic's formula? In a few minutes he was hovering peacefully between waking and sleeping—dovering, his grandmother would have called it.

It was a braw forenoon. He could feel the sun on his face and the cool pluck of the burn water around his ankles and hand as he waited for the trout to nose against it. No one in the village could guddle fish like him, for he had the right touch to caress them under the gills. When he had trapped this one and felt its clammy life twitching in his fingers, he threw it back frantically, unwilling to kill or to watch it suffocate, and yet conscience-stricken in the knowledge that it would have eked out their food at home. He was at one with the purple bens, the puffy clouds sailing overhead, the corbies planing in the breeze and the whops complaining in the heather; he savored the reek of wood fires from the village. . . . They had caught him just after the bell in the playground, and the gang had held him down and sat on him until he choked. "Ha'e ye had enough, Cameron's bastard?" they cried, and he wriggled free and ran for it. As he sped, barefoot, his boots and books slung over his shoulder, the unco-guid minister stopped him to put a sententious hand on his head and bless him, then went home to prepare another sermon denouncing bastardy for that Sabbath.

Handfuls of brown clay clattering on the coffin, the mumbled service and the long walk back, his hand in his grandfather's, the old man's eyes on the ground. "She was too fine a lassie," he was muttering. He stood outside the alehouse and helped him home, crying drunk. No school that day or the next, but he had his own, secret school in the whin and heather a mile from the village. "Naebuddy can tak' what ye carry in your head," his grandmother said. He watched their faces as Cameron's bastard staggered under the books and prizes at prize-giving day.

What were they thinking—that the devil was a rare schoolteacher? Better than the local dominie? Another face: this one a dried fig, eyes like coal and huge earrings; her caravan smelled of sulphur. His mother had come out, beaming. "She says, 'You have a wee boy, and he'll make a commotion with the gift he has in his hands.'" Nobody had thought of him as a surgeon, and he had laughed off the prophecy as Highland superstition.

Now a pair of hands, which he could visualize clearly. Scrubbed until the skin had a flaky, brittle appearance. But skilled. They clipped the needle into the syringe, pierced the rubber bottle cap, then with gentle precision injected the drug which eased the pain of his grandmother's final illness. His eyes followed the syringe into the black bag, the sight of which filled him with incredible awe and mystery. He knew every instrument, from the scalpel to the small scimitar needles; he memorized the colored bottles and the pills. From the cottage window he would spy the doctor's horse and buggy and whiles would hold the horse as the old man unwrapped the tartan plaid from his knees and descended, panting with the exertion. "There now, my callant, these auld banes are no' sae skeigh these days," he would whisper confidentially in his Lowland speech. During the school holidays he would bring his granddaughter with him, an elfin girl with brown eyes, who would sit in the buggy sucking cinnamon and aniseed sweets, watching him but not saying a word. He would catch a glimpse of her at the window or in the grounds of the doctor's mansion when he delivered the newspapers. And he came to associate and invest her with the same air as the black bag. He was relieved that she ignored him, probably condemned him. Had she acknowledged him or even uttered a word, it would have broken the enchantment. What had become of her? The question for him was rhetorical. He never really wanted to know. She had become a thing of his mind; beautiful as a fly in amber, idealized as Greek sculpture. He never wanted to solve human puzzles and thereby end their mystery, their attraction. Another face: this one in his own operating theater, reproach in its lovely eyes, and his hand drawn back to strike it. . . .

He stirred on the divan, summoned back to the present, remembering the dance. Swinging his cramped legs onto the floor, he unwittingly kicked Chula, who squawked her disgust, then lapped his hand with her rough tongue. He poured some milk into a saucer, which she gazed at before squinting at him with an Oriental hint in those blue eyes. "All right, you alcoholic bitch," he grunted, seizing the whisky bottle and lacing the milk with a thimbleful. As she scooped up the liquid, a burbling note echoed in her throat.

His rest had refreshed him, though to steady his nerves, he swallowed a barbiturate tablet before sluicing his face and slipping into his dinner jacket. As he made his way down the corridor, the noise grated, and as he entered the ballroom, the din surged around him, an amalgam of harsh jazz, the strident chatter of five hundred voices and the thudding of feet on the floor; the sound rang like an avalanche of rushing water in his head. Dean Prior came to greet him and introduce him to his guests; he responded politely, and if he betrayed his tension, thank God it did not reflect in their faces. Quickly he did his duty around the guest tables before stepping across to the corner of the hall, where Donovan sat alone. Her quiet eyes followed him as he threaded among the couples. Young or old, her professor still outshone them all. No one wore a dinner jacket with the same elegant ease; no one walked more nobly. In twenty years of knowing him and working for him, she had never known him to commit a mean act. He was loyal; while he could have spent his evening with the nobs, he joined her to chat, have a drink and dance.

For his part Cameron invariably wondered on this one night of the year what compelled Donovan to stay at a place like St. Vincent's. With her qualifications, skill and way with patients, with her good looks and presence, she could have run a clinic or trebled her earnings at half the effort in Harley Street. Even when St. Vincent's was searching for a matron, she could have had his sponsorship and the job; she bridled when he suggested putting forward her candidature.

"Enjoying yourself, Margaret?" he asked as he sat down. Flattered by the rare use of her first name, she smiled and nodded.

"I had a sair fecht to get you this," she said, pointing to the whisky. "I'd almost given up and was going to drink it myself." He raised the whisky and toasted her. She fixed her eyes on him. "Professor, you don't mind if I mention this, but there's a rumor going round . . . they say you're going to retire. I've denied it wherever I've heard it. It's not true, is it?" He heard the appeal, the apprehension in her voice.

"No," he lied. "No truth whatever." She would learn soon enough.

"That's a relief," she cried. "There's been so much clashing in this place about you. . . ." He cut the line of talk short by inviting her to dance. They moved slowly around the perimeter, Donovan keeping at least six inches between them, holding her fair head high and casting her proud glance everywhere.

They had drifted back to their table and taken their seats when one of the medical registrars escorted Frances Tremayne to the table. "Sure you won't change your mind and join us?" he asked, but she tossed her head.

Cameron stood up and acknowledged the girl; they had, he thought, made up their small difference of the other evening in the operating theater. He had never seen her dressed in anything but a uniform before. She was beautiful. The yellow silk evening dress concealed rather than flaunted her figure, though nothing could disguise that. He avoided gazing at the curve of her breasts. She wore a pearl choker and pearl earrings. Her dark hair fell carelessly over her forehead and curled behind her ears. She smiled at Cameron and held out a hand, which lay coolly in his for a second. Suddenly he felt his mouth go dry. "Quiet, you old fool," he muttered to himself. His instinct ordered him to flee; his reason countermanded, whispering that if he did, he would never exorcise the idea of this girl from his mind. He sat down heavily. At all costs he must avoid making an idiot of himself.

"You're not here alone, are you? From the reception I heard them give you I thought you'd have a posse of post-graduate wolves after you."

"She didn't want for invitations," Donovan put in. "Dozens of them."

"I preferred Sister Donovan's company," she said. Cameron guessed that she had sacrificed her own enjoyment for Donovan's benefit. "You do dance, don't you, Professor?"

"Not that palsied stuff," he replied, indicating the twisting, hip-swiveling couples. "At my age it would land me in the orthopedic wing if they didn't chuck me out of the hospital for making an exhibition of myself."

"You're not that old. Would you like to try? I'm an old-fashioned girl anyway." He nodded curtly, and they made their way to the floor. After they had taken several steps, she said, "I wanted to talk to you. I owe you an apology."

"I wasn't aware of it. What for?"

"First of all, for being impertinent enough to put in my stupid word at the clinical meeting after my first few days here."

"You had the right—though it was a daft thing to do."

She let the criticism pass. "There was another thing," she said. "I should not have questioned your judgment in the theater the other morning."

"I'm glad you realize that was impudent," he growled.

"Oh." He felt her hand tighten in his.

"But you're forgiven," he said, and smiled.

They danced in silence for a few minutes. She held her head erect and kept her eyes unflinchingly on his face. That disconcerted him. Her body, pliant but firm, sought contact with his, and he could feel the rise and fall of her breasts. She moved lightly, rhythmically, without swaying, as a ballet dancer would. That sort of pulse and poise is built into some people with their heartbeat, he thought. At that moment he stubbed against her toe and had to apologize, which broke the silence.

"What possessed a girl like you to come into nursing?" he said.

Her brow puckered. "I never gave anything else a thought. Medicine saved my father, and I suppose I was repaying it—casting my bread on the waters."

"What highfalutin gibberish." He laughed. "You might as well have frittered your time away in a convent. Phony idealism—a lot of your sex get carried away with it. You've a good brain and good hands, and if you wanted to stay unmarried and dedicated, you could have done anything—teaching, research. Not that I'd like to see you leave."

"And I thought for a moment that you were trying to get rid of me again."

"Never," he retorted, trying not to betray his hypocrisy. "But take a look at Donovan. She came into this business because some boy jilted her in Airdrie thirty years ago. Now she sublimates like mad and expends all her pent-up emotion on her patients."

"You may be a great surgeon, Professor Cameron, but you're not very good at reading character. Anybody with half an eye can see that she's still in love—anybody but you, that is."

"Why me?"

"Because she happens to be in love with you."

"Havers, woman. Donovan's no more than a latter-day Florence Nightingale. She's in love with the job." She was right, though; he had to admit it. He should have admitted, too, that he probably took advantage of Donovan's love and loyalty.

"Love," he snorted angrily. "What's that anyway but the stimulation of the hormones by sexual excitement? It's a bawdy tune played on the heartstrings or a low fever in the cerebellum. Anything else they say about it is an invention of the poets, who are half cracked in the head, most of them. Or a dodge by the publishing and entertainment industries to boost their takings at the expense of a soft-headed public."

"Am I listening to somebody who either hasn't been in love or suffered too much to be truthful about it?"

"You're listening to somebody who's done surgery on a few thousand hearts and never once seen a new heart produce a change in emotional outlook. When it does, or when I rough up the edge of my knife on an immortal soul, that day I'll believe in love."

"Now you're joking; you're making fun of me."

"There you have the difference between us, Sister—apart from your impertinence, that is. You're taking the conversation seriously, and I'm not." They finished the dance in silence, and he escorted her back to Donovan's table, colliding with couples as he marched quickly through them. He muttered a "Good evening" and strode off to his own party. The presumption of it! To catch him off balance like that, to touch him on the raw, even to tease him and smile innocently. She was clever. If the argument had gone on, by God, she might have defeated him, humiliated him. He knew where she was leading him with all that talk of love; she was trying to vamp him, the bitch. He should have kept his temper, nevertheless.

He still felt angry when he reached his own table. Drawing Maclean aside, he hissed, "When I told you about my possible retirement, it was meant to be in confidence. It's all over the hospital now. What are you trying to do—down me as well as the rest?"

"Keep a calm sough, Murdo. I told no one. It's a rumor like all the others, so forget it."

"If I trace it back to you, Maclean, it's the end of anything there has ever been between us."

"Sit down," the psychiatrist said quietly. The agitation in the surgeon's face and manner subsided, and he slopped into a chair, looking anxiously at Maclean. "Sorry, Alec, my temper isn't what it was. I don't seem to be myself tonight."

"It'll pass, Murdo."

24

? ?
?

The ballroom quivered and thrummed around her. She glided and tripped over the floor, the music enveloping her and giving the impression that it was physically controlling and creating her footwork. The chandeliers swayed and scintillated, reflecting the whirl of bodies below them. Who cared if the perspiration was leaking through her make-up, if she acted a little squiffy, if Ralph was having his umpteenth dance with her? For her last ball, for her last appearance in this grisly old penitentiary, Patricia Holroyd felt she might as well let her hair down. She was going to go out with a bang in more ways than one. The music stopped, and they left the floor.

"Drink?" Conway-Smith asked.

"Just a quickie," she replied, thinking she must not get too tight or leave David sitting on his own too long.

He ordered Martinis. Patricia harpooned the olive, popped it into her red mouth, then said to the barman, "Now fill it up."

"That's what I like," Conway-Smith remarked. "A girl who understands the principle of Archimedes. An olive displaces its own weight of gin—that's what the old Greek said." He looked around the hall. "Ah, I see the Monarch of the Glen has finally honored us."

"The clan's with him," she muttered, following his gaze. Cameron had called David to his table and was chatting with him. Holroyd saw that his cold bitch of a daughter was there as well. They could hardly have timed things better. She appreciated the gamble she was about to take and, for a moment, was stricken with nerves. What if it misfired and she lost everything: David, her dream, her job?

"I think I'll have just one more," she said.

Conway-Smith ordered it. "Don't say he has that effect on you even when he hasn't got a scalpel in his hand."

"I just don't want to feel sorry for him all of a sudden."

"Think of what we all stand to gain and you won't do anything that you'll regret tomorrow," he whispered.

She turned on him almost with contempt, but marveling at his bland nerve. "You mean, don't leave anything undone that *you* may regret tomorrow. Remember it was you who put the idea into my head, and I'm doing your dirty work."

"You want to emigrate in style, don't you?" She nodded. "And if anything goes wrong, you always have me." He grinned as she cuffed him on the shoulder. She knew that he, the eminent Conway-Smith, didn't have the guts to meet Cameron face to face but would stand by and watch the plot that his devious brain had thought up. She swallowed the dregs of her Martini and levered herself off the stool. "Good hunting," he whispered.

Now she was walking, too quickly, too unsteadily, toward the table where Cameron and his party sat. She tried to run over in her mind the opening lines of the scene which she had rehearsed several times, but the liquor had fogged them over in her mind. What was the difference? No one who watched the drama would recall the lines. Only the outcome. She had reached the table. The fat psychiatrist rose to offer his chair, but she waved him aside. Cameron raised his head from his conversation with David.

"Ah, Holroyd. Nice to see you. Sit down and have a drink."

"I didn't come to make polite conversation," she said.

"I understand. You've come to collect your escort. I'm sorry; we got talking shop. He's all yours."

"He's all yours." She mimicked his voice; her own rose in a scream. "He never has been, you old bloodsucker, and you know why. You think you've bought him body and soul, don't you?" David stood up quickly and caught her by the arm, but she broke free. "Leave me alone, darling. It's time we had it out with him. You've said so yourself."

Cameron's eyes narrowed before he saw by her flushed face and swaying stance that she was drunk. He turned to David. "Wilkinson, if you brought this young lady here, I think you should see her home straightway. Some fizzy aspirin and two pints of water and she'll have recovered by tomorrow."

"Come on, Pat," David said.

"No," she shouted. "You've finished taking orders from him." As she worked up her anger, she became aware of the startled faces around the table and the crowd that was gathering. The dean, Lady Fairchild, the governors, that daughter, and Conway-Smith. She had the right gallery. "You've held his hand long enough," she screamed. She mocked Cameron's voice and accent. "Do this, Wilkinson, I don't feel too well—Wilkinson, here's the scalpel, take over—my hand's shaking—Wilkinson, get me the post-mortem report on my last brilliant operation. Well, I have news for you—Wilkinson's had enough. You can do your own dirty work in future. He's leaving for America, where at least they'll give him credit for the work he does."

David stood, silent and anguished, as though the outburst had paralyzed him. Cameron was shaking with fury. He looked at his assistant as if seeking confirmation of Holroyd's attack. Silence seemed to imply assent. "If that's how you feel, you can go," he muttered, his eyes on the registrar's face. "I've been in this profession all my life, and no one has ever thrown such an insult at me, even indirectly. Hold my hand, indeed! I've taught you all I know, and you can still hardly tie the tapes on my gown." David stared at him; he seemed too bewildered by the speed of events to speak.

Maclean grasped Cameron's arm. "Murdo, let's get out of here. This is nothing but a girl who's had too much to drink and is trying to stir things up."

"You keep out of it, Alec—I can handle my own staff. If Wilkinson feels this way and wants to quit, I shall sign him off my staff tomorrow." He drew a deep breath, and to rub home the finality of his verdict, he went on. "Great shame. I thought once he had the makings of a surgeon. . . ."

"It's more than anybody can say about you," Holroyd bawled. "You're finished—you don't even see the mistakes you're making, let alone admit them. You can't see that the doctors here are terrified that you get your knife into their patients. I hope when they have their inquiry, the hospital exposes you for what you are—a fraud and a charlatan." She seized a glass of liquor from the table and hurled the contents into Cameron's face. A gasp went around the circle of onlookers; even the band had muted its sound, since it was playing to an empty floor.

The crack of Cameron's hand on her cheek echoed around the hall. The few people who still had not heard the quarrel turned at the sound and saw Sister Holroyd holding her face and sobbing while the surgeon stood looking shamefacedly at his hand. The silent crowd parted to let Wilkinson lead the girl toward the exit, then closed in on the table to watch what would happen.

"Come on, Murdo," Maclean said, linking his arm with the surgeon's and bulldozing his way through the throng. He felt Cameron's whole body trembling as they left the ballroom and marched along the corridor.

"I had no call to do that, Alec," he kept repeating, his head down and his steps dragging.

"You were provoked, Murdo," said the psychiatrist, wondering who had put that girl up to making the scene.

They arrived at the door of Cameron's flat and stopped while the surgeon fumbled in a pocket for his key. He fished it out and, in the semidarkness, made several futile attempts to insert it in the patent lock. Finally he uttered an oath and handed it to the psychiatrist.

Taking the object, Maclean felt a pulse of horror, as if intuition had suddenly revealed the nature of Cameron's illness to him.

Cameron had not handed him a key at all. It was a surgical instrument. A set of small forceps.

Maclean's fingers identified the scissors handle and the curved blunt ends of the forceps, which he guessed the surgeon carried around in his pocket in order to practice. And he had mistaken it for his key. Why? Because it was dark, and he had to rely on his sense of touch, his discrimination. It capped the whole pyramid of detail Maclean had injected into his mind: the operation lapse, the exaggerated behavior, the loss of smell and memory, the awkward gait. He had pin-pointed the problem.

Without pausing to finish his reflections or to comment to Cameron, he delved into Cameron's pocket, found his key and opened the door. He drew the curtains and switched on the bedside lamp. Maneuvering the surgeon toward the divan, he undressed him, pulled on his pajamas and stretched him out on top of the covers. He picked up the phone and ordered the switchboard to page Sainsbury, wondering as he did why he had not seen the medical superintendent during the incident. As he replaced the receiver, he heard a light rap on the door. It was Donovan.

"Wasn't that just awful, Dr. Maclean? She's no good, that girl. And the professor did so much for her!"

"Never mind, Sister. Where's Stroma?"

"Jean Sainsbury took her to her flat."

"We don't want her here for a while. Tell Jean to send her home, and I'll ring her later. And, Sister, go along to the dispensary and ask them for two hypos—one empty and the other with three grains of Nembutal."

"Is he that bad?"

"Just shocked. The barbiturate will allow him to sleep it off."

In a few minutes Donovan returned with the two syringes. She swabbed the fleshy part of the surgeon's arm with alcohol, and he grunted, as though acquiescing. Maclean emptied the contents of the syringe into his arm and handed it back to Donovan. "I'll hang on, Sister. Tell those people who ask that he's all right." He waited for a quarter of an hour, until the drug had acted, then pushed the surgeon's legs under the covers. Taking the limp right arm, he massaged the veined area in its crook, swabbed it and found a vein with the needle of the empty syringe. He drew off enough blood to fill the barrel. As he finished, Sainsbury entered.

"Sorry, I had to run and missed the drama. An emergency. Jean gave me a blow-by-blow, and I've already got somebody working on Holroyd's cards. I hope he doesn't remember about Wilkinson."

"I hope not." Maclean handed Joe the syringe. He described what had happened with Cameron and the key.

"So you think it may be some sort of brain lesion."

"Anything from hardening of the arteries to a tumor. I've been an idiot, Joe, fooled by my own jargon. I might have caught this a fortnight ago if I hadn't made up my mind that his trouble was purely emotional."

"You're still well ahead of the great minds around this shop," said Sainsbury. He studied the syringe. "What do you want me to do about this?"

"Get them to test it for alcohol level. I don't think he's had much to drink, but it's wise to be sure. And while you're about it, give it to the special department and ask them to run a Wassermann reaction."

"VD?" Sainsbury asked, surprised.

"You never know. It's another possibility we have to

eliminate, and we might as well take advantage of the patient's co-operation."

"I wish he'd be as co-operative as this for a fortnight."

"You know him—he'll be up and about tomorrow."

"Worse luck. I haven't told you my bit of news. In the middle of all this the Right Hon the Lord Blatchford took ill, and I had to argue him into a private room."

"You'll have to argue him into having another surgeon or have him moved to another hospital."

"Can you see me doing that? He's as mule-headed as this man, and it would convince him it was part of the hospital plot." Sainsbury pressed the glowing tip of his stub against a fresh cigarette. "You don't know this man Blatchford. If he had his way, he'd stage the operation on TV at peak hours as part of the 'Your Knife in Their Glands' series. Look at him—he's a Catholic Socialist with a title and cash he won on the stock exchange, and his sense of occasion never fails. He's left the monogrammed shirts, the shoe trees, the twenty suits and his valet in Belgravia. His kit here is a pair of almshouse pajamas, a wash bag and toothbrush. He's ordained Cameron to do his stomach on the Health Service, and that's that. And I suppose, after all, if a man can't choose his surgeon, what rights has he left?"

"We can't allow Murdo to operate on Blatchford alone. If Wilkinson goes, we'll have to cast round for somebody else."

"Who?" Sainsbury ticked the five consultant surgeons off on his fingers. "Not one of them would dare pick up one of his dropped stitches. And it's not on to treat Blatchford with a bland diet and bed rest. He's got an ache in his duodenum, and a couple of days of our grub will set him up for surgery if it doesn't kill him."

"What operation was Cameron going to do?"

"Vagotomy and pyloroplasty."

"You mean the type he did on Fowler's wife?" Sainsbury nodded. They looked at each other in silence. The
surgery would have been difficult enough for a surgeon
with all his skills and an assistant who had done a whole
series with him. But Cameron in his present condition operating alone! To Maclean it seemed that everyone—Holroyd, Blatchford, the governing board, his rivals—had
conspired to knock the surgeon off his eminence. He
wrapped the blankets around Cameron and closed the
door of the flat. It had been a real Walpurgis Night; a
night full of the witches and bogles of his boyhood. He
shuddered and reproached himself for being a superstitious Celtic idiot.

25
? ? ?

With a start Stroma noticed that he had already removed
his card from its socket in the door of his flat. Surely he
could not have quit the hospital so soon, she thought as
she pressed the doorbell. It had taken courage to come
this far, and loss of pride. What was pride if she might
never see him again? Last night, when the others had
kept their eyes on the violent scene between her father
and Holroyd, she had watched David's reactions. She was
certain that both he and her father had been duped by
that girl into quarreling and parting company. At least
she should tell him that she had not been taken in. David
opened the door. He looked weary, as though he had not
slept; his wan face appeared to float above the polo neck
of his sweater. His invitation lacked warmth and grace,

but she walked past him into the flat, her eye taking in the litter of textbooks, surgical and medical instruments, phonograph records and clothing, which lay on the floor beside the two large trunks.

"You don't have to leave today," she said.

"We're not going over all that again," he muttered.

"I'm sorry. Can I give a hand?"

"I can manage."

"Do you mind if I sit down?"

"Help yourself. Have a drink and a cigarette while there's time." He blew the dust off several books and stuffed them carelessly into a trunk. She noticed the surgery manual she had given him.

"David, can't we forget that row? Everybody else has. It was all so stupid."

"Your father, the professor, hasn't forgotten. I had to beat him to the punch by resigning this morning, or he'd have booted me out physically. Oh, I know the dean and Sainsbury and a few others say he'll get over it if I have a fortnight's leave. They've all been here this morning, mentioning sordid commodities like money and talking about the brain drain as though the manhole cover lay under this carpet. I told them no, I was going."

"You've taken the job, then?"

"All I have to do is wire Judson, and I'm an associate professor with money in the bank."

"So she finally forced you into it."

"I would have gone anyway, I think." She noted that his voice carried little enthusiasm.

"My father's going to miss you—he'd be the last person to admit it, but you meant a lot to him, and he depended so much on you."

"Probably why he lost no time in signing me off his firm this morning," he replied sourly.

"You know you could get him to tear up that bit of paper if you went to him and explained things. He'd think no more of it."

"Briefed by you, I suppose. Well, I'm through begging. He knows where I am, and he can knock on my door for a change. I have my pride, too."

"Pride," she cried bitterly. "I seem to be the only person left here with no pride. If it will help, I don't mind apologizing for him. He didn't know what he was doing last night."

He stopped packing and turned to her, as though struck by a new thought or some new aspect of her. "You've got nothing to reproach yourself for."

"Except that I shouldn't have tried to stop your going in the first place."

"And I shouldn't have tried to get back at you. Know something? I don't really think I wanted the job then, even if I griped at the way your old man was treating me. I was all mixed up about him, and you. He was hard to work with, but no more so than many others. I was probably so determined not to lose my identity that I began to resent him. Then you, for siding with him. Now you know why I ignored you, why I behaved so badly the other night."

Her face had assumed the expression he had observed that first day when she had carried her guinea pig in secret triumph out of the animal laboratory. "And you left me with the idea that it was simply because I wasn't as pretty as your girl friend."

"You were jealous of Pat?" he said incredulously.

"How was I to know it was all because my name was Cameron?" she replied. "Now that you're your own boss, you can't object if I give you a hand." She picked up the books, the records and the clothes and began to stow them neatly in the trunks. So preoccupied were they with the packing that they failed to spot Patricia Holroyd until she stood in the middle of the room.

"I see they can't get you off the premises quickly enough, darling," she cried. "What is she—a representative of the eviction committee?"

David went on packing and ignored her. Stroma turned to face the girl, who appeared dressed and ready to leave. When she had found the courage to call on David, the one thing she had dreaded was meeting this venomous creature. It astonished her that she kept so calm.

"How's Daddy this morning?" Holroyd sneered.

"Only sorry he didn't see through your little plot before you forced him to quarrel with someone he had trusted for years. I wouldn't expect anyone as thick-skinned as you to understand or care, but you've probably done more to hurt him than all the letters and rumors."

"Quite a speech," Holroyd said with a laugh. "I should have told him last night he was sick in his mind—though unfortunately not too sick to go on operating."

"It makes what you did all the more odious."

"You'll have me crying in a minute. If you and your wonderful papa both dropped dead today, I wouldn't shed a tear."

"That's enough, Pat—get out," David said very quietly, moving to the door and holding it open for her.

"Aren't you going to give me a lift?" she said, pleading.

"Sorry—no room."

When he had slammed the door behind her, Stroma said, "I thought you were leaving together."

He shook his head. "Just at the same time. Different directions."

"So you knew why she created her little scene."

212

"I'm not that glaikit." Unconsciously he had used one of the Scots words that Cameron would throw at a clumsy nurse or a delinquent house surgeon when things went wrong in the theater. It broke the tension.

"And I was thinking you loved her."

"In my more depressed and stupid moments I thought so, too. That's one thing I can thank your father for— stopping me from making a fool of myself."

"How?"

"By keeping me single long enough to prevent my picking the wrong girl."

"But you wouldn't."

"Until last night and this morning I might've—well, quite a few people do." He looked at her. "After all, she had everything: she was like a glossy magazine ad—the right make-up and layout, bright line of patter, no demands on the intellect, good color and it seemed to fit your home. How do you know until you buy and try the product how well it squares with the promotion pitch? It pays to advertise."

"I tried once," she said. "But the only thing my customer was interested in was champagne."

"I know." He gave her a serious look. "Stroma, why do you bother with a lamebrain like me?"

"Only one reason: I happen to love you."

For a moment she thought he was going to take her in his arms. Instead he picked up the two loose strap ends of a case and buckled them into place, his face distracted, worried.

"I'm all mixed up," he muttered, half to himself. "Things are happening too quickly."

She understood. His life lay around him in disorder, like the textbooks, the packing cases, the bit of paper signed by her father in his pocket. Hers, too, had dramatically turned upside down with the scene at the ball. Time was what they both needed: to put together the broken bits and pieces of their relationship; to erase their vexed hours and the scars on his conscience; to strengthen the fragile bond they had re-created now. Time was what they did not have. Ten short minutes, perhaps.

David was speaking again. "She was right, you know —he is sick."

She nodded. "But he's in good hands." She told him about the weekend and her talks with Maclean.

"But if he operates and makes some fatal mistake, I'd feel responsible in a way. I'd feel I'd left him in the lurch."

"You can still change his mind."

He gazed out the window at the crumbling sandstone buildings, the ancient water tower, the soot-grimed wards and the admin area. "It meant as much to me as it did to him. If he didn't realize that last night, he never will. I can't go and eat dirt."

"He'll come round; you'll see. He'll get in touch with you." Stroma uttered the words as much to comfort herself as out of conviction. Her father—she knew him too well—would never apologize, never climb down. David would go reluctantly to America and, once there, would stay. She felt trapped in the senseless quarrel. They were the two out of her childhood fable who met each other on a narrow bridge, each obstinately refusing to concede, tussling, horns locked, until both tumbled into the river and drowned. They would take her with them, she reflected.

They finished packing. David loaded the car and returned to have a last look around the Spartan room with its bare bookshelves, its table, two chairs and the unmade divan. "I don't think I've left anything," he remarked.

Only me, Stroma thought. It was a moment for honesty. "Wait, David," she said. She hesitated, then burst out, "Do you remember the other night when you said you wanted to seduce me?"

"Yes, but don't remind me of it. I don't know what got into me. I just wanted to shock you, to humiliate you, to prove something to myself. And even then I had to drink so much to pluck up courage that I couldn't have done anything about it. For that I'm grateful."

"Well, I'm not. What I mean is . . . what would you say if I told you that I wanted to be shocked, that I wanted to seduce you, that I had everything planned down to the last drop of champagne?"

For a moment she thought she had ruined everything with her confession. He stood, hesitating, staring at her unbelievingly. "The way things turned out it was a good thing we both botched it," he said.

"But we wanted to then, and nothing has changed it for me."

"Even if we never see each other again?"

"If we love each other, all the more reason," she said, with a logic he did not quite follow. He watched as she went to lock the door, then draw the flimsy print curtains in the denuded room.

Stroma felt her heart pulse in her throat as she came into his arms and let him kiss her and pull her gently onto the divan. She let his slow hands discover her body, her eyes closed, her breathing still, her mind trying to quiet the turmoil of her emotions, to prevent them from surging over her, drowning her in love. "David, this is the first time," she murmured.

His hands lay still. "Are you sure you still want to?" he said.

"Yes," she breathed. She knew there would be pain,

215

but as she felt him enter her, the pain and pleasure fused, and he had to hush her as she cried out with the ecstasy of the moment.

Afterward, they lay in each other's arms, whispering like two people who had come to know each other for the first time. The phone rang; someone tried the knob of the door; they heard voices outside in the corridor. "You must go before they find you here," he said.

"I shall go out with you," she said. "No one here matters to me any more."

They walked to the car. When he made to leave, she bent over and kissed him to prove to anyone who might be watching that they were concealing nothing. Only when the car disappeared around the corner of the boiler house did she sense the tears start in her eyes with the thought that she had won him only to lose him again.

26
? ?
?

If Cameron lamented the loss of his senior registrar, it was not apparent to those who met him the morning following the incident at the ball. Sainsbury encountered him clumping down the main corridor, as though the previous night's drama had been someone else's nightmare or belonged to the apocrypha which attached itself to the surgeon. The blood test had revealed nothing, a fact that sowed doubt in the medical superintendent's mind; Cameron's demeanor, however, made him think again.

"Morning, Sainsbury. You look a bit peaky. Too many fags and coffees in that filing box of yours. Now about

Blatchford—I've just had a peep at his plates and concluded that we must do him quickly—the day after tomorrow in A Block Theater. He's got some *noblesse oblige* bee about eating the hospital slops; then when they've sickened him, he'll go and air his indigestion in the House of Lords about our catering. Get him some food from our mess—it's still mangy, but it's at least hot."

"Shall I brief someone to take Wilkinson's place?"

A frown settled on Cameron's brow, and he shot the medical superintendent a furious look. "All I need is someone to hold the retractors—that's so easy that even you could scramble through it. I'm promoting Collins to the firm and Miss—what's-her-name?—Tremayne to take Holroyd's place permanently. I'll leave you to tell her."

Sainsbury could not avoid thinking that Cameron was treating the difficult vagotomy operation too lightly. He was about to take his leave when the surgeon caught his sleeve.

"By the way, I'm pushing off next week for a bit of a rest. Steele can take over my list for a fortnight. But, Sainsbury—I don't want all this blown into another rumor that I'm giving up the chair, d'you understand? I don't know where these stories originate, though I have my suspicions, Sainsbury, I have my suspicions. In any case I want them scotched. All of them. Understood?"

The medical superintendent glanced at Cameron's livid face and wondered for a second if the professor suspected him; but after his minatory utterance, Cameron merely nodded and stumped off. As Sainsbury went to make the arrangements for the operation and the changes in Cameron's team, his mind was trying to encompass the problem of preventing Cameron from doing anything they would all regret. He and Maclean had already considered one solution. Thinking that Cameron would adopt his normal routine of performing only the more complex surgery and leaving the preparatory and concluding phases of the operation to a registrar, they had taken Steele, a senior consultant who admired Cameron, into their confidence. He would stand by until the professor had quit the theater, then would check that no errors had been made before closing up.

But Sainsbury's meeting with Cameron had changed all that. From his conversation and the fact that he had chosen Collins, a relatively inexperienced registrar, to assist him, the surgeon obviously intended to conduct the whole operation himself. Well, he might get away with it. But if he didn't, his enemies would flock like buzzards, reveling in his own joke about killing a member of the nobility. He, Sainsbury, had not only a professor's reputation to consider; the name of the hospital mattered just as much to him. He sensed something almost inevitable, inexorable, about the situation; his old nose smelled catastrophe. What could he do?

The following night St. Vincent's was settling into its fitful repose. Hardly anything moved as the night staff took over. Cameron had often joked that patients on admission became so many abstract concepts, labeled Broken Leg or Peptic Ulcer, and were treated as though they obstructed the smooth running of the hospital, especially when their maladies refused to comply with textbook patterns. Whatever their condition, they were watered, fed, bedded down early and the lights doused to leave them in no doubt that they and their illnesses had been placed in abeyance until half past six the next morning.

The professor, himself, often prowled quite late through the hospital, as he was doing tonight, to see his own patients. Now, as he reached the main corridor, the waiting room and the consulting rooms were deserted except for the cleaners; the kitchen still emitted that odor, though its doors were shut; and the League of Friends' kiosk had also closed. The operating theaters had finished their day, too, with one exception. A light burned in the room where they carried out those long marathons of neurosurgery. The only noise Cameron heard came from the staff restaurant. Cameron did his rounds, chatting to patients who were recovering from surgery and those on his list tomorrow. He finished in the private room where Lord Blatchford was sitting up in bed, watching a portable TV set he had brought with him.

"Did they mention you?" Cameron asked as the news bulletin came to an end.

"Not a word, Murdo," Blatchford replied.

"Thank God, or they'd have been after me for advertising," Cameron grunted. He glanced at the chart and checked Blatchford's pulse, blood pressure and temperature.

"What's this, the executioner sizing up his victim on the last night?" his Lordship quipped. "Candidly, Murdo, I'm glad it's in your hands," he said as Cameron handed him his sleeping pill.

Cameron had no qualms, either, as he trod his way through the pools of light and shadow in the corridor toward his own flat. Once there he poured himself a whisky and produced his sketch pad. A vagotomy could present tricky problems, the reason so many surgeons avoided the procedure and remained loyal to the traditional excision of most of the stomach. Some of them had also attempted to damn the newer operation, which meant a change of routine, shorter lists and less reward. Cameron had pressed on, and his success could be read about in any medical textbook.

As he sat, sketching the steps of the operation, he could visualize almost every movement he would make the next day: an incision to expose the stomach, the forest of forceps tying off the blood vessels, the division and resection of the left flap of the liver, the mobilization of the lower esophagus and the severing, one by one, of the delicate vagus nerve fibers.

At that point something stopped him. Abruptly his pencil halted on the line of the food tract. Just where those wretches had rumored that he had made a fatal blunder during his last vagotomy. A black shadow descended on his mind as though a light had been snapped off. He sat brooding for a moment or two, then angrily tossed the sketch pad aside. They were wrong, of course. But fear—or was it excitement or resentment?—constricted his throat and spread downward into his stomach. With a start he noticed he had dropped his pencil, and his hand trembled violently. Until now he had conceded no credence, nothing but spite, to the anonymous writer of those damnable letters. But what if they were true and not just blackmail inspired by jealousy? No, he had studied the lab reports. Why did these antiphonal propositions of doubt and certainty oscillate in his mind? He poured himself another whisky. God! His hand left a moist imprint on the bottle. Chula cast him a reproachful glance, whether for his selfishness or self-indulgence no one could guess; she soon gave up trying to wheedle her tot of spirits out of him, sensing his distraught mood.

Mental detachment sometimes did the trick in moments like these, Cameron thought. He fixed his gaze on a spot on the wall and tried to pour all his concentration into it, but he could not sustain the effort; his mind wandered within seconds. Even letting his body go and breathing deeply did nothing to quiet him. Was he really going around the bend? If he were, one man would surely know and would help him.

He seized the phone and ordered the operator to try to

get Dr. Gregor Maclean. "If he's not in Harley Street, he has a flat in Bloomsbury somewhere. You must get him." The switchboard came back in a few minutes, and he heard the voice of that quaint Irish secretary explaining that Maclean was dining with some friends. Cameron's head was now throbbing, but somehow he recalled the psychiatrist mentioning a monthly dinner with some of his cured alcoholics. "Miss O'Connor, this is Murdo Cameron. Please contact him, and tell him I need him urgently." He tried to keep his voice calm, but it trembled audibly. She promised to do what she could.

Restless, he paced the room, watching the phone until he could bear it no longer. His head was bursting; the ceiling and walls of the small room seemed to vibrate and advance inward upon him. Through his headache he had a curious, drunken sensation, as if everything were spinning slowly, deliberately, under his feet. He had to get out. To march. Somewhere. Anywhere. He opened the door and stumbled along the corridor to the hospital grounds. The cool air appeared to steady him, and he paused for a few minutes at the fountain to splash water on his face and wrists. But the buildings . . . When he looked up, they were staggering and wobbling in the twilight, and he had the bizarre impression that they, too, were toppling toward him. Even the moon sagged, ominously red and swollen, in the sky. He was seeing everything as though in a mirror of rippling water. He sluiced his face once again and felt better; everything had steadied around him. He returned to the main building of the hospital. Chula, padding in his wake, followed him through the main block and into the canteen, where some of the staff sat drinking tea.

In the following days they remembered the absence in his face and the agitation in his hands as he drank a mug of tea with his cat perched on his shoulders. He wore, they observed, an old pull-over over an open-necked shirt, the antithesis of the normally immaculate Professor of Surgery. After he left, he must have lost himself for at least an hour among the labyrinth of wings and wards, for Sainsbury, alerted by Maclean, started to search the buildings and found no trace of him. No one ever discovered where he spent that time; he could have prowled through the grounds or made some ghostly round of his sleeping surgical wards.

However, Sainsbury had one clue. When he came to carry out his personal inquest on that lost hour, he was astonished by what he found in A Block Theater, the one chosen by Cameron for his operation on Blatchford. Every instrument which the surgeon would have required for his vagotomy lay on trolleys near the operating table. Donovan would have sacked any new sister who had made such a ham-fisted job. The instruments had been grabbed from their racks in handfuls and piled on the trolleys; suture needles were mixed with forceps, scalpels and retractors were jumbled and swabs and cautery instruments spread haphazardly. No one but Cameron could have visited the theater that evening after the instruments and materials had been autoclaved and the floors and walls washed down. Only Cameron could have prepared thus for the operation; of that Sainsbury became certain when he discovered the surgeon's smock, cap and gloves laid out in the changing room.

Cameron had not consciously sought to evade them. Like a somnambulist, he stepped slowly toward the nurses' wing. There he circled hesitantly around the building before standing for ten minutes contemplating the light in the second-floor window. Suddenly it seemed he had made up his mind. He entered the main door and groped his way upstairs in the dim light until he reached a landing with three doors. He planted himself in front of the center of these, staring at it, as though perplexed by its shape or by his own actions. Impatient at his slow progress and indecision, Chula opened her mouth and uttered a long and deep croaking sound. The door opened.

For several seconds Frances Tremayne could hardly believe what she saw. She gasped at the sight of his disheveled figure and the intense, tortured expression in his eyes. Once before she had seen that look: in the operating theater that morning he had made to strike her. "What's wrong, Professor?" she asked. Cameron ignored her, hobbling past without a word and taking up a position in the center of the room, the cat treading behind him.

Was this where his world, his madness, ended? With her, in this room? The thought overwhelmed him, but strangely enough, he did not question it; he had ceased to care about consequences. She had just bathed. His eyes took in the bathrobe of white toweling and under it the sweep and bend of her breasts; for the first time he could stare without guilt at her body and her face. He marveled at the sharpness of his senses; he might have been studying her under a microscope. He gazed at the sheen and highlights on her skin and at the reflection in the gray flecks of her greenish eyes. He could even smell the sensual, animal odor of her flesh, masking the bath perfume. His shame had vanished, and a calm flooded over him as he realized and admitted why he had spurned her, why he had tried to dismiss her. Without real awareness he had been defending himself against desire, even love.

"I have wronged you," he said, his voice seeming to sigh from the corners of the room. "Through my own weakness and cowardice, I have wronged you. I came to tell you this and ask your pardon."

She shook her head. "No," she said. "If we are both going to be truthful at last, you came to tell me you love me."

"Yes," he cried. "I came to confess it, to lift the shadow from my mind and the pain from my heart. I could bear them no longer. And you were waiting for me."

"From that first day I saw you I have waited."

"We shall go away from here, you and I, and forget everything. Everything except having found each other."

"But first we have to stay and fight those here who have wronged you."

"Wronged me?"

"Your enemies in this hospital. Before, you had no one to help you. You are no longer alone. I am here with you."

"Yes, you are right. I have been alone too long, growing older and more helpless among aliens and tormentors who have heaped sores on me. Trying to heal when I myself was sick at heart. I needed courage when everyone believed I was strong. I needed love when there was no one to give it to me. I thought that the race was to the swift, the battle to the strong, that skill and understanding and compassion were beyond riches. And they were right, and I was wrong." He wanted to weep at the chagrin of those years and the relief of confessing his love; but he held back, even now, afraid she would take tears as a sign of weakness. "Come away with me," he whispered so softly that he scarcely heard it himself. "Come away, and we shall make a new beginning. I could be a sheep farmer, a fisherman. I can grow roses. I've always wanted to give my name to a new variety—a black rose."

"A black rose? You are mocking me."

"A dusky rose, like you. Lovelier than any other. And

you thought I spurned you for your color." He felt tears pricking his eyes.

"No," she said. "I thought you were afraid because admitting that you loved me meant giving part of yourself."

"You are taunting me again about love. Yes, I was afraid—afraid to admit that you were the first person I have ever loved."

"I had to hear it from your own lips," she said. "You needn't be afraid any longer. We have an eternity to love and forget."

Her voice and his jangled in his mind, as if the words were running around inside his skull like so many brightly colored marbles. The background against which she stood had become a quivering, whirling collage of walls, floor and ceiling. The girl stood static in the center, representing his hope, his stability, his sanity. He felt something clawing at his leg; it was Chula. He lifted his foot and struck out at her and heard her squawk.

"You are weary," Frances murmured, moving toward him. He sensed her soft arms around him, her hands caressing the nape of his neck. His head ached no more, as though the odor of her body, the touch of her flesh, the breath of her perfume, the promise of her love, had washed the pain away. She was enticing him gently to the bed from which she had just risen, and he drifted with her, his legs faint, his chest painful, his head bursting with the thought of her. Oddly he felt some relief that it was she who was seducing him, as though some deep moral qualm still disturbed him. "I love you," she whispered in his ear. She offered no resistance as he fondled her, as he thrust the bathrobe back over her shoulders and watched her body reveal itself as the garment slipped to the floor. His eyes took possession of the firm breasts, the narrow waist, the soft flesh of her thighs, and passion poured over him like warm rain, engulfing him; he felt agony and pleasure surge over him. If this was how his world ended, so be it.

27

? ?
?

A good half hour elapsed before Deirdre got in touch with Maclean to pass on Cameron's message. Immediately he left the reunion of some of his former patients. The surgeon would never have summoned him at this hour unless some personal crisis had blown up. He reckoned it would take half an hour to reach the hospital by cab, so he phoned Sainsbury, who promised to search for Cameron. "We'd better alert Frankland in neurosurgery," Maclean said.

"I don't know where he is, but I'll check. I think they packed up half an hour ago."

When Maclean arrived at the hospital, the medical superintendent gave him the scant details they had of Cameron's movements. He thought for a moment, then said, "There's one person who might know where he is, if he's not already with her—Donovan."

Neither man realized that Cameron had preceded them by no more than ten minutes on their journey to the nurses' wing. They hurried to the building and were about to knock on Donovan's door on the ground floor when they heard something between a screech and a squawk ringing loudly from upstairs.

"That's his bloody Siamese cat," Sainsbury shouted, darting upstairs, with Maclean lumbering after him. The scream had come from the middle room. Sainsbury threw the door open. Sister Tremayne was bending over the figure of Cameron, who lay near the bed.

"Professor Cameron," she panted. "He's collapsed."

"Go and phone the Casualty officer and get him round here with everything he's got," Sainsbury ordered. She pulled her dressing gown around her and went downstairs to the telephone.

Cameron lay crouched as he had fallen. Maclean picked up his hand and placed his index finger on the pulse. "Thready and weak as hell," he commented. "High temperature, too." He asked Sainsbury to hold the bedside lamp while he lifted both eyelids. "It's what we thought. See that, Joe—the left pupil's as big as a sixpence. If he's going to have any chance at all, they'll have to work overtime tonight."

"I managed to get Frankland and told him what might have happened. We have Tremayne and Donovan here, and I can rake up somebody from Casualty. And I think he'd like you to give the gas."

Frankland had already scrubbed up when they wheeled Cameron into the neurosurgery theater. The personal antonym of flamboyance, the little brain surgeon rarely squandered a single movement—something of value in a branch of surgery where blood is measured by the drop and even the dust and shavings from drilling into the skull are salvaged and replaced. Never had anyone known him to say anything more profound in the theater than "Scalpel" or "Gigli saw" or "Dural scissors." When things went badly, his pebble-dash complexion would flush, and he would purse his thick lips and hiss through them so hard that his face mask bubbled.

He confirmed Maclean's diagnosis.

"Intravenous saline and mannitol," he murmured. His registrar injected the drug to shrink the brain and relieve the compression while Donovan set up the saline drip, through which they would later transfuse blood. Sister Tremayne was laying out the instruments, her face and movements grave. Maclean had neither the time nor the desire to question her about what Cameron had been doing in her room. He was watching the pulse and blood pressure, checking the anesthetic.

"An arteriogram," Frankland mumbled. "Must make sure." He waited until they had trundled in a portable X-ray machine, then injected a radio-opaque substance into a neck artery. They ran off six plates, then had to hang around, impatiently, waiting for the verdict on Cameron. It was the worst moment. Would it be operable, or would they have to wheel him out to die? As they waited, they took him back into the anesthetic room, where Donovan, moist-eyed, propped up his head and cut his red hair. She bent down distractedly to gather up the clippings and place them carefully on a table, as though they, too, must be preserved. After her went Frankland's theater sister with an open razor, shaving the head clean.

Did Frankland have to peer at the X-ray plates like that? Maclean was looking over his shoulder. "Lucky so far," the neurosurgeon said with uncharacteristic loquacity. "Meningioma." He put his finger on the white "blush" on the plate, revealing the tumor between the frontal lobes. Maclean felt like kissing him.

"You were right," Sainsbury commented.

"A fortnight too late," the psychiatrist muttered. He was crossing his fingers, hoping the small growth which had caused Cameron's troubles would be excised before the brain pressure built up and proved fatal.

Did Frankland have to labor so slowly? Did he have to juggle with the head this way and that, swab the skull with disinfectant, draw that familiar scimitar outline under

228

which he would raise the bone flap? No one could hurry him. For three hours, powerless to do anything but watch, Maclean fumed and fretted; he could have cut those four burr holes and lifted the skull flap in half the time. He might fret, he might sweat in this hothouse atmosphere of humidity and glare, but how could he blame Frankland, who had already spent a long day in similar conditions?

Meticulously the surgeon was snipping through the thick sheath around the brain. This he drew back and for a few moments peered through the glasses on the end of his nose and puffed through his lips; only that and the noise of the suckers clearing the operating field interrupted the silence.

Finally they could see the tumor, lying wedged between the frontal lobes. Like a squashed strawberry, Maclean thought. Frankland had already begun to cauterize the blood vessels around it; then he explored the growth and the small vessels tying it to the brain. In his painstaking style he placed silver clips on these veins before severing them one by one. After what seemed like hours, he grasped the tumor with his forceps, prized it upward and cut it loose. For Maclean the clock had stopped ticking; the mechanism had been defused. He still felt his shirt, under his gown, clamming to his chest and back, and he shivered even in that stifling room.

Pushing through the swing doors, he tugged off his mask, fished out his snuffbox and gave himself a pinch big enough to bring water to his eyes. In the dark he sensed something brush against his legs: Chula. She must have been prowling the corridor for the past four hours. He bent down and ran his hand along her back. "He's going to be all right," he whispered. Cameron had been lucky. The meningioma, slow-growing and benign, would leave behind no permanent effect, no risk of recurrence. Maclean should have spotted it, but such tumors often produced some of the same symptoms as mental illness, like hysteria or even psychosis. You couldn't win them all.

He seemed to have carried some of the tranquillity of Frankland and his team with him. The city slept, except for an occasional car racketing down the street and a tug or some ship hooting on the Thames; above the dark hospital buildings, clusters of stars burned.

"They're closing up." He turned to see Sister Tremayne beside him. The shock of finding Cameron so far gone had almost obliterated the circumstances from his mind.

"Would you care to tell me exactly what happened, Sister?"

"I was sitting in my dressing gown, reading, when I heard Chula crying at the door. I opened it, and there was the professor standing outside. He looked terrible . . . his hair was wet, and he was distraught and agitated. It was as though he didn't realize where he was. . . ."

"So you invited him in."

"I didn't have to. He walked straight past me. I might not have existed. Then he turned and stood staring at me for two or three minutes. Then he just fell, rolled over into the position you found him in, and that started Chula yelling."

"He didn't say anything?"

"He was mumbling. I couldn't catch what he was saying—his voice was so slurred." She paused, then went on. "I did think that . . . that he was going to attack me."

"You mean, rape you?"

"If you want to put it like that—yes."

"But he didn't."

She shook her head. "He looked as if he were moving toward me when he fell."

"You needn't have worried," Maclean said. "In his

230

state he couldn't have done anything desperate. He was merely looking for help. He had been looking for help for a long time."

"I wasn't worried," she said. "But I wonder what I should do now? Do I go or wait until he wakes and finds he collapsed in my room and the gossips get hold of the story?"

"Don't worry about the gossips, and don't do or say anything. Whatever he had in his mind, or his heart, no one will ever know, and himself least of all. He won't remember anything about those hours before he passed out."

No one would ever really know why he had chosen her. From what the surgeon had revealed during the previous weekend, from what Maclean had read into his character, he could guess Cameron had long buried part of his personality and had repressed his frustrations, covering them over with high ideals and hard work. He had everything under control until the tumor began to create changes in the brain and in his personality, which he must have interpreted, like Maclean, as a form of mental illness. Certainly his phone call was the cry of a man who probably believed himself to be going mad. Who could tell, when a man like that lost the place temporarily, how his emotions would erupt through his inhibited thoughts and feelings? They had exploded in lust for Sister Tremayne, but lust he was in no position to satisfy by the time he reached her room. Maclean did not doubt her story. He might have told her, had it helped, that her professor was almost certainly acting out some schizoid episode with her, some hallucination which, fortunately, he would never recall. Like most of the other fantasies and aberrations his tumor had produced, it would be lost.

*

Frankland allowed no one, not even Stroma, to see Cameron for three days. Donovan nursed him personally through the most critical hours, ensuring that he was kept propped up and quite still to give him the best chance of recovery. It was she who reported to Maclean that Sir Kenneth Fairchild had put his head around the door and inquired very kindly about the surgeon. He then spent ten minutes with Frankland, asking about the operation and the surgeon's progress. Donovan had been relieved that her professor, still under sedation, had not met Fairchild. Maclean ventured no comment, though he secretly wished that the two men could have had a few words. He judged that their quarrels had probably made a bigger casualty of Fairchild than of Cameron. Events proved him tragically right.

28
? ? ?

Ostensibly Lady Fairchild had spent the evening at a meeting of the London Microbiological Society for a discussion on cross infection in hospital wards; in fact, she had dined with Conway-Smith at his flat, wrangling for hours over the Cameron affair, sniggering over the fact that he had been picked up, unconscious, in his West Indian sister's flat. Lady Fairchild had always known that sex was at the root of his problem, his strange behavior. And his illness? That lent weight to their argument about deposing him, didn't he see? The hospital and the ministry now had a clear duty to set people's minds at rest by conducting an inquiry into the three cases involving Cameron. Her friend, Conway-Smith, would agree only so far;

he took the more realistic view. "We're tending to omit one factor, Barbara—the man's had a brain operation. For the moment he's the good old fireproof British underdog, and if he slew his friend and eminence the Lord Blatchford on the table with a stab in the heart, the coroner would merely look the other way. Don't worry, there'll be other patients, other opportunities." He uttered the statement without enthusiasm or conviction. Cameron had licked all of them. Conway-Smith was relieved when she ran out of invective and left.

She found the house at Ham in darkness when she returned. She left the car in the drive in case the bang of the garage door might wake Kenneth and give him another sleepless night; she trod lightly up to the bathroom, undressed and entered their bedroom quietly. First she noticed that the bedroom curtains had not been drawn. Her eyes flew to his bed, and she started on seeing it empty. Her mind flashed back to the day her husband had suffered his coronary. Downstairs, through the drawing room and dining room she ran, until she came to his study, where she stopped and gazed at the light under the door. Panic hit her, but she calmed herself with the thought that he must have worked late on his papers and fallen asleep. She pushed open the door.

He lay in a leather armchair as though dozing, except that his arms and legs splayed outward, slack and aimless. She halted for a moment until her composure returned, then drew the curtains before switching on the main light and turning her attention to her husband. Intuition told her it was futile to check his pulse or breathing; it whispered, too, that a coronary attack had nothing to do with his death. She sat down and wept, though not for the figure in the chair.

"You fool," she muttered, apostrophizing him and at the same time reproaching herself. "You stupid old fool."

After a few minutes, she rose and went over to the chair. On the floor by his right hand lay a glass with milk dregs in the bottom. He had always found it difficult to swallow even a single tablet; from the white sludge she estimated that he must have crushed at least twenty barbiturate pills into his final drink. She went to the kitchen, rinsed the glass and wiped it furiously, hardly seeing it through her angry tears. There would be no questions, no talk, no seeking to understand his motives. No inquest. "Killed himself while suffering from depression." In too many hospital minds that would ring as a coroner's euphemism, glossing over a suicide they would read as a form of moral recompense to Cameron. That she would never admit, however valid. From the kitchen she walked to her own small study and opened the bureau drawer with the key. The papers still lay in the small drawer with no sign of having been touched, though she could never say for certain. He knew about them, those copies of the pathology reports on the three cases and the drafts of the letters. Carrying them upstairs to her room, she tore them into shreds and flushed them down the toilet, cursing his final act of cowardice as she did so.

In his study she wondered if she should leave the body where it lay and decided it would be unwise to move it. While deliberating about the people who might help cover up the suicide, she noticed the two letters lying on the desk and seized them. His feathery hand had addressed one to the local coroner; the other, to Cameron, at the hospital, he had even stamped. Thank God he hadn't posted it. Did he really think she would? Viciously she tore it open and read:

"My dear Cameron, I was grieved to learn about your illness but greatly heartened to hear that you had come successfully through surgery and would make a complete recovery. I hope when you read this, you will be on the

234

mend. The last year has been anything but a happy one for many of us at St. Vincent's. In retrospect, one can see the trials you have had to bear and can only admire and commend the manner in which you faced up to them. Some of us have mistreated you abominably, myself more than most. I am satisfied that any allegations about your work at any time are without foundation. Please forgive me. Yours sincerely, Kenneth Fairchild."

To the coroner he had written:

"To Her Majesty's Coroner: I have taken approximately twenty times the normal therapeutic dose of pentobarbital sodium. It may help you in arriving at your verdict to know that I have been suffering from depression and have had treatment for it during the past two years. Kenneth Fairchild."

He had left no note for her, as though condemning her in his typical way by saying nothing, implying everything in the notes she held in her hand. She tore both into shreds blindly, visualizing the face of Cameron gloating as he read the first one and congratulating himself on beating her. He never would. Anger and contempt at her husband's action caused her hand to shake violently as she disposed of the fragments of paper. She searched the study thoroughly before picking up the phone and dialing Conway-Smith's number. Within twenty-five minutes he had arrived.

"I can put my signature on the certificate," he said. "I can even vouch that I saw him in the last fortnight and that his heart was showing signs of stress. But we should have his GP. What's he like?"

"Ellistone at the hospital has looked after him since his heart attack. He's a personal friend. I can ring him in the morning."

"In that case detach your mind. The coroner will treat it as a pure formality and waive the autopsy."

So it turned out. Sir Kenneth's death went unquestioned. The elite of the Royal Colleges, the hospital dignitaries and his many medical friends made his funeral in Woking a big occasion. The minister, for whom he had toiled so diligently, sent his representative. The sorrowful poise of his widow impressed everyone. The hospital staff marveled at her stoicism when she reported back to her department a couple of days after the interment. Only Maclean remained dubious about the whole business. Although he mentioned his suspicions to no one, he felt he could do no harm by talking to the lady. He hated unfinished case notes.

29

? ?
?

Lady Fairchild was bending over a microscope in her fourth-floor office when Maclean knocked and entered. Tragedy had not altered her. Nothing, he reflected, would change those diamond eyes and the hard set of her features.

"Not over to look at the rats again, Dr. Maclean," she said, smiling.

"No, I really came to have a last word with Cameron. My little bit of research work is finished."

She rose and walked over to gaze out the high window. "I hope you agree with me now that he was quite mad and should never have been allowed inside an operating theater this last year, let alone run a department."

"Mad's hardly the term I'd choose. Organic psychosis

—cured as he'd have wished it, with the knife. He had his good and indifferent days."

"You mean he was lucky."

"Luckier than some. I wish we'd been as alert about your husband's condition as we were about Cameron's."

"Don't say they have a surgical cure for coronary as well," she put in, without attempting to hide her sarcasm.

"No." He fixed his gaze on her face. "Nor can we do much for barbiturate poisoning—except spot the potential suicide and keep him from doing anything desperate."

"I find that whole suggestion offensive," she cried.

"I haven't mentioned it to anyone else," he replied blandly.

"The better for you. I should be careful whom you confide your gossip in, Dr. Maclean. Slander is often an expensive way of spreading malice."

"Don't worry. I'm far more discreet than, say, Conway-Smith. Didn't he sign the death certificate? Then there's the small matter of the script in the hospital dispensary and the book recording sixty grains of Nembutal issued to your husband the day before his death. I've made a copy, just in case the record is amended or stolen like some of Fiegler's case notes."

There was a slight hesitation. "That pharmacy entry means nothing. We have as much barbiturate left in the house."

"Why did he clean out his desk at the hospital on the day after Cameron's operation?"

"How should I know? You're our unpaid detective. All this is supposition and speculation by someone who's attempting to blacken the name of a great man."

"Perhaps. But what if the rumor went round the hospital? Or the possibility were mentioned to the coroner? Or an application were made to the police to exhume the body? Or the newspapers got hold of the story? It could be highly embarrassing not only for the dead man's reputation but for a couple of others."

"No one would dare!"

"They smeared Cameron; why not Fairchild?"

"Because he was innocent."

"You ought to know."

"What does that mean?"

"Those three letters—they were written by you. He knew about them and felt involved in the blackmailing business. Fine, as long as he believed the letters justified. But when he realized Cameron's weakness was due to a brain lesion, the thought drove him over the edge. A man with depression doesn't need much of a nudge."

"I suppose you can prove all this?" Her tone had none of its old bite, and she was studying Maclean apprehensively.

"Not directly. But Rothwell is weak and knows much of the story. And, as you know, he's now a patient of mine. Then your friend Conway-Smith. If he believed a scandal about Fairchild might affect him and his big Harley Street practice, his loyalty might get a bit ragged round the edges."

"If you resorted to this form of blackmail, I'd scream the place down. I would throw as much mud back at you, and I would use anyone and anything, lies, influence. . . ."

"I agree, nobody would win. Now, if you want my advice . . ."

"What would that be?"

"If I were your doctor, I'd strongly advise a change of hospital. For your own peace of mind as much as anything."

"I'll go when it suits me, and not before."

"I think a fortnight would give you time enough to

clear things up. The dean will understand your reluctance to remain in a place so closely associated with your husband." Maclean hoisted himself out of his chair and inclined his head as he made for the door. She stopped him.

"You still haven't proved anything," she shouted. "It's all just inference and guesswork." She had lost her control, as she had done that day in the dining room.

"I don't have to prove it. Your husband did that. But when you deal with poison, even the verbal form, you look for a woman as well as for a coward. The trouble was that you poisoned the wrong man. You killed your husband as surely as if you had mixed the barbiturate yourself. If I were you, I'd ask yourself whether you didn't mean to kill him."

In her fury she struck out at him, catching him on the side of the face with the flat of her hand. "You swine," she screamed. Then she put her head in her hands and sobbed.

As he ambled to the lift, Maclean could only feel sorry for her. That guilt would be hard enough on her. He chided himself for planting that last thought in her mind. Who knew? Her frustrated passion for Cameron might have twisted her mind to the extent of wishing her husband dead. He quit the microbiology building with mixed feelings. He had achieved something for Cameron; he had done nothing to save Fairchild. No doctor should drive by, even on his way to another case, and ignore a casualty bleeding to death on the road. Negligence, he reflected, took more than one form.

Walking along the corridor to Cameron's private room, Maclean bumped into Stroma. He would hardly have recognized her as the girl with the strained face he had met just over a week ago. She was smiling, carefree and looked very attractive.

"He's waiting for you," she said. "I'm just on the way to meet David."

"David? Oh, yes, I remember."

"You're an old fraud, Uncle Mac. Didn't you phone him the morning Father came out of the operating theater?"

"Maybe I did. It was a busy morning, and a lot has happened since then. It slipped my mind." He gave her a bland, innocent grin.

"They've made things up," she whispered. "David rang him, and Father wrote him a begging letter, and that must be a record. He let me read it, and then—what did he say?—swithered if he should send it. Do you know how he got round it? He handed it to me and said if I thought it should be posted, I was the one to do it, not him. Of course, I did."

"You've got the rebound phenomenon working for you as well. That girl certainly bounced him off your father. Have you fixed the wedding date?"

"I should discuss that with David, don't you think?"

"I suppose so. Give him till tomorrow, and nail him before your father gets up. Deirdre and I will expect front seats."

She paused a minute. "Uncle Mac, will Father be all right? The operation won't have changed his personality? They tell me nothing here."

"He'll be fine—a different man. Back to normal after a long period of stress, that's all."

She kissed him on the cheek. He was glad she hurried away, or she might have caught him blushing, an emotional response to which any self-respecting psychiatrist with all his complexes straight should have been immune. He marched on toward Cameron's room. The crates of champagne, wine and stout bottles at the door made him shudder involuntarily. Inside, the room gave the impres-

240

sion of a sorting office in one corner, a florist in the other and a liquor shop in between. Donovan was opening telegrams and reading them to the surgeon, who lay entrenched in pillows, his head still bandaged but his face smiling and relaxed. Chula reclined, inert as a duster, at the foot of the bed; she squawked at the sight of Maclean. The surgeon proffered an upturned left hand and gripped the psychiatrist's right until he winced. "Strong as ever," he announced. Maclean spotted a pair of forceps and a pile of paper clips on the bedside table. Cameron was well on the mend.

"Now I know what the full St. Vincent's treatment is, Alec," he said. "It's worse than ten hours a day in theater. Sleeping on the back shift from eight o'clock till dawn, and Donovan choking me with pills and fruit juice and thermometers. But old Prior took the hint and had my food sent in from Chez Some Dago across the street. It's just as bad."

"He's enjoying it," Donovan put in. "Every young nurse in the hospital is drawing lots to look after him, and every patient he's ever had has sent something—a note, flowers, drink." Donovan took her leave of Maclean, as though Cameron had told her he wanted to have a private chat. When she had closed the door, he turned.

"Did I do anything desperate?" he asked, looking Maclean straight in the eye.

"Desperate? You nearly died."

"You ken fine what I mean. If I thought I'd been stupid in any way, I'd never lift a knife again, here or anywhere else."

"You needn't give it a thought, Murdo. There never was any negligence. By your standards most of us would be struck off or in jail. Anyway, if you gave up, where would I or the surgeons I know go if we wanted the best operator in the trade?"

That pleased Cameron. He lay back, picked up his forceps and began to fish among his paper clips. "It's time I eased up, though. I've had an idea lying here. I'm going to put Wilkinson up for a readership and let him take some of the weight off me. What do you think?"

"You should have done it years ago. After all, for an Englishman he's coming along no' sae bad. Properly led, the English are all right."

Cameron smiled. "I've had another daft notion. I don't know whether it's the terrible grub they give us here, but I lie wondering how pease brose and griddle scones taste after all these years."

"They taste fine, the same as they always have. Go up and try them at the wellhead."

"That was the notion."

They sat for a quarter of an hour, a couple of Scotsmen having a crack about the old days. Donovan poked her head around the door and shot a dour look at Maclean, but the surgeon waved her away. "She told me about Fairchild. It vexed me. He took life too seriously. Combination of a weak heart and a domineering wife." Maclean nodded. Cameron had obviously accepted the official story but with his blunt intuition had hit on the right diagnosis.

Maclean rose to take his leave. "I've got to get back to an irate secretary and some of my more genteel and well-pursed patients in Harley Street. I must say, though, it's been fascinating sitting in with Fiegler. But you were right, Murdo—group psychiatry and psychodrama don't work." Keeping a straight face, he added, "It weakens the doctor-patient relationship."

Cameron fixed his blue stare on him. "You're an old twister—always were. I'm not sure it isn't a breach of the ethical code to come barging in and take over patients the way you do, without a by-your-leave. I don't know how to

242

thank you. There's only one thing that puzzles me. How did you learn about my spot of bother in the first place?"

That would have taken too long. Maclean often wondered himself what might have happened had Fowler not knocked on his door, had Deirdre acted her obdurate best, had Bob Hearn's flea not punctured Lady Blye's ego. He grinned. "Put it down to animal instinct," he said.